MAY 2 2 2

The House that Death Built

‡

John Llewellyn Probert

Other Books by
John Llewellyn Probert

The Faculty of Terror
Coffin Nails
The Catacombs of Fear
Against the Darkness
Wicked Delights
The Nine Deaths of Dr Valentine

The House that Death Built

John Llewellyn Probert

METRO VANCOUVER   DOMINION of CANADA

The House that Death Built

First Edition — limited to 100 hardback copies, signed and numbered by the Author and Cover Artist — published October 5th 2012, ISBN: 978–0–9866424–6–3

This Trade Paperback published October 5th 2012, ISBN: 978–0–9866424–5–6

Trade eBook published October 5th 2012, ISBN: 978–0–9866424–7–0

Typeset in Warnock

The "Atomic Fez Publishing" logo and the molecular headgear colophon is designed by, and copyright © 2009, Martin Butterworth of The Creative Partnership Pty, London, UK (www.CreativePartnership.co.uk).

PUBLISHER'S NOTE:
This is a work of fiction. All characters in this publication are fictitious and any resemblance to any real places, homes, or persons — living or dead — is purely coincidental.

ATOMIC FEZ PUBLISHING
3766 Moscrop Street
Burnaby, British Columbia
V5G 2C8, CANADA
WWW.ATOMICFEZ.COM

Library and Archives Canada Cataloguing in Publication entry available upon request

10   9   8   7   6   5   4   3   2

Table of Contents

Dedication   vii

Part One: The Most Haunted House in Britain?

Chapter 1: The Road Back   5

Chapter 2: An Irresistible Offer?   12

Chapter 3: "Touching the Beyond"   18

Chapter 4: Meeting Mr Stokes   26

Chapter 5: An Audience with Sir Anthony   34

Chapter 6: The Old Dark House   41

Chapter 7: Room for One More Inside   50

Part Two: Not a Nice Place to Visit

Chapter 8: Travelling to the Other Side   61

Chapter 9: Getting In…   70

Chapter 10: And Getting Acquainted   80

Chapter 11: A Stroll in the Grounds   89

Chapter 12: An Apparition at Dinner   94

Chapter 13: Coffee and Mints and Esoteric Books   107

Chapter 14: Henderson Waxes Lyrical   112

Chapter 15: Bed and Breakfast   119

Chapter 16: The Music Room   128

Chapter 17: No Way Out   138

Chapter 18: It's Séance Time!   146

Part Three: The Very Worst Place to Stay

Chapter 19: Trouble on the Hill   157
Chapter 20: The House Strikes Again   165
Chapter 21: Worse Things Happen at Sea... Don't They? 176
Chapter 22: Looking for Ghosts   184
Chapter 23: Supernatural Intervention   190
Chapter 24: Something Nasty in the Garden   199
Chapter 25: Something Very Nasty in the House   205
Chapter 26: The Power of Music   212
Chapter 27: Taking Flight   223
Chapter 28: The Dragon Wing of Night   229
Chapter 29: The Suspension Bridge of Disbelief   241
Chapter 30: The Wet and the Wounded   248
Chapter 31: A Coffee Shop in Cardiff   252

Acknowledgements   **259**

About the Author   **261**

Dedication

For my parents, Mair & Graham

Who let me read all those weird books
and watch all those weird films

The House that Death Built

Part One

The Most Haunted House in Britain?

Chapter One
The Road Back

Demons?
  Ghouls?
  Zombies?
Something weirder?
Something worse?

Samantha Jephcott sighed as she drove her little Fiat up the slip road and onto the M5 going north. Of course it wasn't unusual for people to dread going back to work after a holiday, nor for them to wonder what might be waiting for them when they got there, but she was pretty certain that no-one had quite the reasons she did for feeling so trepidant.

She pulled into the middle lane to pass a lorry laden with scrap metal, checking her rear view mirror before she did so and glimpsing the city of Bristol as it receded behind her. She slid the car into high gear and pressed the accelerator pedal, letting the car cruise at a decent speed in the empty middle lane of the motorway.

It had been good to see her mother again, and since it had been well over a year since the last visit, Sam had felt it only fair to spend a week there. Especially as Margaret Jephcott lived on her own and had done ever since her second husband, Sam's stepfather, had died five years ago. It had also been fun to spend a bit of leisure time at her old stamping ground; visiting friends and laying genteel waste to at least one watering hole with her old friends from the gymnasium where she used to work.

And yet, while it had been wonderful to see everyone again, she had been dreading their questions, or more specifically the one question that she had known everyone would ask, and the one question she had lost sleep over wondering how best to answer.

"So, what are you doing with yourself now?"

That was how her mum had put it. Her friends had been more specific. "Where are you working now?", "What have you up to since we last saw you?", and of course the rather more direct "So what exactly is your job at the moment?" had all been levelled at her over glasses of white wine and Italian food. And of course she had fielded them all tactfully, giving them answers she hoped they believed. Not that she had lied to anyone, but she had needed to keep certain facts back to avoid the open-mouthed stares of disbelief, the responses along the lines of "Yeah, right; now tell us what you *actually* do"; and worst of all, the thought that her friends might think she was making it up because she was actually involved in some profession that was so horribly embarrassing and unspeakable that rather than admit to it she had resorted to making up the most outlandish, unheard of, unlikely job she could possibly imagine.

But it was true: for the past year she had been working with the only practising investigator of paranormal occurrences in Britain. At least that was what Mr Massene Henderson called himself. In actual fact, he was more like a private investigator; but instead of infidelities and petty crime he kept himself busy looking into cases of demonic possession, vampiric infestation, zombie curses and worse. Despite the fact that there seemed to be a lot of supernatural phenomena that needed such investigation in the country, people on the whole were still very sceptical, and so it had been easier for her to say that she was working with a private detective. Anyone prying further could then be met with either a change of subject or, if they proved to be rather more persistent than Sam was comfortable with, she could simply say that she was not at liberty to discuss any cases, as everything with which she had been involved so far was strictly confidential. Which also happened to be true, and for good reason.

She had tried to be a little more honest with her mum, though, partly because that was only fair, but mainly because Margaret Jephcott had always harboured what might be considered a housewife's interest in the macabre.

"A 'psychic investigator' you say?" she had said, over tea and Garibaldi biscuits on the Sunday afternoon that Sam had arrived.

"No, mum," Sam had replied. "He's a *paranormal* investigator. He's not psychic." She had left out the part about being the psychic member of the pair, as she thought that might be just too much information at this point.

"That must be fascinating," said Mrs Jephcott, refilling her cup from a teapot in the shape of a little house. "Is he on the telly?"

"No, Mum," said Sam, knowing what her mother was getting at. "We investigate actual cases that happen around the country, and try to work out what's going on."

But there was no stopping Mrs Jephcott once she got going, and she had proceeded to produce a battered copy of a TV listings magazine from a magazine rack that Sam thought was placed precariously close to the fireplace. Sam's mum flicked through it until she reached a full page photograph of an artificially tanned man in his early forties with too many teeth in his smile and far too much dye in his short spiky silver hair.

"He's my favourite," she said. "Is your man anything like him?"

To Samantha, Jeremy Stokes, host of the allegedly popular television series *Touching the Beyond* bore as much resemblance to her colleague as Sam felt she probably did to Angelina Jolie. Mr Stokes' short silver hair suffered from an excess of gel, causing it to bristle heavenwards as if in supplication or alternatively making him look as if he was receiving a mild electric shock (and from the rather forced smile on his face Sam could have guessed where they had stuck the electrodes as well). Henderson's wildly unruly hair always seemed to be in need of a trim. Stokes wore all black, whereas Henderson favoured tweeds and velvet smoking jackets in the winter, and an array of brightly coloured boating blazers in summer. Stokes looked like someone who would sell you a used car; Henderson was the sort of person who would probably buy it.

"Not really, Mum," said Sam, handing back the magazine.

"He's very good, you know," said the old lady. "He talks to people's dead relatives and everything — right on the programme!"

"I'm sure he does."

"And he's found lost pets and valued family objects and once there was this girl and she didn't know who her father was but he was there in the audience and he'd been looking for his lost daughter and he... he..."

Tears were welling in Mrs Jephcott's eyes at the memory of this doubtlessly well-staged and thoroughly manipulative event. Still, thought Sam, if it had provided her mother with a bit of entertainment for an afternoon, where was the harm?

"I'm sure he does a good job, Mum," she said, putting down her cup.

Mrs Jephcott dried her eyes before continuing.

"And what sort of things has your Mr Henderson done while you've been with him?" she said, putting the crumpled tissue back in her pocket.

Sam paused. Over the last year the two of them had fought vampires, ghouls, zombie Vikings, and prevented the destruction of the planet at least twice, but that wasn't the sort of thing you told your mother over tea.

"Lots of things, Mum, but I can't really talk about them, if you know what I mean."

That seemed to satisfy her mother, thank goodness. Unfortunately though, it only led her on to the other question Sam didn't really want to answer.

"And is there anyone 'special' in your life?"

"Not right now, Mum." It was best to be honest about that one, or at least as honest with herself as she could be right now. "I'm still looking for Mr Right," she said with the kind of smile that could have easily have led to a dozen Mr Rights pounding on her door. Until, of course, they found out they'd have to put up with the possibility of being killed by whatever God-awful creature she and Henderson might be dealing with at any particular time. It was difficult to find a man who was willing to do that.

A couple of hours later, she was on country roads, the roar of the motorway far behind her. As soon as she had crossed the border from England into Wales it had started to rain, which hadn't surprised her in the least. She often wished that the huge sprawling manor house where Henderson lived wasn't located in the middle of bloody nowhere. When they had first started working together he had asked if she would like to stay there too, explaining that it would be rather impractical for her to live anywhere else and there was so much room that she could have an entire wing to herself if she liked. Having been used to a two-up-two-down on a modern Bristol housing estate with exorbitant rent and only a job she was swiftly tiring of to keep her there, she had dismissed all thoughts of an ulterior motive from her mind and taken the plunge. She smiled to herself as she took the turn for the tiny road that led up to the house. If Henderson had thought she was suspicious of his motives, he would probably have been mortified — and what's more, it would probably have made him change his mind about her working with him — so she was glad she had never brought the subject up, except in jest; and even then he often acted like a startled rabbit when the slightest hint of mild flirting entered the conversation.

The wrought iron gates of the house were open. As Sam drove in she could barely make out, through the pouring rain, the huge gothic building that was now her home. Built partly into the rock of the mountain it backed onto, Henderson had been remarkably non-specific about who had built it or when, preferring to let her find her own way around and settle in her own time.

She parked the car in one of the garages located to the left of the main part of the house, next to an ancient-looking roadster that had apparently last been used to despatch a creature living in the Severn estuary. "I just drove through it!" Henderson had explained cheerfully, while at the same time steering her away from the runic symbols decorating the paintwork with a muttered "I really must get those covered up."

She pulled her bags from the boot and ran round to the front of the building. She usually used the side door, which was much easier to open, but that was located on the other side of the building and it was raining so hard she didn't mind having to put her back into pushing open one of the heavy oak main doors.

The entrance hall was deserted. The door closed behind her with a slam loud enough to wake the dead, but not a soul came to greet her. She sniffed. Henderson might at least have been here to say hello and help her with her bags. No doubt he was preoccupied with something; either a piece of esoteric lore in one of the myriad volumes he kept in the biggest library she had ever seen, or he was mulling over some aspect of a case that still intrigued him. *Either way, he could have bloody been here to give me a hand*, she thought as she squelched up the stairs, rain dripping from her suitcases onto the deep red pile of the carpets.

Sam's room were located in the west wing and it was with infinite relief that she reached her bedroom. She unlocked the door, dropped her suitcases and went to the window to pull across the wooden shutters that would hopefully keep out the draught. As well as the rain, she noted, as she saw a few drops on the inside of one of the mullioned windows.

She had scarcely thrown the bar across to keep the shutters closed when she heard a familiar voice behind her say —

"Fancy a night in a haunted house?"

Chapter Two
An Irresistible Offer?

Sam turned. In her experience, it was often difficult to refuse the piercingly intelligent blue eyes of the man standing in the doorway, that enthusiastic demeanour, that voice filled with the promise of thrilling adventure.

"No," she said.

But then she had had practice. A lot of it.

Henderson waved the piece of paper he was holding in his left hand and nodded vigorously.

"That's just what I thought," he said, "which is why I was delighted to learn that our services shall be required for at least a week. That should give us a really good chance to tell whether or not all the terrible stories about the place are true."

Sam put her hands on her hips and regarded him. His curly brown hair could do with another trim, he still hadn't taken his brown brogues to the menders, and from the look of the envelopes thrust into the hip pocket of his grey herringbone tweed suit jacket, the bills hadn't been paid yet either.

"Don't I at least get a 'Hello'?" she said.

Henderson looked genuinely taken aback. "I'm sorry?" he said.

"Or a 'Welcome Back'?" Despite her best efforts, Sam could feel herself getting annoyed. "I presume you have missed me? Or has my time away merely proven to you that you can deal with things perfectly well on your own?"

Henderson's eyes narrowed slightly as he tried to read Sam's body language. The smile never left his face as he said, "Now don't be a silly girl." He ignored her swiftly darkening expression and continued. "You know very well that over these last two weeks I have missed you more than anyone I have ever known or been acquainted with. In fact some might say I have missed you to an extent that quite possibly hasn't been entirely good for me. I appreciate that being the woman you are you would like to hear me say these things, but seeing as I could tell from the way you smiled at me when you heard my voice that you had obviously missed me as much as I had missed you, I thought we could dispense with the formalities and get back to what we do best."

Sam felt her frown melt into a smile and realised she was completely powerless to do anything about it. Trying hard to sound cross she said,

"How did you know I smiled if my back was to you?"

Henderson pointed over her shoulder.

"Your dressing table mirror," he said, and then, with a little bow and as formally as if he were addressing the Queen he added, "Welcome back, Miss Jephcott. I have missed you. Very, very much indeed."

Sam resisted the urge to both strangle and kiss him and looked at the piece of paper instead.

"A week in a haunted house?" she said.

"Possibly longer," he said, nodding, "or, at least, that's what I'm going to suggest if we decide to take the case. That should give us plenty of opportunity to get a good feel for the place."

Sam turned her back to him and started unpacking. "Or alternatively to be driven insane by whatever bit of nastiness is causing it to be haunted," she said.

"*Bits*," said Henderson, avoiding a knot of Sam's underwear as it was expertly thrown into a laundry basket by the door.

"I beg your pardon?"

"*Bits*," he repeated. "You said 'bit'. I am reliably informed that there may be more than one evil entity inhabiting the place. Quite possibly several."

Sam fished out her wash bag, unzipped it, then figured she would only be packing it again shortly, so she dropped it back into her suitcase. "I do wish you wouldn't sound so enthusiastic when you talk about these things," she said.

"Why?" came the puzzled reply from the door.

"Because," she sighed, wondering if she would have enough time to wash her favourite black velvet top and get it dry before she'd be setting off again, "I have been with you long enough now to know that your enthusiasm is directly proportional to how sure you are that we're going to encounter something really horrible."

"Somethings," Henderson corrected.

"Oh all right then: some *things*." Sam opened a large jewellery box and selected a black Star of David pendant, a pair of tiny gold crucifix earrings, and a brooch in the shape of a jewel-encrusted ankh. You could never be too careful. "I'm starting to get butterflies already."

Henderson waved the piece of paper at her again.

"You're hardly entering into the spirit of this," he said. "We've been invited to the most haunted house in Britain!"

Sam dropped the jewellery into a small, velvet carry bag and threw it into her suitcase. She took a deep breath and when she turned back to face him her expression was one of dismay.

"Oh God, which one is it this time?" she said, now sounding distinctly unimpressed.

"I beg your pardon?"

"Which one? After all, we've been to a few called 'the most haunted house in Britain' haven't we? All of their owners keen to make out that theirs was the most haunted of all. Some of them rather *too* keen, if you'll recall that rather embarrassing incident at Kempdon House."

"Oh, yes," said Henderson, suddenly remembering. Fortunately after the burns had healed and the local hospital's proctology department had discharged him as fit, Lord Kempdon hadn't been too interested in pressing charges on account of the fact that doing so would have necessitated him admitting to a fraudulent operation dating back nearly twenty years. "But the difference with this one is that while all the others may have held claims to be haunted, and been found to be sadly lacking on our part —"

"Sadly for you maybe," Sam interjected.

"Oh you don't really mean that. Anyway, this one probably is."

Sam snatched the letter from him. "And does this terrifying old pile have a name?" she asked.

"Oh yes," said Henderson. "But I guarantee you'll never be able to read it."

Sam stared at the name on the paper. She hated to admit it but he was quite right. "What language is this?" she asked.

Henderson drew himself up to his full five feet nine and a half inches and assumed an air of pride as he looked somewhere beyond her saying, "Welsh."

"So even if we do find a ghost, we're not going to be able to understand what the bloody hell it's going on about anyway," said Sam with a grin.

"Perhaps not. If it talks," said Henderson. "On the other hand it might just chase you down a corridor, its razor sharp talons poised as it finally finds itself on the brink of tearing free the soul it has been seeking for so long."

"You really know how to make a girl want to come away with you, you know?" she said, throwing the letter back at him.

"Well at least you can't complain that I don't make you feel needed," he replied, stuffing the paper into the pocket bulging with envelopes.

"I hope those aren't bills," said Sam. "And don't say Bill doesn't live here; that would not be in the slightest bit funny."

Henderson plucked the sheaf of envelopes from his pocket as if he had only just registered their existence. He paled as he saw a return address.

"You haven't paid them, have you?" said Sam, trying to keep the exasperation out of her voice.

"Oh, they're not bills," Henderson said, reddening. "They're reminders."

"Reminders of what?"

"Of another case that I agreed we would look at, the day you went away. I imagined I'd have plenty of time to tell you about it when you got back, but then the other case arrived and —" He held up his hands as if to say it wasn't his fault. Which of course, it definitely was.

"And what is this 'other case'?" said Sam.

"Oh, just some television person who seems to be having a spot of bother. He didn't want to discuss it over the telephone, so I said we'd pop over to the studios when he was filming for a bit of a chat."

"Why do I get the feeling that the 'bit of a chat' you mention is scheduled for this evening?" said Sam.

"This afternoon, actually," said Henderson, looking at his watch. "In fact, if we leave now we should get there just in time."

Sam sighed as she bade fond farewell to the bath she had been planning to soak in for at least an age. "And the name of the television programme we are going to have the joy of sitting around for hours on end watching being filmed is?"

"Oh you'll never have heard of it," said Henderson, taking her hand and hurrying her down the stairs. "Some utter rubbish to do with mediums."

Sam grabbed her coat from where she had hung it only ten minutes ago. "And do you happen to know the name of this rubbish...?"

Henderson checked he had his keys and locked the door behind them. "I think the chap said it was called *Touching the Beyond*, whatever that is," he said as they got into the car.

Sam spent the rest of the journey telling him all about it.

Chapter Three
"Touching the Beyond"

They were late getting to the television studios, and Henderson's initial attempts at explaining to a particularly unfriendly security officer that they were 'personal guests of Jeremy Stokes' were entirely unsuccessful.

"They all say that, sir," was the response.

"What, *all* of them?" said Henderson, looking shocked.

The guard looked him up and down with an impassive expression.

"Yes, sir; although they're usually a bit older than you, and a lot more female."

"But I have a letter signed by him," said Henderson, reaching into his pocket and producing a white envelope. The guard took it from him and made a cursory display of reading it before handing it back.

"This appears to be an electricity bill, sir," he said, his expression altering not one jot. "One that needs to be paid by today or you are going to be disconnected."

Henderson tried again, ending up this time with the gas bill. Finally he found the right letter, only for the guard to view it with equal disdain.

"It's typed," the man said.

"Of course it's typed," said Henderson. "What else do you think Mr Stokes would use? Besides, he's signed his name at the bottom."

The security man shook his head. "We get a lot of fakers here, sir. Imposters. Individuals claiming that Mr Stokes has 'contacted' them and made them type a letter allowing them into the studio to see him. Like I said, sir, they're usually ladies, and they usually do a much better job of forging his signature."

Henderson peered at the shaking scrawl at the bottom of the note.

"Well I agree Mr Stokes' handwriting leaves a bit to be desired," he said. "But as I *am* a paranormal investigator and he wouldn't have been writing to me unless he had some kind of problem he wanted me to attend to, and it's quite possible that he was scared when he was writing it."

The guard peered at him again.

"Paranormal investigator, sir?"

Henderson nodded and reached into his pocket to produce a card which turned out to be for a florist's.

"What have you got that for?" Sam asked as he put it away.

"Oh, I was planning to get you some for when you came back, but I forgot," he said with a wry smile. "Sorry."

"Oh that's all right," said Sam. "It was a lovely thought." She turned to the security guard. "Look, I'm terribly sorry we're late. Perhaps a message could be left for Mr Stokes and we could see him after the show?"

The guard made an exaggerated show of radioing through; probably, thought Sam, because he didn't get the chance to do it very often. The man seemed genuinely surprised by the response.

"Well I have to admit, you didn't look like stalkers," he said once the voice on his earpiece had finished talking. "All right, you're to go in. But be quiet; they're taping."

§ § §

Henderson and Sam found themselves squeezed into the back row of the audience next to a blue-haired old lady called Esme who wasn't too happy about having to move further along. Henderson sat next to her and did his very best to be charming. He even promised to look after her if things got too scary, but she only paid him any attention when he said he was there to see Jeremy Stokes after the show. After that her mood improved considerably and she actually became quite chatty, although this abruptly stopped once Henderson explained that no, she wouldn't be able to accompany him backstage.

Contrary to what they had been told, the taping hadn't started yet and the members of the audience — who as far as Sam could tell seemed to be made up mainly of clones of her own mother — were chatting excitedly amongst themselves. The stage was shielded by an immense pair of silver curtains. Sam had assumed there would at least have been some sort of 'warm-up act', but from the way Jeremy Stokes' audience was already behaving, she wondered if perhaps a 'calming-down act' might be more appropriate to reduce the risk of heart attacks.

However, it wasn't long before the lights went down, the signs were illuminated for 'AUDIENCE QUIET' and a voice that seemed to come from somewhere high above them announced, with all the portent of the Second Coming, "Ladies and Gentlemen: welcome to Touching the Beyond!" After this the majestic tones altered to something altogether more hushed and respectful to announce "And now, the man who is going to guide you there: Mr Jeremy Stokes."

The curtains parted to reveal the man himself, standing at the top of a flight of white steps, wearing a matching suit, shirt and tie, and looking for all the world like a cross between an evangelist and a game show host. As he descended the steps, Sam thought the only thing whiter than his suit were his teeth, which seemed to reflect the stage lights almost as much as the subtly reflective contact lenses she was sure he must have had in. The indicator lights out of view of the cameras were telling the audience to applaud but now, instead of the raucous behaviour of before, the clapping that greeted his entrance was restrained and respectful.

"Thank you, my friends," said Jeremy to the now well-behaved crowd as Sam tried hard to see how many elderly ladies were already finding it all far too much to be finally seeing their idol in the flesh. "And a very special hello to all of you at home as well," he said to camera and therefore to Sam's mum. Sam wondered if perhaps she should ask him if he had any spare tickets going, as he began his introductory patter.

"My friends, we are all of us on a journey. I am. You are," he pointed at an grey-haired lady in the front row who tittered and squirmed. "So are you," a large lady three rows back who seemed to melt into her chair. "You are too," he said, pointing to a birdlike austere-looking lady on the end of a row who, when he raised his finger in her direction, looked as if she was about to burst into tears. "Yes, my friends, a very personal journey, for each and every one of us. A journey filled with hills to climb and hardships to overcome. But also moments that fill our hearts with joy, moments that we treasure and return to when we need help to get us through times of hardship."

"He certainly knows how to control a crowd," Henderson whispered to Samantha.

"Manipulate, more like," Sam replied.

"Will you two be quiet!" Esme said, as Stokes continued.

"But, my friends, that journey does not end when life ends. Today, in this studio, my sincere desire is to prove that to you all, and along the way provide a chosen few of you with some more of those special moments of joy to treasure as you walk the rocky road that is our time on this planet."

"Reminds me of P.T. Barnum," whispered Henderson.

"Or that evangelist bloke: Billy Graham," said Sam.

"True," came the reply. "Mind you, he's in his nineties now so who are we to say he might not have a point?"

"If you two don't shut up, I'm calling the security man," said Esme, more loudly than she intended and earning a black look from the blue-haired lady sitting in front of her. She returned the look with the practiced glare of someone who has served fifteen years on a local village church flower committee, folded her arms and returned her attention to the stage.

Stokes had now moved on from his introduction and was beginning the first of his 'readings'. "I can feel this room bursting with spirits eager to contact people here tonight," he said. "In fact, this chamber is so replete with friendly faces that I almost wonder if there might not be a spiritual contact for everyone here this evening."

There was a collective intake of breath from the audience.

"Wonderful way to include everyone," said Henderson.

"Or just to keep their attention," said Sam.

"But, dear ladies and gentlemen, I have delayed things long enough." The lights went down and a single spotlight focused on Stokes centre stage, as he closed his eyes and began to massage his temples. "The first spirit tonight is a man. He's got a little bit of grey hair. Sometimes wears glasses, and his name begins with either an N or an M." More hands than Sam could immediately count went into the air. "Actually it's an M," said Stokes. Half the hands went down, most of them reluctantly. "Probably a Michael." That felled the remainder by just over a half, still leaving ten hands in the air. "A Michael who passed away recently." Three hands.

"In the last week." Two hands. "In an accident." One chubby female hand was slowly lowered — seeming to almost bunch itself into a fist as it did so — leaving a final frail elderly arm still in the air.

Stokes opened his eyes and gave the little old lady sitting on the far right of the auditorium a warm smile as he called her up to the stage.

"More time wasting," said Sam.

"But the audience are loving it," said Henderson. "It's amazing how you can give people what they think is their money's worth without actually doing very much."

Once the woman singled out by Stokes had finally been helped onto the stage, he asked her name.

"Ada," she said in a voice quivering with nerves. "Ada Jenkins."

"And Ada, how old was Michael when he was taken from you?"

"Eighty-three," she sniffed. "He'd had a good life, really."

"And he's still having a good life now," said Jeremy. "A good after-life." Sam winced at that. "And he wants you to know that he's very, very happy; and that he's waiting for you in a place filled with flowers and lovely memories; and when you're reunited you'll both be remembering them together as well as creating new ones."

"Really?" The old lady's grip was so tight that Sam could spot Jeremy wincing, even if no-one else could.

"Oh yes," said Jeremy with a smile. "So you mustn't be afraid when your time comes. Just remember that your Michael is waiting for you." He produced a white handkerchief with a repeating 'J' motif woven into the silk for her to dry her eyes. "Now don't you worry about a thing. Go and sit back down and enjoy the rest of the show." He turned back to the audience as Ada was led away. "A big hand please for lovely Ada!"

The audience responded wholeheartedly. Over the next forty minutes Stokes essentially reproduced the same act with only minor variations, but his audience never seemed to tire of it.

"I'd get bored doing that," Sam whispered to Henderson as the show neared its end.

"That's why you spend your time with me fighting horrible things," was the reply.

"More like running away than fighting," she said with a giggle. "At least that's what it feels like half the time." She ignored Esme's black looks and crossed her fingers that Stokes' summing up patter on stage was signalling the end of the programme.

"Finally," he was saying, "before I leave you, I have one more message." Stokes closed his eyes once more and pinched the bridge of his nose with his right thumb and forefinger in the most deliberate and theatrical way possible.

"I've really had enough of this," said Sam, starting to fidget.

"We can't leave now!" said Henderson. "We'll miss his last message."

"It'll be about donations to his 'worthy cause'," said Sam.

But it wasn't.

"I have a message for..." said Stokes opening his eyes and looking to the far back to the auditorium. "Mrs Esme Cannon."

The lady sitting next to Henderson leapt to her feet with such unnatural vigour Sam swore she could hear her bones creak.

"Is it about my sister Mary?" she said. "Oh, Mr Stokes, I miss her so much. Is she happy?"

"Mary is very happy, Esme, very happy indeed," said Stokes. "But this message isn't about her."

"Who, then?"

There was a pause, during which Stokes' entire face seemed to change. Gone was the calculated expression of the professional television presenter, and in its place was something more innocent, more honest. "This is about Derek," he said. Sam frowned while Henderson leaned forward with interest. Even Stokes' voice seemed different, somehow more sincere and yet also nervous. For a moment Sam almost believed him.

"My husband?" said the old lady. "But he's not dead. I've left him watching *Countdown*."

"No, he's not dead," said Stokes. "But treasure him while you can." Then, within the blink of an eye, he was back to the professional television psychic routine, holding his arms out wide as if to embrace his audience, both in the theatre and over the airwaves. "All of you," he said "treasure those loved ones of yours who are still with you. They need you more than the spirits of the beyond. And now, until the next time, farewell!"

There was a puff of smoke littered with silver glitter and an exaggerated musical chord, as Jeremy presumably disappeared through a trap door in the stage.

"Utter crap," murmured Sam.

Henderson was already getting to his feet to avoid the rush. "Come on," he said. "It's against my principles to push ahead of ladies, so if we don't get to his dressing room now, we may have to wait all night."

Chapter Four
Meeting Mr Stokes

It turned out that they didn't have to wait at all. A well-dressed middle-aged woman with shoulder length black-brown hair and wearing a navy trouser suit met them as they were leaving the auditorium and introduced herself as Mags Parkin.

"I'm Jeremy's agent," she said. As she was shaking Henderson's hand Sam noticed the woman had far too many rings on her fingers. "To be honest, I can't say I agree with him seeing you, but he wouldn't listen to me. I think he needs to see a proper psychiatrist."

"Oh I'm not a pretend psychiatrist," said Henderson as they were led backstage. "I'm —"

"I know who you are, Mr Henderson," said Mags as they bypassed the queue of autograph hunters, "or rather *what* you are. Let's keep any further conversation until we get to where we're going, shall we?"

Sam and Henderson exchanged weary glances as their route took a discreet left turn between a couple of security guards and away from the overexcited crowd, down a narrow flight of stone steps, and along a musty-smelling, airless corridor lit by fluorescent strip lights. Mags knocked on the last door on the left and waited only seconds for a reply before going in anyway. She beckoned for Henderson and Sam to follow.

The dressing room was almost bare, yet it still felt cramped; especially now there were four people in it. Jeremy Stokes was sitting in a battered armchair in the far corner. As soon as they came in he got to his feet, the glass of milk in his hand looking jaundiced next to the brilliance of his suit, the jacket of which he had discarded.

"Mr Henderson! Miss Jephcott! I'm so glad you came!" He shook both their hands and offered them a drink, which they politely declined as they squeezed themselves onto the tiny sofa adjacent to the door. Mags stayed standing. Sam took out her notebook with some difficulty, while Henderson asked what it was Stokes felt they could do for him.

"Did you see the show tonight?" he asked.

Sam was about to say something, but Henderson got in first. "We did, Mr Stokes. I can't say it's the kind of entertainment I usually watch, but then I don't make a habit of watching television. I must say, however, that it all looked very professionally executed."

"You're not a believer, then?" said Mags from across the room.

Sam gave her a piercing look and was about to say something rude when Henderson prevented it. "I find it odd that you should ask that question, considering what you said to me in the corridor," he said. "What is it *exactly* that you think I do?"

"Your card says 'Paranormal Investigator'," said Mags. "But that could mean anything. I was the agent for a couple of them in the late nineties and neither would have recognised a real ghost if it had come up and bitten them on the arse."

"Well we've dealt with plenty," said Sam, obviously having trouble containing herself as she looked to her colleague. "Can *you* remember when our last arse-biting case was?"

Henderson tried laughing but when that didn't lighten Mags' dark expression he added, "We haven't actually dealt with any 'arse-biting cases' yet, Miss Parkin." He looked from an irritated-looking Sam to a worried-looking Jeremy and asked in a very serious voice. "Is that the problem you have here?"

Mags gave Henderson the look of someone who has no sense of humour whatsoever, prompting Jeremy to intervene.

"What Mags meant, Mr Henderson," he said, "was: do you believe in what I do? In the ability of an individual to contact the dead and communicate message from the beyond?"

"Oh yes," said Henderson. Mags and Jeremy visibly relaxed, only for them to tense again almost immediately when he added "I don't believe *you* can, though. The medium I use for most of that sort of thing is called Greta. Lovely little lady from Hungary who lives in the village at the bottom of the hill near my house. She's very good. She's also much like other mediums I've met: a shell of her former self, because of the ability she cannot help but channel whether she wants to or not, and over which she has little control. In return for her occasional help, I have been trying to heal her a little from the more deleterious effects of contacting the afterlife, which are many and which you, Mr Stokes, do not seem to display any of, despite your having been in your chosen profession for sufficient years that you should now be a shambling wreck. So, therefore, I would be very grateful if you would stop wasting our mutual time and tell us precisely why we are here."

Jeremy had been sinking lower and lower in his chair while Henderson had been talking. Now the detective had come to a pause, he took a final swig of his milk and looked at Mags, who nodded.

"Of course you're right, Mr Henderson," he said, looking sheepish. "I can't contact the dead. I never have been able to, but I like to think I offer comfort to those who need it, and Heaven knows there are enough of them around."

"I would imagine if Heaven knows about you, Mr Stokes, you probably won't be going there anytime soon," said Sam, visibly prickling.

Judging from Stokes' reaction to Sam's comment this obviously stung. "Do you really think so, Miss Jephcott? Do you really think that making elderly people smile and feel comforted is really such a terrible thing to do? Because I don't. And if it's a choice between doing this and stacking supermarket shelves, I think I'm actually doing more good *here*."

"But what exactly is your problem?" said Henderson.

Stokes returned Sam's ambivalent look before answering the question. "Mr Henderson, I freely confess that my television programme is based on cold readings and a television presence that seems to be what the general public want." He looked at Mags. "My problem is that for some time now I seem to have actually developed some kind of psychic ability. I have to confess, just as you implied, that it is starting to drive me crazy."

"Well you've been doing a very good job of covering it up," said Henderson, now sounding more sympathetic. "What form does this ability take?"

"To be honest, it might even be a curse or some kind of divine punishment, considering the kind of audience I usually have," said Stokes. He paused for a moment. "You see, Mr Henderson," he said finally, "I seem to have acquired the ability to predict when people are going to die."

"What, *everyone*?" said Sam.

"No," said Stokes, "only some people, and only if they're going to die in the next fortnight or so. But you can imagine that in one of my shows there's always someone who falls into that category."

Henderson leaned forward, obviously interested. "And what do you do?"

"The same thing I've always done," said Stokes. "Try to give them comfort and reassurance. After all, now I'm dealing with people who are really going to need it. You remember Ada, that first lady I picked from the audience; the one who I told her husband is waiting for her?" Henderson nodded. "Well she's going to die of a heart attack this Friday," he said. "I didn't tell her that, of course, partly because it wouldn't make good television, but mainly because I don't like upsetting people."

"No," said Sam, still very much unimpressed. "You prefer to make money off people's misery and false hope."

"I used to," said Stokes with an apologetic shrug. "I used to and didn't give it a second thought. I justified it by telling myself I was comforting the audience members I chose, while at the same time entertaining the viewers at home. I do have a lot of viewers and," he said in an aside to Henderson, "as a rather pleasant side effect making quite a lot of money in the process. But how this thing has happened, I have no idea. All I do know is that I need help or I'm going to go insane."

"How long has it been going on?" Henderson asked.

Stokes leaned back in his chair

"I've never been able to do any of that contacting the dead stuff, but about a six months ago I walked into the studio, faced the audience, and realised I knew the future of the woman sitting three rows back. I knew she would be visiting the grave of her dead husband on the weekend. I could even read the words on the gravestone."

"And you told her?"

"I told her what I could read. For the first time in my entire life I wasn't guessing. I knew when he had been born, when he had died and that he was a 'beloved father', so I took a guess on her having at least one son and I was right."

"But you can only see about two weeks into the future?" said Sam.

"It varies," was the reply, "and along with that variance I also don't have any control over whose future I get to see." He paused and looked at the stained red carpet tiles. "But there is one thing they all have in common."

"They're all going to die," said Henderson, his face grim.

"Exactly," Stokes looked at the two of them, his face a mask of desperation, "I don't know what to do or why it's started happening, but I need it to stop or the next future I'll be seeing will be my own."

Henderson asked him if anything special had happened to him six months ago, but Stokes shook his head. "You didn't visit anywhere unusual?" Henderson persisted. "Or buy or take something, a curio or collectible, that caught your eye?"

"Nothing," said Stokes. "Believe me, once I realised what was happening, any doubts I might have had about the paranormal vanished. I've gone over and over all my actions in the couple of weeks leading up to this change, but I can't remember doing anything out of the ordinary. I wish I could."

"Well, that does make it rather more difficult," said Henderson, scratching his head. "And unfortunately we do have another rather pressing case that is probably going to occupy us for the next couple of weeks. On the other hand, it will give me a chance to think the problem over. I'd suggest you take a break from making your programme, though; it doesn't seem to be doing you any good at all."

"He's had to keep going until now because of contractual obligation," said Mags. "But that's okay: today was the last one, which is why he was so keen for you to be in the audience."

"What are you going to do now?" asked Sam.

"Get myself as far away from people as possible until I hear from you again," said Stokes. "But I would ask you not to take too long; and I'm being serious when I say that money's no object. I know it's not the most reputable of professions, but I have made a lot of money out of what I've been doing, and if you can cure me I promise I'll be able to make it worth your while."

Mags showed them out, while Stokes readied himself for an autograph signing session.

"I do hope you'll be able to help him," she said as she pulled open an exit door that led onto a side street. "He really isn't himself anymore."

"You mean he isn't quite the meal ticket he once was," said Sam before she had a chance to bite her tongue.

The older woman scowled. "We all have to make a living, Miss Jephcott," she said.

"Do you believe he's begun to see how people will die?" said Henderson, giving Sam a reproachful look which was ignored.

"It's not important what I believe, Mr Henderson," Mags said. "I'm a businesswoman. If he was a magician and spent his days turning children into Afghan hounds, it wouldn't matter to me whether he could really do it or not, as long as it turned a profit. Just make him better and we'll all be able to do well out of it."

She shut the door with a clang, leaving the two of them standing in the street.

"I think it's going to rain," Sam said, looking up.

"Nonsense," said Henderson, looking up at the blobs of cloud gathering in the otherwise blue sky.

They looked about them to get their bearings. "You weren't very nice to her," he added as they realised they had no idea which side of the television studio they were on.

"Not my sort of people I'm afraid," said Sam. "Not him and most *definitely* not her. Sorry, but I did do my best to rein it in."

"Yes, I noticed that, well done," he replied, spying the clock tower they had passed on the way there and guiding her towards it. "I'm afraid I'm going to have to ask for your promise to behave yourself at the meeting I've scheduled with Sir Anthony tomorrow."

"Sir Anthony who?" said Sam, leaping back as Henderson did his best to lead her straight into oncoming traffic. They both ignored the beeping of horns.

"Sir Anthony Calverton," he replied.

Sam looked blank.

"The exceedingly wealthy industrialist?" he prompted.

Nothing.

"I suppose you're going to tell me he owns the most haunted house in Britain," she shouted above a crack of thunder, as they finally found a crossing and Henderson pushed the button.

"As a matter of fact he's just bought it," he said, as the red man turned to green and the sky turned from blue to black.

Chapter Five-
An Audience with Sir Anthony

"You didn't tell me you would be bringing a woman."
Sir Anthony Calverton must have been close to eighty years old, and while his three-piece pinstripe suit had no doubt been made to measure, the way it hung on his bony form made Sam wonder if the measurements had been taken from somebody else. His head resembled a dried turnip whose sagging skin was trying desperately to stay attached to the desiccated flesh beneath. *An upside-down turnip, in fact*, she thought, with the few wiry hairs that crowned his yellowing pate looking like rather sad examples of roots. He coughed, sipped at the whiskey that, at ten o'clock in the morning, was presumably brunch rather than breakfast, and repeated his statement while at the same time regarding Henderson with eyes that were as alert as the detective's.

"I think you'll find I did," said Henderson, tapping the document on top of which Calverton had now rested his whisky, "just as I very much suspect you already knew that Miss Jephcott was my assistant."

"Oh I knew that," the elderly man spat, shifting in his wingback leather armchair and making a noise which Sam hoped was just the leather creaking.

If it wasn't, there was no-one else to object. At that time of the morning the lounge in which the conversation was taking place was empty save for a young waiter dressed immaculately in the club's green waistcoat, red tie and white shirt who came in to check from time to time to see if they needed anything.

"The Welsh flag," Sir Anthony had rasped, as Sam had gratefully accepted a cup of coffee on their arrival.

"I beg your pardon?" she had said.

Sir Anthony had gestured to the swiftly exiting waiter. "The colours they're dressed in. To emulate the Welsh flag." Then he had leaned forward and peered at her. "You do know what the Welsh flag looks like, don't you?"

"Of course she does," Henderson had interrupted, in case Sam was going to say she didn't just to see what sort of an effect it would have on their prospective employer. Sir Anthony hadn't appeared convinced and he had expressed surprise at Sam's presence probably just to be annoying while she had done her best to ignore this silly old (but obviously very rich) man and instead gaze at the opulent surroundings in which they had found themselves.

The Cardiff branch of the Diverticulum Club (or *Clwb Diverticulum* to its Welsh speaking members) was located in the middle of the city, close to the castle. After getting off the train and taking an improbable detour through several of the shopping arcades off St Mary Street they had finally arrived at their rather innocuous-looking destination. Between an antiquarian bookshop that was closed despite it being the middle of the week, and a designer shop that seemed to specialise in selling one single type of silver shoe, was a white-painted six-panelled Edwardian door with an ornate brass plaque to its left and a bell pull to its right. A confident tug from Henderson had summoned a severe looking man dressed in red and green who had led them through into the members' lounge, which was where they were now sitting and where, Sam observed, Sir Anthony now seemed to be attempting some sort of character assassination of the two of them.

"What kind of a name is Massene, anyway?" he barked, having taken the file from his drinks table and flipped it open to peruse Henderson's CV. He pronounced it in three different and increasingly creative ways before allowing Henderson to reply.

The detective did his best to look mock offended but Sam knew his feelings ran deeper than that. "Don't ask me," he said. "I'm not the one who gave it to me. Even I don't know how it should properly be pronounced. It's not a name that's used much."

"Certainly not by you, eh?"

"Oh, you know," said Henderson, ignoring the old man's cackling. "My parents were never around much and, of course, once I started school I was never referred to by anything other than my surname; as were all the boys. So over the years I've almost forgotten I have a Christian name. Certainly it's not something I encourage the use of."

"Not one for familiarity, I suppose?" Sir Anthony gave a little cackle and rocked back and forth slightly. "Good! If it's one thing I can't stand it's all this friendly touchy-feely let's-all-call-each-other-by-our-first-names nonsense. I mean," he said gesturing around him, "do you think this magnificent building was constructed by the kind of people who gave each other a group hug?"

No, thought Sam, *but they might have got up to other things at the end of the working day.*

"What are you smirking at, young lady?"

Sam suddenly felt very small and very young under the older man's gaze.

"Nothing," she said, shocked that she was having to fight to suppress the desire to say "Sir". Even at his age, Sir Anthony was still sharp, and she made a mental note to keep her thoughts to herself.

"Good," was the reply as the old man turned his attention back to Henderson. "You say you're an investigator of paranormal occurrences."

"The only one in the country," said Henderson with pride, "as far as I am aware."

"What about all those johnnies on the television?"

"Not quite the same thing. They look at often unsubstantiated and unproven phenomena for the sake of entertainment. I, on the other hand, tend to require at least some evidence of supernatural involvement in a case before my interest is piqued."

"You may not be interested in this case, then," said Sir Anthony, reaching under a chair and producing a heavy manila document.

"I didn't say that," Henderson replied, eyeing the bulging file with trepidation.

"But you've all but implied it," said Sir Anthony

"I prefer to make up my own mind whether I wish to take a case," said the detective, reaching for the file.

Sir Anthony snatched it back.

"Oh, for Heavens' sake behave yourselves, both of you!"

The two men turned to Sam, feigning expressions of shock at her outburst.

"Miss Jephcott." Sir Anthony turned his attention back to the file that had been put together for him about them. "Miss Samantha Jephcott. The two of you met at a gymnasium, I believe?" They nodded. "Where you Mr Henderson were employed on a case in which as far as I can see absolutely nothing happened."

"Ah, but it would have if I hadn't been employed," said Henderson. "You see, the spirits of three witches were murdering the staff."

Sir Anthony turned over several pages of foolscap.

"I see no records of death here," he said.

"That's because we were able to reverse time and stop everything before it happened," said Sam.

"Absolutely," added her colleague. "In fact the only person who should have been able to remember what actually happened is myself but Miss Jephcott here exhibited such tremendous powers of recall that I was convinced that she must have some degree of psychic power herself, which indeed she does and that is why I have kept her on as my associate."

Sir Anthony didn't look at all convinced. He withdrew a stapled sheaf of papers and waved it at them. "Then there's the case of a man who doesn't live too far from here." He showed them a photograph of a battered musical instrument. "I understand you smashed up his daughter's grand piano?"

"A soul sucker," said Sam. Sir Anthony raised his eyebrows.

"I beg your pardon?"

Henderson did his best to explain.

"The instrument was possessed by a soul sucker," he said. "They hide inside objects that can produce strong emotions in an individual, and when things all get a bit intense they jump out and eat you. I found one inside a copy of *Wuthering Heights* once."

"And did anyone else, other than the two of you, see this 'soul sucker'?" asked Sir Anthony. They shook their heads. "And in fact all the Truscott family found the next day when they returned to their home was their piano gutted of its wires and the lid nailed shut?"

"I do find it best to keep the general public out of the way when dealing with a case," said Henderson, starting to sound annoyed. "At best they only get in the way and at worst they get turned against us."

"Yes, well, in that case I'm not even going to ask about your involvement in all that trouble at St Joseph's Cathedral last year, or that business in Bristol with the meteorite buried in the Severn estuary that drove people mad."

"All sorted out now, I think you'll find," said Henderson with a look of smug satisfaction on his face.

"Yes, well, you seem to believe what you're doing, even if no-one else does." Sir Anthony sniffed, put down their file and picked up the document he had teased Henderson with the offer of before. "But as I said, if you need some sort of proof before you're willing to take on a case, I'm not sure if I'm going to be able to interest you with this, which is a shame. You're the only people I've met so far who profess an interest in the paranormal, don't dress as if you live under a bridge, and are also capable of maintaining a semi-coherent conversation."

"Perhaps," said Sam, realising that the situation called for her absolute charming best, "if we might be told a little about what you were thinking of employing us to do, we might be able to tell you whether or not the case would suit us?"

For the first time since they had met him, the old man smiled and Sam could see a vestige of how charming he must have been when he was a younger man.

"Very well, my dear," he said, "but only because I like your face." He put the files away, emptied his glass and rang for the waiter to fetch him another. He offered Sam and Henderson one as well, but they both declined. "Are you sure?" he said. "this is going to take a little while to tell."

"Then it's all the more important that all our faculties are at their most acute to absorb what you are going to say," said Henderson.

That made the old man nod in agreement.

"Well at least you've got the right idea about how to go about a job of work, I'll give you that," he said, making himself comfortable. He waited until his drink had been served before he began. "It's all to do with a house I have acquired," he said.

"Haunted?" said Henderson.

"How on earth should I know?" snapped Sir Anthony. "That's partly what I want you to find out. But you're causing me to get ahead of myself, so if you would kindly keep quiet, I will tell you a little bit about it." His eyes glittered and Sam could tell even before he started that there was something terribly wrong; that for some reason Sir Anthony Calverton, magnate of industry, was extremely worried, perhaps even terrified. And now he was going to tell them everything he knew about it.

"That terrible place...." he began.

Chapter Six
The Old Dark House

"It was built," Sir Anthony said as the two of them sat listening, "by someone who didn't believe in the supernatural. But he wanted to, by God he wanted to. Not that he had appreciated the full ramifications of what he was in store for, if the supernatural really existed."

"Does this place have a name?" said Henderson as Sam flipped open a notebook.

"Oh it's had many names over the years," Sir Anthony said, leaning forward. "But the locals in the nearby village still call it *Y Maenor Tywyll*, or in English —"

" 'The Dark Manor'," said Henderson, starting to look interested.

"You've heard of it?" said the old man, visibly annoyed that he had been interrupted again.

"To be honest, Sir Anthony," said Sam with her best situation-defusing smile, "Mr Henderson would hardly be the man to investigate your haunted house if he *hadn't* already heard of it, would he?"

"But only as a myth, a legend," said Henderson, "something whispered in pubs all over Wales, or mentioned in hushed tones over Welsh cakes in tea shops. I don't even know where it is."

"Do you know Monmouth?" said the old man. Henderson nodded. "Do you know the back road that takes you to Raglan?"

"Not the A40, then?" said Henderson as Sam scribbled.

"No, of course not," Sir Anthony snapped. "Since when was a dual carriageway with a service station a 'back road'? No, I'm talking about the road that winds through the countryside until you get to a place that I will have to write down for you. Then you turn left and drive for about a mile and a half until you see an overgrown gateway on your right. If you go through there you'll soon find yourself at 'The Meadow of the Grave'."

"That's what it's called?" said Sam.

"In English," said Sir Anthony, "the actual Welsh name is *Yr Ynysyrwyddfa* but that's a close enough translation and probably easier for you to spell."

Henderson shot a glance at Sam to warn her off saying anything.

"So, you've told us where it is," he said. "When was it built?"

"Nineteen hundred and forty one. Amazing, isn't it, that a house only seventy years old should become the most wretched, evil, haunted house in Britain. Of course, one shouldn't be surprised seeing as that was the intention of the man who built it."

"He deliberately built a haunted house?" said Sam

"Oh yes, young lady. He began by choosing the site very carefully and decided that a stone circle would be the best place to build it. He even used the stones themselves in the building's construction."

Henderson raised a hand to pause the old man.

"I'm sorry to interrupt you again, Sir Anthony, but who exactly are we talking about here?"

Sir Anthony drained his glass and called for another before continuing.

"His name was William Marx and he was a very, very rich man. Quite how he came by his fortune is a matter for some conjecture; but before the outbreak of the war he had never been heard of, and a couple of years into it he was one of the richest men in Britain, so it is assumed that his acquired fortune probably had something to do with the arms business. Which, in a way, was also his undoing."

"How do you mean?"

"William Marx lived in Bristol with his wife Sally and their three year old daughter Jessica. On the night of June 19th 1940 he was away when bombings occurred over Avonmouth and to the north at Filton."

Sam looked up from her notebook.

"...and Sally and Jessica were killed?" she said.

Sir Anthony nodded. "Exactly, Miss Jephcott. Exactly. And when Mr Marx was informed of their demise, he went mad with grief; mad enough that he left his business concerns to run themselves and took himself off to God knows where with the sole intention of finding a means of contacting his dead wife and his dead child again. He tried everything: every piece of advice he was given, every scrap of information he could glean from books, but nothing worked."

"By 'everything'," said Henderson, "I presume you mean mediums, séances, card readings —"

Sir Anthony waved a hand to stop yet another interruption.

"I mean *everything*, Mr Henderson, such that in the following year he had decided that the only way to contact the spirit world was to bring the spirit world to him and make damned sure they bloody well listened."

"So he built a house on the site of a stone circle," said Henderson. "It's been done before, you know."

"Oh no it hasn't, Mr Henderson, and to prevent this discussion from degenerating into some sort of pantomime, I tell you it had never been done on this scale before. He built the house on a stone circle and used the stones in the foundations, yes, but that wasn't enough. He became convinced that everything the house was built from needed to be saturated with psychic power, which therefore meant..."

"...all the building materials had to have been exposed to evil?" said Sam, trying to keep the tremor out of her voice.

"Strange isn't it, that evil should be thought to infuse itself into objects and items far more than good? But that appears to be the way it is, or at least that was the way William Marx saw it. And so, for the walls he took the bricks from Dorringborough Asylum two hundred miles away."

"Didn't they need them?" said Sam.

"Dorringborough was closed down in 1935 for 'severe and savage mistreatment of its inmates'," said Henderson.

"Oh you *do* know your stuff," said Sir Anthony. "Perhaps I have the right man after all. Yes, he took the bricks from the asylum, then for windows he paid an inordinate sum to have some imported from a seventeenth century French monastery where local girls were apparently taken and afterwards were never the same again."

"You mean violated," said Sam, aware that Sir Anthony was pulling his punches for her benefit, and wasn't in the least impressed by his behaviour.

"Seeing as you asked, my dear, I mean violated *repeatedly*. After each amputation, if you must know.

"Once the building was complete, he made sure every room was laid with rugs and carpets woven by slaves who had been beaten and castrated before being put to work at the looms. Not exactly 'fair trade', if you get my drift. Anyway that's the way it went. He even had a children's nursery on the first floor filled with toys that had caused the deaths of little boys and girls: a skipping rope that had got wound round some unfortunate little fellow's neck, a jigsaw where one of the pieces had caused some little kiddiewink to choke to death; that sort of thing. Then, once everything was in place, William Marx sat in the great library — in a chair allegedly upholstered in the skin of maidens from the West Indies — and waited."

There was a pause before Sam asked. "What for?"

"To receive a sign," said Sir Anthony. "To learn — in some shape or form — that the supernatural existed, that it could be contacted, that he could interact with it. For in so doing, he might be able to communicate with his dead wife and daughter, or at least know that they might all be reunited in the afterlife."

"Well it makes a change from just going to church and hoping," said Henderson. "So what happened?"

"I have no idea," said Sir Anthony. "No-one does. William Marx disappeared and unfortunately," he threw a weathered leather journal at the detective, "that's pretty much where his diary ends."

"How did you get that?" said Sam

"It had been lodged with his solicitors to be delivered into the hands of whomsoever purchased the property," said Sir Anthony. "Which would be me."

"How did *they* get hold of it?" said Henderson, opening the cover and catching several loose leaves as they tried to escape.

"One presumes he posted it to them before he commenced his vigil in his house of horrors," said Sir Anthony. "One also presumes such an act implied he was not planning on coming back."

"Presumably not." Henderson cautiously laid the volume beside his chair, half-expecting it to start crawling away if he took his eyes from it.

"I used to be like that with it as well," said the old man, gesturing at the book. "Despicable bloody thing. Reminded me of a dried out slug. I used to come home sometimes and I would swear the damned thing had moved during the day."

"Why did you buy the house?" said Sam.

"Oh, curiosity, mainly," was the reply. "You see, since Mr Marx disappeared, there have been a number of curious occurrences either in or close to that house. Some no doubt are hearsay, but others have the verification of the local constabulary. When I bought it a couple of years ago the place had fallen into ruin, but strangely enough odd things didn't start to happen again until I'd had the place tidied up. Perhaps the ghosts can't stand mess."

"You believe in them, then?"

"That's your job young man: to tell me whether I should believe or not. I am a lifelong cynic with two deceased ex-wives and the thought of them waiting for me on some nether plane of astral existence fills me with a horror far more unspeakable than whatever might be waiting for you in that house. But forewarned is forearmed as they say, so if you can prove to me that the Dark Manor really is haunted, I can at least make some preparations before I head for the grave. Do we have a deal?"

"Of course," said Henderson, barely able to contain his enthusiasm.

"Er... not until we've discussed the little matter of our fee?" said Sam, tearing a sheet from her notebook on which she had written a figure she thought reasonable for what might be the most horrendous job of work they had yet taken on. She handed it to Sir Anthony, who took one look at it before crushing the notepaper with one withered claw.

"Ridiculous," he said.

"I'm sure my colleague was overestimating," said Henderson, flashing Sam a scowl which she immediately returned with twice the vehemence, "perhaps if we could discuss —"

"If you really *are* going to charge me such a paltry sum," the old man continued, "perhaps you aren't quite the experts I had been led to believe."

"That's the deposit," Sam chipped in before Henderson had a chance to say anything. "Ten per cent now and the rest when we deliver our results."

Sir Anthony raised his eyebrows.

"Ten per cent, young lady?" he said.

Sam held his gaze, determined to stare him out, and permitted herself the tiniest of nods. "Until you know: one way or the other," she said.

Sir Anthony laughed.

"Under the circumstances I suppose that's quite reasonable, although are you sure you don't want a greater proportion of the money now? Say, twenty per cent? After all, once you come out of there you may not be in any fit state to enjoy it, neither mentally nor physically."

"It sounds to me, Sir Anthony," said Henderson, "as if you already know the answer."

"Not at all," was the reply. "I just know what has already happened to the individuals who have tried to spend a night there."

"All of them?" the detective breathed.

"The ones they found," said Sir Anthony with the trace of a grin. "Now, are you quite sure you want to take on this particular case?"

Sam got to her feet. "Well perhaps we should talk about it first."

"Most definitely," said Henderson, shaking Sir Anthony's hand. "I take it you'll be supplying us with all the necessary documents and background information?"

Sir Anthony smiled but there was no warmth in it. "Of course," he said. "I'll get them couriered to you. Oh, and one other thing. You won't be the only people I'll be sending in there. Thought it best if I had a bit of a team, so you could all look after each other, so to speak."

Henderson's eyes narrowed. "Who are the others?"

"Well I'm not entirely sure just yet." Sir Anthony rubbed his chin. "You're the only two I've formally interviewed and gained an acceptance from. The only other definite is my grand-daughter, Madeleine."

"You grand-daughter?" said Sam.

"Yes, my dear. You see, she's convinced that she's a medium; thinks she can 'channel the dead', in her own words. Or so her psychiatrists have told me. Load of bloody nonsense if you ask me, but one of the reasons I bought the place was because I thought it might help her."

Sam looked shocked. "How?" she said.

"Well with any luck, it'll make her realise that it's all a load of rubbish."

Sam bit her lip so hard that she winced. "Or make her realise that it isn't," she said.

Sir Anthony folded his arms and gave her a cool look. "Well if it isn't, Miss Jephcott, then don't forget you're going to need to convince me of that too, thus giving one particular grandfather and grand-daughter a never before experienced degree of mutual understanding that will hopefully give a warm glow to both your little hearts, as they take you away to the kind of place Madeleine has been in and out of for the past five years."

"Have you thought about anyone else?"

"A scientist perhaps; a physicist most likely, or perhaps a biologist if there's going to be lots of that ectoplasm stuff around. I also thought a doctor might be useful, in case of minor injuries, wounds, that sort of thing."

"An architect might be helpful."

Sir Anthony paused by the door. "You know, it's funny you should say that," he said. "I sent an architect in there a couple of weeks ago — to look for secret rooms, hidden floors, that sort of thing."

"And did he find any?" asked Sam.

"I have no idea," Sir Anthony replied. "No-one has seen him since."

"Have you contacted the police?" said Henderson.

"They are specifically the people who *haven't* seen him, despite searching the place from top to bottom. Well, from top until they got scared, not that any of them would admit to that, but I could see it in their eyes." Sir Anthony looked from Henderson to Samantha. "You can tell a lot from someone's eyes, you know. For example my dear, yours are quite beautiful."

"Thank you," was all Sam could think of to reply.

"Oh yes. It would be shame if you were to end up stumbling out of that house with them torn from that pretty face of yours, but I suppose that's the kind of risk you take in your stride all the time. Good day."

Chapter Seven
Room for One More Inside

Sir Anthony's package was delivered to Henderson's house by a disgruntled-looking courier early the next morning. Sam searched for a pair of scissors while Henderson continued to munch on toast. Once she had cut the parcel open he reached across the breakfast table to take it from her. "Oh no you don't," she said. "You'll get marmalade all over everything."

Henderson wiped his hands and did his best not to bounce up and down with excitement.

"What's he sent us altogether?" he asked.

"Well, we've got Marx's diary," said Sam, holding up the journal bound in worn red leather. She emptied the sheaf of documents that comprised the rest of the package onto the kitchen table, well away from the loganberry jam. "Otherwise it looks like some old police records, some building blueprints, and photocopies of newspaper reports of weird goings-on in the area."

Henderson swigged coffee and, realising his fingers were still a bit buttery, resisted the urge to join in the inspection. "Any of them worth hanging onto?"

Sam leafed through the photocopies. "Not really, but the locals must really have overactive imaginations if these are anything to go by. It looks as if someone at some time has seen everything from a wispy wraith to a 'black carriage drawn by four horses and driven by a winged demon the size of a helicopter'."

"That's a good one," said Henderson with a grin. "I'd like to see that."

Sam tried to bat him over the head with the report, but he was too quick for her. "I know you would. Sadly, Hollywood movies and CGI haven't just raised the expectations of cinema-goers have they? And don't ask me what CGI is because I know you know and I also know you'd only be asking me to appear charmingly out of touch which — while it works — isn't something you should overdo or I might get fed up with it."

Henderson gave her a big grin. "Goodness me!" he said. "That's a bit of an outburst for a Thursday morning! Is everything okay?"

Sam tidied the papers, made sure they were on a crumb and jam-free area of the table, and sat next to him.

"Yes," she said. "I suppose so."

"Only suppose?"

"Well," she said. "It's silly, but…"

"It's not silly if it's bothering you," said Henderson.

"I just keep going back to that supremely horrible image that Sir Anthony left us with, of me crawling out of that house with… you know."

Henderson grimaced.

"I do indeed," he said. "And for what it's worth, I agree that it wasn't a very nice thing for him to say at all. But I get the feeling that our Sir Anthony was doing his best to unnerve us; either to see if we were up to the job, or perhaps solely because it amused him. Either way," he said, looking her in the eyes, "we're not going to let a mean old man get in the way of us defending the world from horrible nasty things, are we?"

Sam squeezed his hand and smiled. "Of course not," she said. "But if I freak out a few times on the way there, now you'll know why."

"I would have known anyway," said Henderson with a grin. "Now, while I wash my hands and have a look through these papers, why don't you make a start on the recommended reading I've put together for you?"

Sam pointed at the pile of documents on the kitchen table. "You mean this isn't it?"

Henderson shook his head and got to his feet. "Oh no. Before we go anywhere near Sir Anthony's Dark Manor I want you to become fully acquainted with the scariest haunted houses imaginable. Which is why, before we get going, I want you to read Shirley Jackson's *The Haunting of Hill House*, Richard Matheson's *Hell House* and for good measure Stephen King's *The Shining*, even though that's actually about a hotel."

"But those are all made up!" said Sam.

"The very best haunted house stories are," said Henderson, "and hopefully they'll prepare you for what we might encounter where we're going. You should be able to find copies of all of them in the library. If you could take them from the 'Reading Copies' section, I'd be grateful. Some of the first editions will hopefully provide for me in my old age."

Sam rolled her eyes while making a note not to touch anything she found in the library that wasn't a paperback. "And do you seriously expect me to read them all before we leave?" she said.

"I very much suspect you won't want to read them once we're in there," said the detective with a twinkle in his eye. "Once we're actually inside *Yr Ynysyrwyddfa*."

"Bet you can't say that twice," said Sam.

"I might be able to," said Henderson and took a final swig of coffee, "but I'm not in the habit of courting disaster."

"Oh yes you are," said Sam, as she wandered off to the library.

Henderson collected up the papers and winced as he realised that he had, despite all his efforts, managed to get marmalade on them. As he leafed through them himself, he was pleased to see that Sir Anthony had included a list of the other individuals who would be joining them, with a note written in green ink saying that if Henderson wished to bring anyone else along who might assist in the job at hand that would also be acceptable.

Henderson wondered if the old man had meant in addition to Samantha, or instead. But the old man had seemed quite taken by her, his spiteful sense of humour aside. Although, perhaps that was why he didn't want her to go.

His thoughts were interrupted by the ringing of the telephone. It was Jeremy Stokes.

"I was wondering whether or not you had decided to take on my case," said the nervous voice at the other end of the line.

"I'm afraid I haven't been able to give it much thought," said Henderson as he re-read Sir Anthony's letter. "We're right in the middle of something else now and so it's going to be a little while before I'll be able to devote my time fully to your problem."

That obviously wasn't what Stokes had wanted to hear: the voice on the other end of the line assumed a tone that was almost pleading.

"Mr Henderson, I know it's only a couple of days since we met, and I appreciate that you probably have a lot of other urgent pressing matters, but I'm willing to top what anyone else is paying you right at this moment."

You might find that harder than you think, thought Henderson with a grin and then quoted what Sir Anthony was planning to pay them.

"And that's just ten percent," he added.

There was a pause.

"I'm sorry, Mr Henderson," Stokes said eventually, his voice if anything even more nervous and with a definite touch of humility to it now. "I had no idea you were so highly sought after. I'm sorry to have wasted your time. I'll try and find someone else."

"Now don't be silly," said Henderson. "Besides, as far as I'm aware, there isn't anyone else."

"Well, if you could at least suggest something for me to do," said Stokes, an element of tired humour creeping into his tone, "that would be a real help. I've never been much good on my own and it's only been a couple of days but I'm already starting to climb the walls over here."

Henderson looked at Sir Anthony's letter again, and at the green scrawl the millionaire had added as an afterthought. He licked his lips. It was either a ludicrous idea or a brilliant one, and hadn't so many ideas in the past actually been one and the same?

"Mr Stokes," he said. "Right now the only thing I can suggest for your case is some occupational rehabilitation."

"I don't understand," said a confused-sounding Jeremy.

"You will. I have to be honest with you and say that at the moment I have no idea how to treat your problem. Certainly there have been documented cases in the past of people possessing similar abilities to yours, but on the whole those individuals were never 'cured', as you might like to put it. Rather they had to learn to live with their abilities. Probably the best thing for you now is to improve your feeling of self-worth. If nothing else it would help you to come to terms with this admittedly rather peculiar ability of yours."

The other end of the line went quiet for a moment.

"So what are you suggesting, exactly?"

Now it was Henderson's turn to pause. What he had intended to suggest was already sounding like a bad idea. "Never mind, Mr Stokes. That was just me thinking aloud. I'm afraid you've rather caught me off guard. I'm never at my best first thing in the morning."

"It's half-past eight."

"Exactly," said Henderson, nodding even though there was no-one around to see it. "An idea had crossed my mind but I have to say it's rather extreme and could possibly put you in danger, so please forget we even had this conversation. I'll be in touch once we're back from our current assignment."

With that he put down the receiver. Two minutes later the phone rang again. Henderson answered, hoping all the noise wasn't disturbing Sam who was hopefully in the library speed reading. It was Stokes again.

"Listen, Mr Henderson, I fully appreciate that you have my best interests at heart," he said. "But I would like to say that I've made some inquiries and I can match your current employer's fee."

Henderson took a deep breath. Perhaps he was in the wrong line of work after all. "I'm sorry, Mr Stokes," he said. "Once we have agreed to a contract we cannot renege on it, even if we receive a better offer. It's just not the done thing."

"Well at least tell me what your idea was," the voice implored.

As soon as he began to speak, Henderson knew he was quite possibly making a terrible mistake. "I was going to suggest that you accompany us on our current case, Mr Stokes. We've been asked to investigate the most haunted house in Britain as part of a team recruited specifically for the purpose. It crossed my mind that it might be very useful to have someone along who could predict if any of us were in imminent danger of expiring, but giving it a little more thought I now realise that it could place you in quite serious danger."

This time there was no hesitation on the other end of the line.

"I'll do it."

Despite the fact that still no-one could see it, Henderson shook his head. "No, Mr Stokes, you don't understand. I've already decided that at best it's a bad idea, and at worst it's positively reckless."

"Mr Henderson, I have a problem. You are the only one who can help me. Your suggestion that I might be of some help dealing with the real paranormal — as opposed to the fake one I have made my fortune with — is the most perfect I have ever heard. Please let me come."

"No."

"I am willing to pay you for the privilege."

"No," said Henderson, "absolutely not."

"Very well," said Stokes. "Here is my final offer: I am willing to match what you are being paid for this investigation and throw in my services at the same time, which means — if it's of help to me — you have the double satisfaction of a job well done and having been paid handsomely for it; and if it all comes to nought, at least you will have been rewarded for your trouble. Oh, and I'm willing to sign whatever you want me to saying that if I die it wasn't your fault."

Now it was Henderson's turn to pause. It might actually be helpful to have Stokes along: if Sir Anthony had employed a medium, Stokes would probably be pretty good at spotting if she was a fake. Then there was the ability he claimed to possess, which could actually come in useful. Henderson had no idea if he was doing the right thing, but if the house did turn out to be haunted then an extra pair of hands on their side wouldn't go amiss either. He took a deep breath and crossed his fingers, which was quite difficult to do when he was holding a telephone receiver.

"If I give you the address of the house and the time we're all meant to be there, can you make your own way?"

He could hear the delight in Stokes' gleeful 'Yes!', and the man's anticipation was almost palpable as Henderson gave him the details.

"I'll see you there, Mr Henderson; and thank you, thank you so much."

As Stokes put the phone down, Henderson wondered if the man would be thanking him by the end of it, or cursing him for ever having suggested the idea.

Part Two

Not a Nice Place to Visit

Chapter Eight
Travelling to the Other Side

Sam was running in darkness.

The annoying thing was she knew perfectly well that she was asleep; just as she knew that the steady rumbling she could just about feel was the car making its way south from Henderson's mansion in the North Wales mountains. But this didn't make the thing that was coming after her any less frightening.

She couldn't even see it, whatever it was. Whenever she stopped to look back, all that met her gaze was a hazy dimness in which something huge was making its inexorable way towards her, slavering and slithering, the beat of its heavy footsteps causing the ground beneath her feet to shake, the heat of its breath burning her skin even from a distance. She could run but it would never give up. She could halt but then it would definitely have her. The inevitability and the frustration and the terror, most of all the terror, made her cry out, but even her screams weren't loud enough to drown the noises of the thing that was almost upon her.

"Would you like an ice cream?" it said in Henderson's voice.

Sam opened her eyes. They were in a car park. Sam blinked and read the words 'Magor Services'. She shifted in her seat and realised she was damp with perspiration.

"Where are we?" she said.

"Just over the Severn Bridge," was the reply. "You did your usual thing of nodding off once we got going and I thought it would be kinder to come straight down the M5 rather than subject both of us to the horrors of the A roads of mid-Wales. Unfortunately an accident had closed off the M50 so we've had to go the long way round. And now that you've had the traffic news, would you like to tell me what all that was about?"

Sam pushed her hair out of her eyes.

"Oh, nothing really," she said. "Most likely the late night and those bloody books you wanted me to read."

"Ah yes," said Henderson. "Well, I thought they might help to prepare you. Anyway, rest assured you didn't make that much noise." Sam breathed a sigh of relief. "And you didn't dribble much either."

Sam's fingers flew to her lips before she saw the huge grin on Henderson's face. She had nothing to hit him with and so felt entirely justified using her hand.

"Just my little joke," he said once the beating had ceased. "And now, as I said in my gentle efforts to rudely awaken you, would you like an ice cream?"

Sam opened the car door and got out. The day was warm, even for the middle of June, but the journey and the dream had left her appetite somewhere outside Birmingham.

"No thanks," she smiled. "Besides, I'd rather keep an empty stomach for when we get there, just in case there's anything horrible waiting for us."

Henderson took the file Sir Anthony had sent them from the back seat.

"It says here that he will have 'made all the appropriate catering arrangements'. Whether that means food will be brought in or if some lovely old Welsh lady will be there baking us cakes I have no idea."

"If there's a lovely old Welsh lady there I'm going to assume she's some ghastly creature in disguise until proved otherwise," said Sam. "In fact it might be a good idea if you suggest we all go out for our first night to get to know each other a bit better outside the confines of the place."

"A splendid idea," said Henderson. "I'm glad to see that whatever nightmare you may have had, it hasn't distracted you from the fact that we have Sir Anthony's expense account to avail ourselves of."

"Indeed," said Sam. "And that, combined with your knowledge of where the best restaurants always are, means that hopefully our first night on the case shouldn't be too distressing."

"I know the very place," said Henderson, dropping the file onto the back seat. "I was going to suggest we eat there before arriving, but that's a much better idea. How are you feeling now?"

Sam smiled, realising the entire stop had been for her benefit.

"I'll be fine," she said. "And don't worry, I'm not planning on nodding off again. We shouldn't be far away from it now anyway."

"About another thirty miles," said Henderson as Sam got back in the car. He started the engine. "Now it's a beautiful day, so just sit back and watch out for little people."

"That's not a very nice thing to call your countrymen," Sam said as they slipped back onto the M4.

"That's not what I meant," said Henderson. "We are now on the borders of Machen country, and before you ask: Arthur Machen was a Welsh author of the late nineteenth century."

"Who presumably wrote about little people?" Sam asked as they came off the motorway at the Coldra roundabout and took the A449 going north.

"These lands are rich in myth," said Henderson as the dual carriageway cut through some of the most gently beautiful countryside Sam had ever seen, "including tales of primitive races that existed before what we know as 'man', and which may exist still."

Sam looked around her. It was hard to believe that such creatures could still exist in between power stations, industrial farms and factories, and yet the land through which they were currently passing gave her the impression that yes they could, that it was man and the modern insults he had made to this land that would be cast out long before any of the elements that belonged there would be forced to leave. Suddenly she realised why William Marx had decided to build his house in this part of the country. Even though they were in a modern car on a modern road, she could feel the vibrations of the land around her, steeped in history and charged with power. She turned to Henderson.

"This might actually turn out to be quite scary, you know," she said.

Henderson nodded.

"Just remember that I'll be there with you," he said. "And if at any time it gets too much for either of us, then we'll leave."

"If we're allowed to," came the sullen reply.

"You know, I do believe it's your ebullient optimism that's the reason this partnership of our works," said Henderson, doing his best to avoid the inevitable blow. "And for the record our dear Mr Machen also happened to write about impromptu brain surgery on an unwitting young girl so there's always that for me to bear in mind if you don't behave yourself."

Rather than sulk Sam, preferred to think she was merely ignoring him for much of the rest of the journey. By lunchtime they had reached Monmouth, successfully found the minor road that took them through the village of Mitchel Troy, and followed Sir Anthony's directions to find themselves driving down a narrow lane. High hedgerows on either side merely added to the feeling of confinement as the sun did its best to glare at them through gaps in the overhanging tree branches.

"Not the best road to have to pass something on," said Sam as the road narrowed even further and she began to hear the sounds of twigs scraping against the car's paintwork.

"I think we're meant to turn off it in a bit," said Henderson. "What do the instructions say?"

Sam looked at the typed sheet of A4 once again.

"It says to carry on down here until we see a farm."

"Like that one up ahead?"

Sam looked up to see the dung-smeared walls of what was quite possibly the least friendly rural building she had ever seen in her life.

"Perhaps," she said with a grimace. "If it is, then there should be a right turn just after it."

Henderson slowed down once they were past the farm.

"There's no road here," he said. "Just a dirt track leading off between the trees."

"That's it," Sam said, nodding. "It says here the trail should lead us up to the house. It's also the bit of the instructions I presume you didn't read as it says we need a four-wheel-drive to get there."

"Ah, now, I did read that," said Henderson, indicating right so at least the sheep regarding them from the open gateway of the farm knew of their intentions, "but I thought it would be very unlikely that we wouldn't be able to get down it in this."

Sam braced herself as the car went over the first of many bumps and her head hit the ceiling.

"You mean you thought this beaten up old wreck of a car that I keep telling you we should trade in for something rather more roadworthy would be perfectly capable of getting down a dirt track in the middle of Wales that hasn't been used in years? Ouch!" Henderson had spotted another deep gouge in the road but, in trying to avoid it, had merely succeeded in almost driving the car into a ditch on the left hand side.

"Sorry!" he said. "I'm sure it's not far now, and you have to admit, there seems to be plenty of life in the old girl yet."

"Well there's not going to be much left in this one," said Sam as they turned a shadowy corner and almost ran over a petite girl with shoulder length black hair carrying a rucksack. Henderson braked a little too enthusiastically and once again the car slid perilously close to a ditch. Sam was still catching her breath when the girl tapped on her window.

"Are you all right?" the girl asked in the kind of posh accent Sam thought had only ever been used in black-and-white British public information films.

"Fine thanks," said Sam, pretending she wasn't shaking at all. "We're just finding the road a bit treacherous, that's all."

"You should have a four-by-four for this," said the girl. "After all, for all you know there could be half a mile of mud to get through further on."

"Is there?" said Henderson.

"No idea," said the girl. "But as long as there isn't, would you mind giving me a lift? I presume you're headed for the House of Horrors?" Sam nodded and the girl slung off her rucksack and jumped in the back. "I'm Maddy by the way," she said, "Maddy Calverton. If you're part of the group, you probably had to endure talking to my grandfather Sir Anthony."

"Oh we did," said Sam, introducing the two of them as Henderson crossed his fingers and threw the gears into reverse. There was a degree of protest from beneath the bonnet before the car shifted and they were able to get back on the trail.

"Your grandfather told us he wanted you along for your psychic abilities," said Henderson, once he was happy that the car wasn't going to slide away from his control.

"You're very polite, Mr Henderson," said Maddy, "but I'm sure that's not how he put it. He thinks that a spell in a house miles away from anywhere, whether it's haunted or not, might be good for me. Mind you, his benevolence didn't extend to getting me here: I had to take the train to Abergavenny station and then hitch-hike from there. I normally don't mind that sort of thing, but no-one ever comes down here, and did you seen the state of that farm back there?" Sam nodded. "Bloody scary or what?"

"Do you have any idea how far down here we have to go?" Henderson asked.

"Actually," said Sam. "I think we're here."

The track had come to an end. To their right there was a gap in the trees where two huge rusted wrought iron gates had been propped open against lichen-encrusted pillars. The towering stones were crowned with the eroded remains of winged beasts whose heads had long been lost to the ravages of too many Welsh winters. The dirt road continued between them.

"You'd think he'd have built a better road to get to the place," said Maddy as the car bumped and protested along the rutted road.

"Maybe he didn't want anyone else coming here," said Sam.

"Either that," said Henderson with a sigh of relief, as he felt the car gain purchase on a more substantial road surface, "or there's some reason we can't use the main drive up to the house."

The road had widened and was now paved with what looked to Sam like flagstones. They began to climb, spiralling to the right around the side of a hill, the trees still providing thick ground cover with only a momentary break in the foliage to reveal the view over the valley below. As they reached the top, the house came into view.

Sam was glad they hadn't arrived when it was getting dark. Even seeing it at its best, in daylight and bright summer sunshine, the building ahead of them seemed to be made of black stone. Either that or it was in shadow. Perched on the hill as it was there was nothing to block the sun's rays. *Nothing but the spirit of the house itself,* she thought.

At the front of the house a broad gravelled area peppered with weeds allowed them to bring the car to a halt. They got out and Sam shielded her eyes from the sunshine as she gazed at the view. Beyond where they had parked, the ground dipped suddenly; the once immaculate lawns that stretched to the forest through which they had driven, now wildly overgrown. Further still, she could see the mountains making an uneven horizon, one on which she could see no buildings or other signs of life.

Henderson's stomach gave a tiny gurgle.

"You're really hungry, aren't you?" said Sam.

The detective pulled a face. "I have to admit I could do with a spot of lunch," he said.

There was a tapping from behind them.

"Are the car's back doors still dodgy?" said Sam

Henderson grimaced. He had been supposed to get them fixed while she was away.

They both apologised to Maddy as she stumbled from the car. "I'm sorry to be a nuisance," she said, "but I was getting a bit claustrophobic in there." She dropped her rucksack on the ground and stretched her arms above her head, which only served to emphasise her petite figure. "It's a lovely day, isn't it?" she said. "A shame we have to go in there, really."

The three of them turned to look at the house.

The double doors that led into the building had been painted a deep red and were crowned with a gothic arch. Either side of the entrance were two rooms with huge windows whose ten panes, in two rows of five, had been filled with stained glass. Try as she might Sam could not work out what image was meant to be conveyed in any of them. Flanking these were the wings of the house, stretching towards the forest that surrounded the house on three sides. Each floor was pockmarked with tiny windows that reminded Sam of a Victorian asylum. From the centre of the main building arose a lofty tower crowned with the charcoal grey crenulated slates that covered the rest of the roof.

But the thing that really gave Sam the shivers was the masonry from which the entire edifice had been constructed. There was not a cloud in the sky and yet the building still looked as if it was in shadow, the black stone that made up every wall swallowing up the light of day and giving none of it back. The broad wings either side of the main building made Sam think of a vast slumbering beast that even in sleep, or death, still defied her to look at it. She shuddered. If ever a house could be alive, it was this one.

"Not very pretty is it?" said Henderson.

"It wasn't meant to be, Mr Henderson," said Maddy, suddenly much more serious. "It was built to serve a purpose. And our job is to find out whether or not the man who built it actually succeeded. Shall we go in?"

No, thought Sam.

"Yes," she said.

Chapter Nine
Getting In...

Henderson selected the most likely looking key from the bunch Sir Anthony had included in his package, and rattled it around in the lock with little success.

"The house doesn't want to let us in," said Maddy. "I suppose that's hardly surprising, really."

"Oh I don't know," said Henderson, trying the next key along on the heavy ring and failing miserably with that one too, "if I was reputed to be the scariest house in the country, I should imagine I would be delighted to welcome some new victims that would allow me to cement my reputation further."

"Do you really think this house cares about something as small-minded as reputation?" Maddy closed her eyes and laid the palm of a tiny hand on the pillar to the left of the door. She closed her eyes and shuddered. "It knows we're here," she said, swaying slightly. Henderson saw Sam was about to say something but motioned her to keep quiet for now. "We beg entrance to this place," the girl said in a half-whisper. "We beg entrance and promise that we shall cause no harm here."

"I'm going to have to stop you there," said Henderson, realising the third key wouldn't fit at all. "I've always found it a very good idea not to promise anything to forces you don't know anything about."

"Me neither," said Sam, aiming a pointed toe of a black designer boot at the door and giving it a hefty kick.

The door creaked open.

Maddy drew breath, opened her eyes and grimaced.

"The house didn't like that, you know," she said, sounding quite indignant. "It didn't like that at all."

"Maybe it did and maybe it didn't," said Sam, returning the girl's scowl. "But at least now we can go inside, can't we?"

Maddy pushed past the two of them and stepped into the entrance hall. The door swung shut behind her.

"Was that such a good idea?" Henderson hissed to Sam once the girl was out of sight.

"I can't feel anything," said Sam. "No presence, no supernatural forces, nothing. If I were you I'd take everything little Miss Calverton says with a ton of salt."

"I'm starting to get the feeling you don't like her," said the detective with a grin.

"I'll have you know, I'm merely giving you my professional opinion," said Sam, returning his smile and squeezing his arm.

There was a scream from inside.

Henderson pushed at the door, half expecting it to refuse to budge, but it swung open easily. Maddy was standing in the centre of the hall, hugging herself and shivering.

"There's something here," she said.

"Something?" said Henderson, staying where he was. "Or someone?"

"I can't say," said the girl. "Only that I felt a presence as soon as I entered."

Henderson looked at Sam, who gave him an 'I have no idea what she's going on about' shrug. "Well let's just stick together for the moment, shall we?" he said. "After all, there *are* meant to be other people coming here. Maybe it's one of them you can feel."

"Yes," said Maddy, as if she had completely forgotten that anyone else was meant to be meeting them there. "Sorry."

"Nothing to be sorry about," said Henderson. "To be honest, stepping in here would be enough to give anyone a shock." He looked around him. "Although I have to admit I wasn't expecting it to be quite so..."

"...tidy?" said Sam.

Henderson nodded as he took in the rich carpet on which they were standing and which continued up the twin staircases that led to the first floor, their balustrades and banisters highly polished.

"It looks as if Sir Anthony spent some time getting this place tidied up in preparation for our arrival," said the detective. "How jolly thoughtful of him."

"It wasn't him," said Maddy, shaking her head. "My grandfather may be ridiculously rich but I'd be surprised if he was able to get anyone to stay here long enough to get this place looking like this. No, this is the house's way of welcoming us."

"After I kicked the door in?" Sam was starting to feel confrontational again.

"Well, whatever the reason, it's nice to have such a warm welcome, don't you think?" said Henderson, rubbing his hands together enthusiastically.

"You know, I hate it when you do that," said Sam. "Because it means you've spotted something that probably means trouble."

"Oh I don't know about that," said Henderson, looking up at the balcony above them. "But I think I just saw something move up there. Fancy coming to have a look?"

Sam looked at Maddy, who wasn't saying anything. In fact she seemed to have closed her eyes and gone into a trance.

Good thing too, Sam thought and then wondered if the girl had been able to pick that up. "No," she said. "I think I'll wait for you to get thrown back down the stairs and then I can say I told you so."

"While tending to my wounds, I hope?" asked the detective, setting foot on the left hand staircase.

"You should be so lucky," came the reply. "And why do you have to tempt fate by going up the left side?"

"It's always more fun that way," said Henderson, gingerly placing one brown brogue in front of the other on the plush crimson carpet.

"You know, I think Sir Anthony must have had this place refurbished," he said as he made his way up. "This carpet's top quality."

"Maybe he's thinking of making the place into a hotel." Sam called up. "Can you see anyone?"

Henderson reached the top of the stairs and was making his way along the landing staying close to the balcony before he spoke again.

"There's a long corridor leading off into the house," he said. "But I can't see anyone."

"No," Sam called back. "I'm not surprised."

"Why? Because you doubt my observational powers?"

"No," she said. "Because they're coming down the other staircase now."

Henderson dashed along the balcony and headed back down the right hand staircase. He was about halfway down when he collided with Jeremy Stokes, who yelped in terror. The cry broke Maddy from her trance and she screamed again and pointed at Jeremy.

"That's who I thought I saw when I came in!" she cried, turning to Sam. "Please, tell me you can see him too!"

"Yes," said Sam, resisting the urge to roll her eyes. "We can all see him. He's meant to be here as well."

"Although we weren't expecting him until a bit later on," said Henderson, accompanying a shaken-looking Jeremy down the stairs. "I'm most terribly sorry for frightening you like that," he said once they were all back together in the entrance hall.

"That's OK," said Jeremy with a brisk grin. "I've had worse."

"Who are you?" said Maddy, looking Jeremy up and down with obvious disdain.

"If you don't already know, then I don't think you'll be very impressed," he replied.

"Maddy, this is Jeremy Stokes," said Sam, and when the girl's face registered a blank she added "he's a television psychic." Having lit the blue touch paper, she then retired to a safe distance to watch the fireworks.

"Oh for goodness' sake!" Maddy looked indignant. "I thought this was supposed to be serious undertaking." She looked around her. "Where are the cameras then? Where are all the bloody cameras?"

"There aren't any," said Jeremy. "That's not why I'm here."

"Then why exactly are you here, Mr Stokes?" said Maddy with an indignant glare.

"For the same reason we all are," said Henderson. "To determine whether or not this house is actually haunted."

"Doesn't seem to be so far," said Jeremy. "I got here about half an hour ago and all that was waiting for me was that letter from Sir Anthony saying he hoped we had a fruitful stay and that we found the place comfortable. Oh, and he'd also included the number of the local hospital."

"Very thoughtful," said Sam. "Although knowing us, I suppose we may well need it. Where did you put it?"

"On that table to the right of the front door," said Jeremy. "The one the telephone's resting on."

The telephone looked as if it would probably have been considered an antique sixty years ago, and was so ornate that it probably belonged in some old lady's boudoir rather than as the main communications device for a manor house. The black marble-topped table on which it rested was similarly decadent.

"Well it's not there now," said Sam, checking behind the table as well just in case it had fallen on the floor. "No sign of it anywhere." She picked up the telephone receiver, put it to her ear and gave the group a resigned look. "And guess what?" she said. "No dial tone either."

"Oh that's all right," said Jeremy, taking out his mobile and frowning as the little grey bars failed to materialise on the screen.

"We're in Wales, Mr Stokes," said Henderson, "a country that is often less than friendly towards such modern-fangled devices."

"Yes," said Sam at Maddy and Jeremy's reaction. "In case you were wondering he often talks like this."

"But what if we need help?" said Jeremy, giving his phone a little shake in case violence might succeed where the might of a multinational telecommunications company had so far failed.

"I think that's one of the reasons Sir Anthony wanted a doctor here," said Sam.

"But she's not here, is she?" said Jeremy, giving his mobile a final shake before returning it to his pocket. "I'm already starting to think coming here was bad idea."

"I was already thinking the same thing," said Maddy "About you I mean."

"Okay that's enough," said Sam. "Rather than stand here bickering, don't you think we could more profitably use our time getting our luggage in and finding out which rooms we've been allocated?"

"According to the letter my dear grandfather sent me, mine is down there," said Maddy, turning to face away from the front door and pointing to the corridor straight ahead of her.

"And I've already found mine," said Jeremy, holding up a key.

"Well in that case, Henderson and I will go and find out our rooms while you two stay here and get to know each other better," said Sam. "I can see you're dying to."

Henderson followed her out to the car.

"Wasn't that a little bit harsh?" he said, opening the boot.

"Probably," said Sam, turning and pointing at the house. "But look at this place, Henderson. I know nothing's happened yet but just look at it. It's bloody terrifying. And it was built *deliberately* to be bloody terrifying. And while our first few tentative steps inside haven't been met with anything horrible, I don't doubt for a second that by the time we leave here we're probably both going to be slightly different people for what we've seen here. And the last thing I need is to be around people who exhibit all the maturity of a dim-witted five-year-old who has been deprived of his favourite, brightly coloured, bouncy object by an uncaring world."

"Sam, we'll be okay," said Henderson, turning her to face him, holding her gently by the shoulders and speaking with all the reassurance he could muster.

"There's always the chance we might not be," said Sam.

"Of course," he said, his grin broadening. "But I thought you might like to hear me say it anyway."

Sam gave him the kind of smile she knew grown men had been tempted to kill for.

"You know I did. And you know I wouldn't come within a hundred miles of a shitty place like this if you weren't with me." And then the moment, whatever it might have been, was over.

"Come on," he said, "let's find out what the rooms are like that Sir Anthony has had fixed up for us."

"Has *hopefully* had fixed up for us," said Sam as Henderson dragged their cases back to the house.

"Ever the optimist," he said. "That's one of the things I like about you."

"Oh," she said, "in that case, we must go through some of the others sometime."

Henderson held the door open for her as she helped him drag the bags inside. "If you don't behave, I might be more tempted to go through the list of things I don't like," he said.

"Don't you dare," said Sam.

"Well, we're only here a week so I don't think we would have enough time anyway," Henderson replied before dodging the inevitable blow.

When they got back inside, Jeremy and Maddy had vanished.

"Do you think they've gone to kiss and make up?" said Henderson, dropping the cases and consulting Sir Anthony's letter.

"More like hiss and make documentaries. Separately, of course, although I wouldn't be surprised if Mr Stokes turned out to be the voyeuristic type."

"Well your guess is infinitely better and possibly more experienced than mine," said Henderson. "Either way, let's leave them to their own devices." He looked from the letter to the balcony. "It would appear that our rooms are on the first floor."

Sam helped him drag their cases upstairs, insisting they go by the right hand staircase this time. From the landing a broad corridor led off into the depths of the house. Its wood-panelled walls were scratched with paler oblongs along its length indicating where pictures must have once been hung. The carpet was much older here, although still of good quality, but Sam got the distinct impression that any refurbishment that had been undertaken had been limited to the part of the house they had just seen. The far end of the passageway ended in an ornately carved door with their rooms just before it on either side.

"Opposite each other," said Henderson. "How thoughtful. Do you want to swap?"

"We haven't even looked inside them yet," said Sam, dropping her case and going to inspect the door at the end.

"I know," he replied. "But yours is on the left side."

"True," said Sam, resisting the urge to run a fingertip over the door's centrepiece. The monstrous fanged visage looked so lifelike, and so aggressive, that she could almost imagine it rearing off the door and biting her. So it probably wasn't a good idea to even think of it. "But if we look at it from the opposite direction, the 'running away and out of this house as far and as fast as possible' direction, it's on the right, so I'm happy."

"That's a jolly interesting-looking door," said Henderson. "I wonder where it leads?"

Sam tried the handle only to find it locked.

"A wing of the house where we are *Not Meant To Go,*" she said in spooky voice.

"Or an old cupboard," said the detective.

"Or better still," she said as he nodded with a knowing grin, "a cupboard that becomes a room but only on certain nights."

"All waiting for us to discover," he said, rummaging through the envelope to produce two small keys. He handed the one with the blue fob to Sam before going into his own room.

Sam took one more look at the carved thing at the end of the corridor before sliding the key into the lock of her own door. The creature already seemed nearer than when they had first seen it, and she did her best to dismiss the desire to try and find a room somewhere else in the house. The other rooms probably all had scary things in close proximity to them as well, she thought. But still, she really didn't like the idea of that thing coming to life in the middle of the night and trying to break into her room.

She didn't like it at all.

Chapter Ten
...And Getting Acquainted

A t least the bedroom was big.
Unfortunately, no matter how hard Sam tried, she couldn't find much else to commend it. There was a decent-sized window opposite the door, but its mullioned panes were too small to offer her an escape route (over the past year she had got used to checking every room she stayed in for escape routes, something that had occasionally produced a look of concern from whichever chain motel superintendent happened to be showing her a potential bed for the night). The view was fairly dismal as well. After a lot of thumping she was able to get the rusted handle of one of the tiny window panes to finally shift with a protesting creak and puff of rusty dust. Poking her head out, she was greeted to her left by a view of the west wing of the house that effectively blocked out any sunlight her room might otherwise get from that direction. To her right, the main part of the house extended for another twenty feet or so — meaning that the hideous door at the end of the corridor definitely had to lead to something more substantial than a cupboard — before ending just before the surrounding forest began. If she looked straight down, her gaze was met by flagstones that may once have formed part of a rear courtyard, but which were now so overgrown that

they were only just visible through the tangled morass of thorny weeds which covered them. Even if you could get out of the window, she thought, a fall from that height would result in a couple of broken limbs before whatever might be living in the undergrowth came to eat you.

She turned back to survey the rest of the room. Opposite the door was a slightly dilapidated-looking double bed, the edges of its carved wooden headboard cutting into the fading red flock wallpaper that covered the walls, in some areas none-too-successfully. She gave the bedspread a punch, and breathed a sigh of relief when a cloud of dust failed to erupt from the ancient-looking coverings. On closer inspection the sheets actually looked new, and further exploration revealed that the mattress was in fact perfectly capable of supporting her weight, even when she subjected it to a savage, prolonged, and rather unfair bout of bouncing.

Next to the door was a wardrobe, and beside that a tallboy. Both had been fashioned from mahogany and had seen far better days. An experimental shove revealed that, if necessary, the wardrobe could also serve to barricade the door, although Sam would need a minute or two to get it into place. The drawers of the tallboy were spacious and smelled pleasantly of furniture polish, so she elected to put all her clothes in there and leave the wardrobe empty just in case some added security was required.

The taps on the sink next to the window offered a choice of either reasonably cold or very cold water. She was already imagining how Henderson would probably tell her that he had stayed in far worse Welsh boarding houses when he was younger, when she was distracted by a crash from across the hall.

Henderson's door was ajar but the detective was already on his feet again by the time she entered the room. The bed, however, looked like a lost cause.

"Did your bed do this?" he said, coughing amidst the dust.

Sam looked at the sorry excuse for a resting place that had caved in in the middle.

"No," she said. "Even though I gave it a pretty stressful testing."

"Well I'm relieved to hear that at least, although perhaps your somewhat lighter form may have been more suited to this room," he said, looking round for something to prop the middle of the bed up with.

The room was similar to Sam's. Henderson's window had a view looking out towards the east wing, but was otherwise similarly depressing. The wardrobe leaned to one side a little and Sam suspected that if you tried to shove it across to block the door it would probably collapse before you got it there.

"Completely unsafe," said Henderson, pointing to it. "I tried seeing if it would shift and the thing threatened to collapse on me."

"Do you want to try another room?" said Sam, taking a handful of the tattered hardback books from the shelves near the bed to shove underneath the sagging bed base. They lacked dust jackets and Sam had to squint at the gold lettering on the spines to see what they were.

"Nothing interesting I'm afraid," said Henderson, lifting the bed up. "I've already checked."

"So no *Revelations of Thingie*, then?" said Sam, getting on her hands and knees to push the books into the place where there probably should have been a couple of supporting legs.

"No," said Henderson, "no sacred texts, no Latin tomes, not even *The Diary of the Naughty Chambermaid Who Lived in a Haunted House*."

"Stop looking at my bottom while you say that," said Sam from under the bed.

"I can assure you that, if my eyes happen to have gravitated in that direction, it's purely out of concern for your safety," said Henderson. "You are under a bed that might have an unpleasant history, you know."

Sam crawled back out and got to her feet, brushing dust from her clothes.

"Has this place even got haunted beds, then?" she asked.

"According to the account Sir Anthony sent us, everything in this house is meant to have some connection to unpleasant and quite possibly supernatural events," said the detective. "For all we know someone could have been stabbed to death on that."

"Well it might explain why it's in such a terrible state of repair," said Sam. "But you're right; I suppose in this place it's far more likely to be that than any more fun reasons. What are you going to do about the wardrobe?"

"A-ha," said Henderson. "I've weighed it down." He opened the door to reveal three velvet jackets: one burgundy, one blue, and one a variety of green colour which Sam really hoped he wasn't thinking of wearing. "Luckily my tailor always uses the heaviest material and this cupboard is so flimsy they should do the job nicely. And of course when I change for dinner, this tweed I'm wearing will perform the job even more satisfactorily."

"I wonder what arrangements have been made for dinner?" said Sam.

"Good point," agreed Henderson. "If it's all the same to you, I don't fancy having to negotiate that slippery road again unless we really have to."

"I don't know," said Sam. "It might be a good idea to get some practice in, just in case we have to get down it very, very quickly indeed."

"True," said Henderson, looking at his watch. "Although..."

"Although what?"

"Well I have to say I'm a bit disappointed that we've been here for over half an hour now and nothing out of the ordinary has happened. I was rather hoping to be met by howling phantoms brandishing swords or furry monsters with tentacles."

Sam raised an eyebrow. "Fur *and* tentacles?"

"Yes," said Henderson with the boyish enthusiasm she tried hard not to let worry her, "I've never seen that, you know. Wouldn't that be interesting?"

"Well I suppose 'interesting' might be one word to describe the experience," said Sam. "Anyway, according to that Maddy girl the house has already performed some kind of manifestation by looking neat and tidy for our arrival."

"Yes," Henderson said with a smile. "I take it by the way you say 'that Maddy girl' that you're still not exactly endeared to Miss Calverton?"

"You've noticed that, then," said Sam.

"Oh indeed," said the detective. "But no matter how you might feel about her, try not to wind her up. I presume you've felt nothing since we got here?"

Sam shook her head. "Absolutely nothing at all, which in itself is a bit weird. Usually wherever we go I feel something, although usually it's just background noise, emanations, vibrations of people long gone or of events that were powerful enough to leave an echo of their happening. But here there's nothing at all."

"That is odd," said Henderson. "I suppose it's possible that something could decide to channel any psychic forces or phenomena through a certain individual of its choosing, but to do that it would also have to expend a huge amount of energy preventing you from picking up anything, which hardly seems likely."

"More likely Maddy Calverton's full of shit," said Sam.

"Now, now," said Henderson, wagging his finger. "You behave yourself. It might be that she has different sensitivities to your good self."

Sam didn't look convinced. "More likely she's making it up," she said.

"Well let's wait and see," said Henderson.

"Or it's just going on in her head. Maybe she's a couple of sandwiches short of a picnic."

Henderson regarded his companion gravely. "We're not feeling threatened, are we?" he said, swiftly adding, "Whatever she might turn out to be, the one thing we don't want is an uncontrollably upset and hysterical girl on our hands, understand?"

Sam resisted the urge to pout.

"Okay," she said. "But I don't like her."

"That much is obvious," said Henderson. "Plus, you have already stated the fact. Several times."

"And between her, Jeremy, and me, there do seem to be rather a lot of potentially psychic people here," she said.

"Agreed," said Henderson. "But you're the only one that I will ever trust. Why are you smiling like that?"

"Oh no reason," said Sam, feeling much better now Henderson had finally said the right thing. "Shall we go downstairs? I think I hear voices."

§ § §

The couple standing in the entrance hall were bickering in that resigned, understated way that couples sometimes do when they have been together for too long. Sam would have preferred to wait and see what it was they were arguing about, but Henderson was already bounding down the stairs, his right hand outstretched in greeting.

"Hello!" he said, a little too enthusiastically. "My name's Henderson! I'm the paranormal investigator who's been recruited by Sir Anthony Calverton for this little expedition, and this is my assistant Samantha Jephcott."

"Alan Pritchard," said the man, returning Henderson's handshake. Pritchard looked about the same age as Henderson, and his worn, green corduroy jacket (with elbow patches) and open-necked check shirt which didn't match gave him the air of an academic. "I'm the physicist," he said, confirming Sam's suspicions.

The woman with him was the complete opposite, wearing an immaculately tailored blue wool suit, the skirt of which came down to just below the knee and, Sam noted with a hint of jealousy, a pair of black Jimmy Choos that must have cost her a pretty penny. Her raven black hair had been neatly but expensively styled to contribute to the overall impression of a no-nonsense career woman.

"Dr Helen Pritchard," she said, in the manner Sam assumed she used to greet her patients. "I'm the medic."

"I am a doctor as well of course," said Alan, looking uneasy, "but of physics. It always confuses people so I don't tend to mention it."

"But you just have my darling," said Helen, eyeing up Henderson in a way Sam didn't like at all. "Now, I don't suppose you can tell us where our room is?" she said. "I'm afraid my husband forgot the letter with the details on."

"I'm afraid I've no idea," said Henderson. "Sam and I have the rooms at the top of the stairs but there aren't any others up there."

"The two of you aren't sharing, then?" said Helen as Alan tried not to look embarrassed.

"A business partnership, yes," said Henderson, "anything which could ruin that partnership, no."

"Well that sounds rather dull," said Helen, letting her eyes roam around the hall before settling back on Henderson. "So let's keep our fingers crossed that something interesting happens before the end of the week, or we may well all die of boredom."

"I imagine there'll be plenty to occupy us before then," said Henderson.

"Oh I do hope so," said Helen.

This increasingly uncomfortable situation was thankfully relieved by the sound of footsteps from behind them. They turned to see Jeremy emerge from the corridor directly below the one on which Sam and Henderson's room's were located.

"Ah, Mr Stokes," said Henderson, introducing everyone. "Sam and I were wondering where you had got to."

"Just checking out my room," he said, pointing back the way he had come. "It's next door to Maddy's down there on the left." He turned to the Pritchards. "I think yours is on the right because I went into it by mistake when I was looking for mine, but Maddy soon put me right."

"Well that's our first mystery solved," said Helen, picking up her suitcase. "What time is dinner?"

Henderson shrugged. "I'm afraid I have no idea," he said.

"I seem to remember our letter saying we were supposed to be in the dining room at seven," Alan piped up, "which I think was marked on the plan of the house?"

The others nodded.

"Well at least that'll give me a chance to get out of these clothes and into something a bit more presentable," said Helen. "Come on, Alan, let's see what kind of a room we've got."

"They aren't going to like it," said Sam once the Pritchards had disappeared.

"No," said Jeremy. "I don't think they are. Which side is your room on?" he asked her.

"The left," Sam replied. "Why?"

"Oh, just that my room might be underneath yours then," he said, and then with a grin directed at Henderson, "and I think they are probably under you."

"Good job I'm not a light sleeper then," said Henderson, "although I have to admit to now being a little worried about the week's events."

"Why?" said Sam.

"Because if I were a ghost I would need to be made of very stern stuff indeed to even consider trying scare Mrs Dr Pritchard," he said with a grin.

"Well, even though they're settling into the room opposite mine, I think I might follow Maddy's example and have a bit of a snooze before dinner," said Jeremy. "The last couple of weeks have been a bit punishing as you know," he said, "and I have to admit I'm rather hoping nothing does happen while we're here so I can have a bit of a holiday."

"I think that's unlikely," said Henderson.

"I know," said Jeremy. "In fact if I was to be as serious as you appear to be right now, I'd be telling you that the reason I'm going to try and get some sleep is that it might be the last chance I get for the next seven days."

Sam knew he was right, just as she knew that, as Jeremy Stokes wandered back to his room and the two of them were left alone, it was time to go exploring.

Chapter Eleven
A Stroll in the Grounds

*E*verything should look lovely on a sunny afternoon in *Wales*, thought Sam, *even haunted houses built from former torture dungeons.* As they stared up at the Dark Manor's façade before them, she realised that the house was doing its very best to prove them wrong.

"Astounding how innocuous it feels inside compared with out here, isn't it?" said Henderson, taking care to stay out of the shadow cast by the spire that emerged from the building's central tower. The part of the building presumably accessed by the door next to their bedrooms. The one they had found to be locked.

"Not really," said Sam. "I think it wants us in there. Now that we've come outside again it's glowering at us because it knows we still have a chance to leave and it doesn't like that one bit. Do you?" she addressed the house, and for a moment the blackened stone seemed to assume an even darker shade.

"Well if that's the case it's probably best not to upset it," said Henderson before directing his words at the building in front of them. "Especially as we are not leaving, we just thought it might be useful to have a little look around."

"Do you really think it can hear us?" said Sam

"I have no idea," said Henderson. "You're the one who started talking to it. I assume you can feel something that caused you to say what you did?"

Sam nodded.

"Oh yes," she said. "It's weird but when we got here with Maddy I couldn't feel a thing, which is partly why I was very cynical as to what she was harping on about. But now we're out here, on our own, on a hot summer's day…"

"Now you can feel something?"

"Let's just say I wish I'd packed my winter clothes," Sam said with a shiver. "Before you say anything, I promise I'm going to be very, very careful, but I can already tell you we'd probably need more than a week here to document everything that I'm getting impressions of right now."

"In which case we already have an answer for Sir Anthony," said Henderson. "But of course we'll need proof." He sighed. "You know, I've always regretted that there isn't some sort of machine that could just extract whatever you're thinking from your head and preserve it for anyone to see."

"Er… I'm quite glad there *isn't* something like that," said Sam. She could still feel the house glaring at them. "Shall we go for a wander?"

They set off to the left, keeping close to the wall of the east wing, despite Sam's protestations, because Henderson wanted to see if there were any obvious symbols or phrases carved into the stone.

"This is one of the wings from that old asylum," he said, as they moved less quickly than Sam would have liked. "In fact, I think our Mr Marx arranged for the exposure of just what had been going on inside it, just so it could be closed down and the stone transported here."

"I know I'm going to regret asking what sort of things went on," said Sam.

"You might, actually," said Henderson with a wink as he trod over ground which was becoming distinctly marshy. "Apart from the usual beatings, tortures, and humiliations to help pass the time, the warders would force the inmates into playing rather cruel games: ones where the loser would end up either dead or horribly mutilated. There was a whole room filled with contraptions that resembled a cross between a children's playground and a medieval torture chamber: see-saws with razor blades, slides with sharpened spikes, roundabouts with ropes designed to cut off the circulation as they were turned, that sort of thing."

Sam breathed a sigh of relief as the ground began to get too wet and they were forced to move away from the house.

"I don't suppose Mr Marx had the bad taste to keep any of those?" she said.

"I've no idea," said Henderson. "But while we're on the subject," he pointed to the first floor, "don't forget that somewhere up there is apparently a children's nursery, filled with toys that had all in some way caused the death of a child."

"Charming," said Sam. "You mean the skipping rope that might have strangled someone."

"Or a small toy that might have caused choking, toys with sharp barbs that led to tetanus infection, all kinds of things. I dare say we'll get a chance to look at them all eventually."

They had reached the end of the wing. The forest began only a few feet away but they were able to squeeze between the thorny undergrowth that heralded the trees and the marshy ground encroaching upon the building, to find themselves around the back, which was just as overgrown as Sam had thought it was from the view from her window.

"At least it's drier here," said Henderson, shielding his eyes from the sunlight and looking off into the distance. "There are some buildings further back there as well; shall we take a look?"

They set off and quickly realised that the reason the ground was so firm was because they were walking on flagstones.

"This whole area behind the house was probably a courtyard," said Henderson, kicking the worst of the brambles out of the way, "which means these buildings back here were probably stables."

To Sam the tumbledown brick buildings, with their collapsing corrugated iron roofs, looked more like the remains of a concentration camp. Almost directly behind the row of huts the forest craned over them, extending claws of branches that looked poised to tear them from where they stood once they were within reach. She really hoped horses hadn't been made to live here.

They were making their way back around the west wing, when Henderson tripped over something and almost fell, putting his hand out to steady himself on an upright pillar to his left.

"Funny thing to have out here," he said as he took a closer look at what he was leaning against. "But then again, perhaps not."

Sam looked at where he was pointing. She could just make out a few tarnished words set in slate into the stone. " 'In Loving Memory'..." she read aloud before rolling her eyes. "So there's a graveyard here as well."

"I knew there would be," said Henderson, nodding far too enthusiastically for Sam's liking. "That's the main reason I wanted to come out here. I probably tripped over one as well; ah, yes, I did. I wonder how many others there are out here?"

"And who they were," said Sam, convinced that they were probably standing in a cemetery filled with murderers, rapists and torturers. "Can we go now, please? I've been doing my level best to not be too sensitive to all this but, not to put too fine a point on it, my head is bloody killing me."

Henderson's face fell.

"I'm terribly sorry," he said, taking her arm. "Come on, let's get you back to the house."

She batted him off, not really angry with him, but she hated being treated like an invalid. "I'll be okay," she said with a brave smile, "but let's get out of here, shall we? And I won't be offended if you want to come back on your own to have a better look at whatever horrible people must be buried here."

"I just might," said Henderson as they made rather swifter progress back to the front of the house, "and of course there's the question of whether or not there are actually people buried there, or whether it was considered sufficient just to bring their grave markers here, especially the really old ones whose bodies would have crumbled to dust anyway."

"Enough talk," said Sam as they went back inside. "Time for a bath and dinner."

"Oh, does your room have a bath?"

"No," said Sam. "What I meant was, time to find a bath, have one, and then have dinner. And I'll find the bath on my own, thank you; I don't want to get waylaid by us coming across a bakery full of evil bread-making implements, or a music room filled with instruments made from bits of old bodies."

She left Henderson to ponder the glorious possibilities while she went in pursuit of cleanliness.

Chapter Twelve
An Apparition at Dinner

The dining room was located in the west wing at the front of the house, off a mahogany-panelled corridor that led from the entrance hall, and probably stretched for the whole of the wing. It was the first room Samantha and Henderson came to as well as being the only one with open double doors and a circular table set for six in the centre of it. The wall opposite the door boasted double rows of bay windows with gothic arches, the glass thankfully bereft of the strange designs present in the windows in the front hall. Even though it was only early evening, the sun was already almost hidden by one of the higher mountains in the far distance.

"One of the unfortunate consequences of being situated in an area riddled with valleys," Henderson remarked.

The countryside did look lovely though, thought Sam, the fields below them tinged with the gold of a summer's evening, the few tiny farm buildings she could see burnished with a coppery glow. In fact she was so taken with the beauty of it all, that she almost failed to notice the absence of any roads.

"Bit odd, that, isn't it?" remarked Henderson, after he had pointed it out to her. "You'd expect to see the headlights of at least a few cars winding around the lanes, or at the very least some evidence of what might pass for the remains of rush hour on that dual carriageway we came in on."

"Maybe the roads are too well hidden by the countryside," said Sam.

"They might be," said a voice from the door. "On the other hand, it may just be that the house doesn't want us to see them."

At first Sam thought this was someone they hadn't met yet, perhaps one of the staff (if there were any). But it only took her a second to realise that the girl standing at the entrance with her hair piled on top of her head was Maddy. She wondered how on earth the girl had managed to cram what looked like a Victorian governess' dress into her rucksack, just before wondering why someone like Maddy would even want to wear it.

"It was in the wardrobe in my room," said Maddy, the black material of her swirling skirts whispering as the heels of her Victorian boots made little indentations in the carpet as she stepped forward, "along with the shoes. I've no idea if they were meant for me or not, but after seeing the rest of you I thought I'd probably better dress up a bit for dinner; all I had was the stuff I came in and some changes of underwear."

Too much information there, thought Sam, and if it had been for Henderson's benefit she knew it would have passed him by totally. More likely he was wondering who that dress had originally belonged to, which was probably a very useful thing to be wondering.

"May I say, Miss Calverton, that you look quite exquisite," said Henderson, clicking his heels and giving a little nod of appreciation. Sam, in her rather more modern — and she hoped rather more fetching — black cocktail dress that came down to mid-thigh, resisted the urge to proprietarily clutch his left arm as Maddy gave a little smile of acknowledgement and came closer before turning to look at the table.

"That's a bit more lavish than I was expecting," she said, eyeing the silver cutlery which suggested at least three courses and possibly four. Each place setting had also been provided with four different glasses, presumably for red wine, white wine, water, and the fourth one looked to Sam like a champagne glass. Perhaps spending a week here wasn't going to be quite so arduous after all?

"I wonder who set all this up?" said Maddy, picking up one of the individual salt shakers with which each place had also been provided, and holding it up to the light. It appeared to be made from silver and had been fashioned in the shape of a raven's head. Shaking it caused salt to pour from its wide open beak. The pepper shakers were in the shape of tiny black cats.

"I think someone likes their Poe references," said Henderson with a grin. "The question is, is this all just to get us in the mood, or do all these items have some possibly unpleasant connotations as well?"

Maddy was putting the shaker back into its appointed place as Alan and Helen Pritchard entered the room. Helen had changed into a figure-hugging evening dress of purple satin which Sam very much suspected hadn't been found hanging in the wardrobe of their bedroom. Alan Pritchard was wearing the same clothes he had arrived in.

"You see?" said Helen to him but for the benefit of everyone. "I told you we'd be expected to dress for dinner."

"Not necessarily 'expected'," said Henderson, keen to defuse the situation before it had the chance to become explosive. "Samantha and I didn't feel like wearing the same clothes we'd been tramping around the grounds in, and Maddy here actually found her evening wear in her wardrobe."

"Was that in your wardrobe?" Maddy asked Helen, eyeing the purple number with something approaching disdain.

"No," said Helen, doing her best to remain polite. "I took one look at the collapsing horrible old thing and decided my clothes would start to rot if I put them inside it. So at the moment they're hanging all over the room."

"So in fact, it's just as well I didn't bring many," said Alan with a slightly forced laugh.

"It can't be as bad as my room," said Jeremy Stokes as he came in, dressed more casually than any of them in an open-necked shirt, jeans and a crumpled navy linen jacket that had seen better days. "I swear to God if any ghost does set foot in there it'll be more likely to commiserate with me than try to scare me!"

For the next ten minutes they all made the kind of pleasant introductory small talk common to groups of people who aren't at all well acquainted but who know they are soon going to be working intimately together. Topics such as the journey there, the weather, and the aforementioned less than luxurious state of their rooms, were all rapidly exhausted as they each began to wonder what was meant to happen next.

"Do you think we should sit down," Alan said, leaning on the back of one of the chairs, "or are we supposed to wait for someone to come and show us where to sit?"

"I would imagine that if someone has gone to all this trouble to set up the table, if they wanted us to sit somewhere specific, each place would have its own name card," said Henderson. "But there doesn't seem to be anything of the sort."

"It would be nice if they'd at least left us with some drinks," said Alan.

"Drinks will be served with the meal, sir."

They all turned in the direction from which the voice had come. The far wall, adjacent to the right side of the window, was panelled in the same manner as the corridor. A door had now opened two-thirds of the way along it, and standing in the doorway was an elderly man in formal dress. He was so tall he had to stoop to get through. Sam was surprised he didn't bang his bald head on the lintel as he came in.

"Who are you?" asked Jeremy as the man approached them.

"My name is Arthur Wakehurst, sir. I and my wife Philomena have been employed by the man who sent you here to take care of you, so that you can all devote your energies to that which he has employed you for."

"Philomena's a charming name," said Helen.

"Thank you," said Arthur with the hint of a smile. "My lady wife shall be taking care of the cooking and of other sundry household chores. She has been left strict instructions to leave your bedrooms entirely undisturbed, however. I believe this is so that any alterations of your personal items will either be that of your own doing or of any entity which might be thought to inhabit this house."

"Do you think there's something here, Arthur?" asked Alan.

"Oh for Heaven's sake," said Helen. "He wouldn't be here if he thought the place was filled with monsters, would he?"

"I believe my views on the matter are of little import," said Arthur, "but my wife and I have only taken the positions on the strictest of understandings that we leave before midnight, that and we do not return until daylight is once more filling the valley. Now, pray be seated, I believe Mrs Wakehurst has prepared a duck pâté for starters." He looked at Maddy, "except for you, young lady," he said. "We have been informed that you are of the vegetarian disposition and therefore something else has been arranged for you."

Arthur disappeared back into what they presumed was the kitchen and they all sat down, Henderson and Sam sitting next to each other and Alan and Helen sitting across from them, leaving the other two to fill in the spaces. Maddy took the seat between Henderson and Alan, while Jeremy sat between Sam and Helen.

"Well I wasn't expecting him," Jeremy said.

"No," said Helen. "But I have to say it's a huge relief. I was half expecting to be living off tuna sandwiches and fizzy water all week."

"Well, rooms aside, Sir Anthony does seem to be doing his best to make us comfortable," said Alan, unfolding his napkin. "Perhaps we should just sit back and enjoy it."

"Have you brought any equipment with you, Dr Pritchard?" Henderson asked. Both Mr and Mrs Pritchard looked up at once, and Henderson indicated with apologies that he had meant Alan.

"It's *Professor* Pritchard actually," the physicist said, fiddling with his cutlery. "For my work on magnetic resonance imaging."

Helen explained that was how they had met. "At the time I was involved in research in the imaging of certain tumours," she said, "and Alan was the man I was advised to approach to discuss field strengths and radiofrequency signals, and we just hit it off."

"As you do," said Jeremy, but everyone ignored him.

"Of course!" said Henderson, realisation striking as the first course was served. "I'm familiar with your work, Professor Pritchard, in fact I wondered if you might be the same Pritchard who published that very interesting paper on *Imaging of Otherwise Unobserved Phenomena*."

"Yes, well," said Alan, obviously a little embarrassed. "It was very much a sideline to my main research work, you understand. That's not why I was granted my chair."

"Splendid paper, though," said Henderson, smearing a piece of brioche with duck, "the first proper piece of scientific work I've read that attempts to quantify the imaging of possible supernatural apparitions."

"You mean like *Ghostbusters*?" said Jeremy, showing signs of relief as his wine glass was filled.

"If you like," said Alan, assuming a faintly patronising tone. "But it was very much basic science research and the funding for that is non-existent. I had hoped that the paper would have helped raise interest, but sadly not."

"What did you do?" Sam asked, indicating to Arthur to fill her glass with red wine.

"I applied a set of sequentially incremental radiofrequency impulses under a variety of field strengths and т-weightings to test subjects to determine if any paranormal activity could be detected at the point of expiration."

"You did *what*?" said Maddy, toying with her salad.

"He scanned cockroaches to look for their ghosts," said Henderson with a grin. "Simple really; put them in the MRI scanner, add a puff of insecticide and switch on the machine. He used different settings each time to try and get the best images. I thought it was a very elegant experiment indeed."

"Thank you very much," said Alan appreciatively.

"That's horrible," said Maddy, who at the mention of cockroaches was now searching her lettuce for signs of anything moving. "Did you just kill cockroaches, or did you move onto anything else?"

"Nothing else, I'm afraid," said Alan. "Unfortunately I couldn't get permission and, as we had no money, that was the end of that."

"But it's brought you here," said Henderson. Alan nodded enthusiastically. "But presumably you haven't been able to bring an MRI scanner with you."

The two of them and Helen laughed at what must have been the obvious lunacy of such an idea.

"No," said Alan. "But I *have* been able to bring a portable field generator adjusted to the setting I think may yield the best results."

"Did your experiment with the cockroaches show something then?" Sam piped up.

"Only on one particular setting and even then all we could detect was a very vague shape hovering somewhere near the body," said Alan. "But the important thing was that it was reproducible. Every time an insect died that shape appeared, enough to suggest a significant connection."

"So we may actually get to see some ghosts this week?" said Jeremy, who had already drained one glass and was motioning Arthur to refill it.

"I hope so," said Alan. "One way or another."

"I very much imagine *that* will be up to the house," said Maddy, sipping at her glass of water and looking around her.

"If there *are* actually any ghosts here," said Henderson. "After all, just because you build a place to be haunted it doesn't necessarily follow that you're going to end up with a house of horrors."

"I don't believe William Marx's intention was to create a 'house of horrors', Mr Henderson," said Maddy with a glare. "He was simply so desperate to contact the spirit world, to contact his own wife and daughter, that he thought using materials saturated with the essence of strong emotions would be more likely to create a house on the border between this world and the next."

"You may well be right, Miss Calverton," Henderson replied as he was served what looked like a lamb shank of the most excellent sort. "However even the best of intentions can have unfortunate consequences; and you have to admit that if there ever was a formula to create a haunted house, then this one ticks all the boxes."

"Do you *all* know the history of this place then?" said Helen, emptying her wine glass. "Unfortunately, I didn't have time to read any of the notes I was sent before we had to come here, and Alan wasn't terribly helpful."

"Only had a chance to skim them I'm afraid," said the professor with a sheepish shrug. "I've been terribly busy completing grant applications and had to get the last one in yesterday evening."

"What about you?" Sam asked Jeremy.

"I was rather hoping someone might be able to give me a potted history," said Stokes, looking less uncomfortable now that he knew others around the table were as in the dark as he. "I'm used to researchers doing that sort of thing for me."

"In that case," said Henderson, tucking into his main course, "once we've had dessert, I think it might be time for a history lesson."

"Thank you, Mr Henderson," said Helen, "but I think we're all quite capable of reading up on the subject for ourselves."

"Oh no, you're denying him his moment of glory," said Sam with a smile. "He's just dying to tell you all about this place."

"How about a quick résumé?" said Stokes, looking around the table. "I'm sure no-one will mind if you start before the puddings get here."

Henderson reached for his wine glass, but Sam took his wrist and directed his hand to the water.

"You'll thank me in the morning," she said.

Henderson took a mouthful of water and then began.

"Well from the notes we were given, I would assume that the room we're sitting in now was part of the old Dorringborough Asylum, dismantled and then rebuilt here. In fact I very much suspect both the east and west wings were originally part of that structure, and this very room may have been where the inmates were tortured to help the warders pass the time. Sam and I did a little exploring today and certainly the flagstones of the courtyard look as if they were derived from the stone circle that originally stood on this site. As for the buildings at the far back close to the forest, they look like stables but, as they look mid-twentieth century in design, I wonder if they might have originally been used to house German prisoners in the Second World War. I have no idea what our bedrooms originally were, but between mine and Sam's is a room that's locked and has the most fascinating design on it. I've not seen it before and for all I know it might even have been taken from some Black Magician's house. I can't wait to find the key."

"Perhaps he knows where it is," said Jeremy as Arthur filled his wine glass yet again.

"Do you know where the key to that room might be, Mr Wakehurst?" said Helen.

The butler shook his head.

"We opened all the rooms we had keys for when we arrived yesterday, Dr Pritchard," he said.

"And did you see any ghosts last night?" Jeremy asked.

"No sir, but then we had gone before evening had fully descended," said Arthur, before explaining that although it was only a little past eight o'clock he and his wife would now be on their way. Dessert was limited to cheese and biscuits which, along with coffee and port, had been placed in the drawing room for when they retired there.

"It's the house," said Maddy, after he had gone. "It wanted to wait until we all arrived."

Jeremy snorted "Well it hasn't exactly got off to a flying start now we're all here, has it?" he said. "I don't know about any of you, but I've not seen anything the slightest bit scary all day."

Which is when all the lights went out.

Later none of the women would own up to who had actually screamed; but Henderson believed Sam, who had certainly been in more perilous situations and hadn't made the kind of strangled gasp that someone had uttered in the darkness. Besides, far more important than who had screamed was the reason why.

A shape was floating high over the dining table.

It was difficult to make out what it actually was, even though in the absence of any other light, the nebulous, ethereal, intertwining wisps of its form were suffused with a silvery glow. Henderson warned the others to stay still and not to get up from where they were sitting.

"But what if it tries to hurt us?" hissed Helen as the knots of glowing tissue resolved themselves into a gossamer-thin glowing dome resembling an ectoplasmic jellyfish the size of the dining table at which they were sitting.

"I think if it wanted to it would have already done so," said Henderson. "Besides, for all we know it was here when the lights were on, we just couldn't see it."

"What does it want?" said Jeremy as the shape began to descend, drifting down until it was at eye level.

"I think we're about to find out," was Henderson's reply as the ethereal apparition began to tip over until its convex surface faced him. It stayed in that position for ten seconds and then moved to his left to face Sam, doing the same thing to each of the people sitting at the table in turn, before floating back up to the ceiling and disappearing.

Which is when the lights came back on again.

"What on earth was all that about?" said Helen, visibly shaken.

"I've no idea," said Alan. "But its luminescence in the absence of any obvious energy source would certainly suggest a possible supernatural origin."

"I agree," said Henderson.

"Either that or some extremely elaborate special effects trick," said Jeremy, trying to sound unconvinced.

"Oh for Heaven's sake!" said Maddy. "Isn't it obvious?" The others turned to her. "The house was saying 'hello' to us, greeting us individually in turn. Couldn't you feel it?"

"I didn't feel anything," said Jeremy, reaching for his wine. The glass shattered at his touch.

"Interesting," said Henderson, reaching for his and getting the same result. It took him few seconds to recover before he turned to Maddy and said "Maybe the house doesn't like us."

"Well that would hardly be surprising, would it?" said Maddy just before the tumbler before her shattered, spraying her with droplets of mineral water that fizzed on the material of her black dress.

The others shielded their eyes as their glasses broke in quick succession. Red and white wine bled into one another on the tablecloth as they all jumped to their feet.

"What should we do?" Jeremy asked Henderson, and the others turned to look at him expectantly.

"It would probably be best if someone checked the door," said Henderson, meaning Sam, who backed away from the table.

"You mean in case it's locked?" Helen asked.

"Yes," said the detective, "just to make sure this whole room hasn't been transported into another dimension, that sort of thing."

"It does happen," said Sam with an apologetic smile.

"I hope not," said Alan. "I've left my detecting equipment in the car."

"I don't think it's needed right now anyway," said Jeremy.

Sam was able to confirm, to a collective sigh of relief, that neither was the door locked, nor did it open onto some fiery nether land.

"Thank goodness for that," said Alan.

"Yes," said Helen, acidly. "They're probably giving you a chance to drag your instruments in before they do anything really horrible to us."

Sam opening the door seemed to have calmed things. The group waited in silence for something else to happen until Henderson's sigh of relief signalled that they, too, could relax.

"Are you all right?" said Henderson, meaning Sam.

"Yes," Maddy replied from across the table before Sam had a chance to open her mouth. "I think so. But I need to talk to you about what happened at the table, when this house's apparition faced me." She paused, as though trying to make sense of what she thought had happened. "I think it was trying to communicate with me."

"Because you saw something in it, you mean?" said Jeremy. The girl nodded. "Thank God," he said. "I thought I was the only one."

"Did we all see something when it came to our turn with that ectoplasmic entity?" said Henderson. He looked around the group to be rewarded by a nod from each of them. "Excellent!" he said, rubbing his hands together. "Then we have something to talk about over coffee and mints!"

Chapter Thirteen
Coffee and Mints and Esoteric Books

The drawing room was next to the dining room. It was dimly lit, lined with bookcases crammed with crumbling volumes and, despite the warmth of the summer evening, rather chilly. Arthur had seen fit to light a fire before he had left, and the girls grabbed the chairs nearest to it while Henderson and Alan saw to the drinks. Jeremy, too jumpy to sit down, peered at some of the volumes.

"Who on earth would want a book called *The Achievement of Death*?" he said with a frown.

"Probably someone who wanted to understand more about it," said Maddy, refusing the offer of port.

"*Esoteric Orders*," Jeremy read, "*Elements of Mysticism, Unveiling the Ungodly...* "

"That last one sounds more like my cup of tea," said Helen, making an elaborate show of crossing her legs before warming them in front of the fire.

"I imagine the books are, like the rest of the house, intended to attract and cultivate a supernatural atmosphere," said Henderson, sipping at his port and pulling a straight-backed chair which he placed facing the rest of them. "And judging from what we've just seen, it may well have worked."

"What have we just seen?" asked Sam.

"Why don't we start with you?" he said, looking at her kindly. "I know what I saw, but it would help to know if everyone saw the same thing."

"You mean once that floaty thing was in front of my face?" said Sam. "Well, at first it just looked blank, like a very thin white sheet, stretched very tightly, as if it was almost at breaking point."

"Exactly what I saw," said Henderson nodding as the others looked on, "and what then?"

"Well, it was so thin that it was easy to see beyond it," said Sam.

"Even though it was dark?" he asked.

"I'm coming to that," she snapped, but not unkindly. "Stop interrupting me. As I said: it was so thin I could see beyond it, which was weird because the only light in the room was coming from the thing itself. Even so, I thought I could see across the table to Maddy, at least I did at first. Then I realised it wasn't her at all: it was someone else, someone I've never seen before. And there was something with her."

"You mean *someone*?" said Alan.

Sam shot a glare at him. "I mean some *thing*," she said, looking back at Maddy. "I thought it was you at first because she was wearing the same kind of dress: very austere, with a high collar, the sort of thing a Victorian governess might wear. But she was young and had a very pretty face. I don't mean that you don't, I mean she looked different from you. Anyway she was pretty, or at least she would have been pretty if she hadn't looked so stern. In fact, I would almost have called her frightening if she hadn't paled into insignificance beside the thing that was sitting next to her."

"What was it?" Henderson said, very gently.

Sam closed her eyes tight.

"I don't really know. It was short, squat, hairy, and it was crouched low to the ground. Or perhaps its legs were very short, I'm not sure. I also couldn't tell how many legs there were. I didn't get a look at its face either because it was blurry and I didn't have time, but I got the impression that whatever it was, it was holding her hand."

Sam shivered and Henderson put an arm round her.

"You're freezing, you know," he said. "Get nearer the fire."

"A bit more of this will help I think," said Sam, knocking back her port and holding out her glass for a refill.

"What did you see?" Henderson asked Jeremy, once he had replaced the decanter.

"I was so weirded out by the whole thing I didn't really concentrate on it," said Jeremy with a sheepish grin. "It might well have been what she said. All I saw were a couple of blobby shadowy shapes, but I guessed they was just part of that jelly thing."

Alan and Helen testified to seeing something similar.

"I did my best to look at it as carefully as possible," said Alan, "but I certainly didn't pick up any of that kind of detail."

"I did," said Maddy, pointing at Sam. "It was like she said but with one difference. I saw a young woman wearing a dress like mine but she was standing next to a child, a little girl in fact. But I'll agree that neither of them looked very happy."

"So only those with psychic sensitivity saw anything more than a few shadows," said Henderson, "which, incidentally, is what I saw and nothing more. I wonder if it might be Marx's wife and daughter?"

"If it is we should try to bring them back," said Maddy.

Alan suggested setting up his portable detection equipment in the room above the dining room. "Whatever it was may have come from there," he said, "and if we see it again tomorrow night, at least then everything would be in place for me to get some data."

"That's a good idea," Henderson agreed. "Of course we don't have any guarantee that it's going to reappear at that place and time, or indeed appear again at all."

"There's one way we could make sure there was the best possible chance of it appearing," said Maddy. Her eyes were bright as she jumped to her feet and approached Henderson as if asking her head teacher for special permission to get out of a particularly hated lesson. "I'd like to hold a séance."

"What, now?" said Jeremy, scratching his head. "Would that be a good idea?"

"I think Maddy means tomorrow night, Mr Stokes," said Henderson as Maddy nodded. "We've all had quite enough for one day. I would suggest that we retire once our drinks are finished, and use the daytime tomorrow to prepare us for whatever we may experience then."

"How do you know nothing will happen during the daytime?" Helen asked.

"I don't," Henderson admitted. "But all the other documented hauntings only occurred during the hours of darkness so I imagine whatever we're dealing with won't make any special exceptions for us."

"I don't suppose you could enlighten us as to some of these 'documented hauntings' could you?" asked Jeremy, pouring himself another drink and sitting down next to Sam. He looked around him. "We're probably better off knowing as much as you do about it."

Henderson rolled his eyes. He had quite forgotten that none of the others had managed to find the time to go through the information that Sir Anthony must have sent them.

"You really haven't read about *any* of them?" he said.

Sam reached out a calming hand as his outburst was met by four apologetic looks. "Maybe just before bed isn't the right time," she said, doing her best to defuse the oncoming tirade.

"No," said her companion, drawing himself up to his full height and addressing Sam, but glaring at the sheepish looking group before him. "They all agreed to come here. How can they possibly expect to deal with what might be lurking here if they have no idea of the things that have happened to those who have preceded them?" He paused. When no-one dared break the silence he carried on. "Are you all sitting comfortably?" he said.

Silence.

"Then I'll begin."

Chapter Fourteen
Henderson Waxes Lyrical

"William Marx's wife and daughter," Henderson began, "were killed in a bombing raid over Bristol in 1940. From that moment it's very likely that he became a changed man, although because the war was on, and because of certain business interests he was making a considerable amount of money from, he carried on with his life more or less as normal for the next couple of years. The invoices and records sent by Sir Anthony testify to that. However, during this time Marx started to travel much more widely and I don't doubt that the purpose of these trips was to seek out the building materials for this house. His diary details several trips around the United Kingdom, and even a very interesting map detailing what he thought were the most potent sites of supernatural activity in the country. Some of that part makes very interesting reading, especially his charting of the war effort mainly out of concern that the main site he was considering might get hit and he would have to settle for one less satisfactory.

"Fortunately for him, this part of Wales never attracted the interest of the Third Reich and by 1945, once everyone was sure the war was truly over, he was able to start planning this house. By this time he had already made a trip to the southwest of France to buy, from a private collector, the stained glass recovered from Le Monastere de Saint Benedict de la Malediction."

"I can't say I've heard of that," said Professor Pritchard, interrupting and glancing at his wife, "and we know France pretty well."

Henderson nodded. "It's unlikely that you would have. It was an institution devoted to the worship of something extremely un-Christian-like, until the terrible things going on there were discovered — by someone much like me, who put a stop to it all. But to continue, he had also learned that, after the scandals that had caused it to be closed down in 1935, Dorringborough Asylum had been lying empty, and that the building itself was still structurally sound, so he bought that as well. Now he had enough materials to begin construction. He would use the standing stones already on the site for the foundations, and the materials from the buildings he had plundered for the walls.

"It took nearly seven years just to dismantle the wings of the asylum and bring everything here. The stonemasons needed to take the building apart brick by brick were expensive, but that was not the problem. It was rather that there were so few of them trained in what was admittedly a rather esoteric request that it was more of a manpower issue."

"I get the feeling our Mr Marx probably wasn't sitting around while all this was going on," said Jeremy, stretching his legs.

"No, he wasn't," said Henderson. "During this time he was travelling the globe, collecting further items. While he was away, he received a communication to say that the blocks obtained from the standing stones would not be sufficient to build the central part of the house. It doesn't say in his diary exactly how the problem was resolved, but a clipping from a newspaper article seven months later details how the bodies of seven children who had been abducted over the previous months had been found buried at strategic points in the grounds of Llanfair Castle just a few miles away from where construction was taking place. Of course, in those days historic buildings like that were subject to far less protection than they are now and the government was far too busy trying to rebuild the country to worry too much about them, so when a substantial part of the castle was taken away no-one of any importance really noticed; and even if they did, I think Mr Marx would have been able to sufficiently reimburse them for their concern that they kept their mouths shut."

"That's *horrible*," said Maddy, and the others nodded.

"It is, isn't it?" said Henderson with a gleeful beam. "Over the following seven years, work on the main part of the house was completed. In fact, it's very interesting just how often the number seven keeps cropping up and I'm sure it's not coincidental. By 1960, the building was ready to be furnished. And goodness me, had Mr Marx collected some interesting items to furnish it with, not the least of which was a very interesting collection of books which now grace the shelves in various rooms."

"You mean like *Rites and Rituals of the New Guinea Primitives?*" said Helen Pritchard.

"Or *Time Lapse Photography of the Dying Child* by Wolfgang someone-or-other?" said her husband. "We seem to have both of those in our room."

"Wolfgang von Schmidt," said Henderson, eyebrows raised. "I had no idea any copies had escaped the ovens. I'll have to come and have a look at those later, although I suggest that you don't unless you have very strong constitutions indeed."

"Don't worry," said Helen, "we have no intention of going near the grubby-looking things."

Henderson looked down at his feet. "Most of the rugs and carpets on which we tread were woven under the most extreme of conditions, and I don't doubt that a few of them have blood mixed in with the fibre, either deliberately or as the result of blows received from cruel masters in the sweatshops where they were made. The curtains in many of the rooms were purchased from some of the more decadent brothels to be found in Tangiers and Bangkok. It would seem that violence was not the only extreme emotion that Mr Marx hoped would attract the interests of supernatural forces. I do wonder if that's where he got the beds from as well."

Henderson trailed off for a moment, as if lost in thought, or perhaps trying to put those thoughts in order. "And so finally, by about 1961 the entire project was completed, twenty-one years after the event which had caused Marx to start it. Again, I suspect that twenty-one being the product of three times seven is significant also. His diary leads up to the date of the third of July (three times seven again, you see) in 1961, then it stops, and as we know his body was never found. I suspect he saw it coming, as prior to taking up residence here he had alerted his solicitors that they should receive a communication from him on the last day of every month. Therefore, sometime during the first week of August an exhaustive search of the building was undertaken, but to no avail. Consequently, and again according to Mr Marx's wishes, many of the items in the house were taken away and put into storage to prevent the attentions of other collectors. They were also left with strict instructions that neither the property nor its contents were to be sold until a period of at least forty-nine years had passed, or seven times seven if you prefer."

"Which brings us up to now?" said Sam.

"Exactly!" her colleague replied. "And Sir Anthony Calverton buying everything outright for what amounted to a song, partly because there was a strict stipulation that the house contents were not to be sold individually but as part of a whole that included the building itself, and partly because the house has garnered such a reputation over the years that any self-respecting property developer has probably quite sensibly reasoned that the place would be more trouble than it was worth.

"You see, in the years since William Marx disappeared, there have been a considerable number of strange stories associated with this place. As is always the case, the vast majority of them have been of only the most minor interest: strange noises, a light in one of the upstairs window seen in the depths of night by unreliable observers, and so on. I know it's already been suggested that I shouldn't send you all to bed with nightmares but if you really haven't read the most pertinent cases associated with this house I do think it's only fair to us all if we *all* know what we might be up against."

"Do I really want to hear this?" said Helen.

"You might not," said Alan, "but I do."

"I have a feeling Mr Henderson is going to tell us anyway," said Maddy, looking at Jeremy, who merely waved his hand in a gesture to 'please continue'.

Henderson poured a glass of port and took a sip before continuing. "About ten years ago, during a party that was being held locally, a young lad and his girlfriend studying at the college in Newport were dared by some of their friends to spend the night here. They'd never heard of the place, but sufficient beer had been consumed and the couple were of a rather cynical bent anyway, that they quickly agreed to the terms: to spend one night at the manor and in the morning to receive their reward from their colleagues, who would come to pick them up. They were dropped off at the front door at just before half past one in the morning. Their friends had made sure the door opened and that they could get inside the building. Then they left them there and that was the last that was seen of them. Almost. The next morning, when it was time to leave, their sleeping bags were found, as was evidence that they had bedded down for the night. Their clothes were there as well, but of the two of them there wasn't a sign. Now you may say that the couple ran off intending to play a trick on their colleagues and met with some accident at the bottom of one of the valleys that riddle these parts, or perhaps even a lake or river, but despite the police initiating a search of the county, nothing was found. Of course, that's not the strangest part. After all, they could just have easily been intending to run off to sunnier climes and realised they had been given the ideal opportunity to do so.

"Because that didn't explain the scratch marks, the ones that covered the walls either side of the entrance and the heavy wooden door itself, the ones that those who had left the couple there testified weren't present at half-past one that morning. But of course drunken students are hardly likely to be reliable observers, especially at a late hour and in semi-darkness. No, it was the forensic findings that got everyone worried and which gave the case a considerable degree of notoriety. You see, scratches were not the only clues the front door had to offer. Embedded in the wood, by the cold light of day, the police found fingernails — seven of them to be exact — heavily varnished and dug so deeply into the wood that they had been torn out by the roots when the owner's hands must have been wrenched away."

Henderson paused, letting the details of what he had just said sink it. This time there were no interruptions, no questions, no comments, just quiet contemplation by a group of people, some of whom were only just beginning to realise what they had let themselves in for. He gave them a moment and then carried on.

"The blood traces found matched the blood type of the missing girl but despite an investigation, which is still officially open, no other evidence was found, nor did they ever find any trace of the missing boy. In fact the only item of interest was the discovery of some bones in the outhouses at the back, where Sam & I were exploring today."

"And were they the bones of the missing child, Mr Henderson?" Helen Pritchard asked, her eyes bright with fear.

Henderson shrugged. "Apparently it was difficult for the medical examiner to reach any definite conclusion as to what they were," he said. "They were too old to be considered relevant to the case, and while they could have belonged to a child they were so warped that anyone possessing such a bone structure should not by rights have been able to live for more than a few days."

Chapter Fifteen
Bed and Breakfast

"Henderson, I think that's probably enough for now," said Sam, who knew full well that her companion would have been completely oblivious to the growing discomfort among the group as he had related the history of the house.

"But I haven't had a chance to tell them about the strange animal tracks that have been seen near here," he said, with all the verve of a political dissident knowing he is about to be repressed. "There's even a plaster cast of one in the Monmouth Museum; a great, three-toed, taloned thing apparently."

"You've not seen it, then?" said Alan.

Henderson looked sheepish. "No. It's not on general display and when I rang them, the lady I talked to denied any knowledge of it." He took a deep breath and then another sip from the glass Sam had recharged for him while he had been talking. "Tomorrow," he said, finally picking up on Sam's non-verbal cues that he really ought to be changing the subject, "I would suggest we explore the *rest* of the house, either as a group or in pairs. It probably wouldn't be a good idea for anyone to go wandering off on their own. I have to say I'm particularly looking forward to seeing the Music Room."

Helen got to her feet and shivered. "Well, I've had quite enough for one evening," she said. "I think I'm going to go to bed before Mr Henderson starts telling us about all the wild and wonderful body parts the instruments have been made out of."

"Not all of them, actually," said Henderson, oblivious to Sam's poke in his ribs. "Apparently there's a clarinet that is alleged to have belonged to a serial killer and he used to play it as his victims bled to death. Marx's diary claims the killer's dream was to play Mozart's 'Clarinet Concerto' in its entirety while someone slowly died in front of him. But apparently he was never able to make it to the end."

"Bed sounds like a good place for me, too," said Alan, rapidly following his wife to the door.

"We will be conducting the séance tomorrow, won't we, Mr Henderson?" asked Maddy.

"If everyone is amenable, Miss Calverton," said Henderson, all too aware that it hadn't been a request.

"In that case I shall see if I can find anything suitable to aid us in communicating with the supernatural," she said and with that she, too, was gone, closely followed by Jeremy, stifling an overly dramatic yawn.

Sam put her hands on her hips and sighed. "Well, you certainly know how to clear a room," she said.

"I just thought it important that they know a bit about this house," Henderson replied. "Some of them don't seem to realise how dangerous it might be. I can't believe they didn't read up on it before they came here. And the look on their faces when I was just trying to be helpful!"

Sam shook her head. "They didn't do the kind of exhaustive background research that you consider routine, because that's not the kind of people they are; not even Alan, who I suspect is far more obsessed with his magnets than he is with the idea of ghosts actually existing. And they didn't want to listen to what you were saying because right now most if not all of them are going through a phase best described as 'I don't think I realised what I was getting into when I signed up for this and now I'm not sure I want to stay'."

"Oh," said Henderson. His face fell, and then he looked at Sam. "That's not how *you* feel, is it?"

She smiled. "I've been through enough weirdness with you that at the moment I can safely say this is feeling like one of our milder cases, so don't worry. That horrible thing I saw in that ghost jellyfish thing has me wondering, though."

"Me too," Henderson agreed. "I'm sure the others saw it as clearly as you did, they just didn't want to acknowledge it."

Sam nodded. "Quite possibly, but I'm not altogether sure a séance tomorrow night is a terribly good idea," she added with a frown.

"I know what you mean," agreed Henderson, "though I don't think there's going to be any stopping Maddy. All we can do is stay on guard and keep our fingers crossed that she doesn't stir things up too much."

Sam did her best to yawn without making too big a show of it.

"Do you think there's a lot here to stir-up, then?" she said as she left the room to go upstairs.

"Oh yes," said Henderson with a big grin as he followed her out. "Lots and lots and lots."

§ § §

At eight o'clock the next morning, those who had already managed to make it down to breakfast had little to report in the way of supernatural phenomena during the night, although not everyone had enjoyed a good night's sleep.

"I kept expecting something to come through the wall," said Helen, drinking her first cup of black coffee in one gulp and immediately pouring herself another. "I'm amazed I got any rest at all."

"Me too," said Alan, who had arrived with her. "But then I turned my mind to how I might adjust my detection devices to best image what we saw last night and before I knew it I was out like I light."

"Yes," said Helen with a barely veiled sneer as she buttered a piece of toast in the most vindictive way possible, "you were, weren't you? From the sound of your snoring I imagine if all the hounds of Hell had raced through our bedroom they wouldn't have disturbed you, deep in your physics wonderland."

"Well I read a book for a bit," piped up Jeremy, "and then lay there, staring up at the ceiling for God knows how long until I eventually drifted off, and before I knew it the sun was up."

"How about you, Miss Jephcott?" asked Alan, helping himself to a croissant and ignoring Helen's pointed look at his waistline.

Sam wondered what to say. After she had got upstairs to her room she had spent the best part of half-an-hour moving the dresser in front of the bedroom door, and then another wondering whether she should nail the window shut (she always carried a few essential tools in her luggage based on past experiences) before deciding that, even though there was quite a drop, its value as an escape route just about outweighed the risk of anything trying to get in through it. After that she had taken a piece of chalk from her bag and, using the method Henderson had demonstrated to her many moons ago, drew a protective pentacle around her bed and tried to get to sleep, unsuccessfully.

"Oh, very quiet," she said with a smile as she refused the cooked breakfast Arthur was about to place before her. "Just coffee for me, thanks," she said.

"You should probably eat a bit more than you usually do, Sam," said Henderson from the doorway, "After all, you are going to need to keep your strength up!"

"And here he is," said Alan with a mouthful of bacon. "The very man responsible for all our sleepless nights!"

"Oh I'm sure I can't quite claim responsibility for that," said Henderson, sitting down. "This house has to shoulder some of the blame for being actually haunted, as we all witnessed last night." He inspected the three ramekins that had been arranged next to the toast rack. "Three different types of marmalade?" he said. "How splendid!" Henderson reached for a slice of toast and began buttering it enthusiastically. "So where's Miss Claverton, then?" he said, pointing to the solitary vacant space at the breakfast table. "Has she already been and gone?"

The others looked at the untouched, pristine napkin and the unused cutlery.

"Maybe she likes to sleep late," said Jeremy, wiping his mouth and getting up to leave. "Well that's me finished, so I hope the rest of you don't mind excusing me," he said. "I'm going to grab a shower to make myself feel more human. Don't worry," he winked at Sam, "I'll keep an eye out for any ghostly maniacs with knives, although I imagine they'd be more likely to come after you."

"Not if they know what's good for them they won't," said Sam under her breath.

"So what's the plan for today?" asked Helen as her husband nodded yes to a second helping of sausage.

Henderson grabbed the greengage jam. "As I explained last night," he said, "I think we should get a better idea of the layout of the house during daylight hours and fortunately with it being summer that means we have plenty of time to map this place out today. We could all go together, but I was thinking if two of us took the west wing, another two the east, and then the final pair explored outside in more detail, by mid-afternoon we should be able to meet back up here and share any interesting finds we've made."

Helen leaned over the breakfast table to take the jam from Henderson in a manner Sam thought unnecessary and rather excessive. "And how do you suggest we pair up, Mr Henderson?" she asked.

The detective took a sip of tea, frowned and returned the sip to its cup in as refined a manner as possible.

"Sorry," he explained. "Earl Grey; can't stand the stuff. I think our group has three natural pairings. Ideally one of each pair needs to be sensitive and we have Samantha, Madeleine and, in a different way I appreciate, your husband with his detection devices."

"They're not terribly portable, I'm afraid," Alan interjected.

"Nevertheless," said Henderson, "If you come across something unusual presumably you can set up your device at that spot to see if it picks anything up?" Alan nodded. "Excellent! Then there we are. I suggest Sam and I take the west wing, the two of you take the east and when Maddy comes down I'll ask her to look around outside with Jeremy."

"You may as well ask her now," said a voice. The four of them turned to see Maddy, now attired much as she had been when she had arrived yesterday, standing in the doorway. Draped over her arm was what looked like a long black tablecloth. "It'll do very nicely for our séance tonight," she said, opening it out and nodding with satisfaction when she saw that it would easily cover the dining table. "I also found some fantastic candlesticks in a trunk in my room — six of them, which is rather a nice coincidence, don't you think?"

Henderson didn't look convinced.

"I don't suppose there were six black candles in close proximity to the candlesticks were there?" he asked.

"I was going to keep that a surprise until tonight," said Maddy, looking surprised. "How on earth did you know?"

"Oh, just an educated guess," he replied. "I have a feeling you were meant to find all those things."

Maddy glared at him. "Are you suggesting we shouldn't continue with the séance?" she snapped.

Henderson shook his head. "On the contrary," he said. "I very much suspect we are going to have little choice in the matter, which is why it's all the more important that we have a good working knowledge of this entire building and its grounds in case we end up having to do a lot of running about once whatever it is has arrived tonight." He turned to Alan and Helen. "We'll meet in the drawing room at three o'clock this afternoon, okay?"

Helen nodded, the trace of a smirk on her face, and Alan gave a little salute.

"Who went and put him in charge?" said Maddy once Alan and Helen had left.

"Oh no-one," said Sam, "but it always seems to end up that way and trust me, it's better that it happens sooner rather than later. He gets unbearable the longer things don't happen the way he knows they should have from the start."

"Only because I'm usually right," said Henderson defensively, as Sam laid a calming hand on his arm.

"Trust me, Maddy," said Sam. "I've been with this man long enough to listen to what he says and if you don't go along it will just spell more trouble for all of us in the end."

"Besides," said Henderson, "it's not as if I've forbidden you to do what you wanted. All I'm suggesting is that your will may not be entirely your own at the moment."

Sometimes Henderson had no tact at all. Sam cringed in expectation of an outburst and was very surprised when the girl remained calm.

"You may say that, Mr Henderson," said Maddy, "but I'm telling you now that I know my own mind and that I would have planned a séance during our stay here irrespective of whatever else might or might not have happened. I do agree with you, however, that we should explore the house and I don't doubt that in your plans you have paired me up with that television presenter, the one who thinks he can 'predict death', and seeing as the rest of the group seem to be going along with you for the moment, then I suppose I must play along as well." She folded the tablecloth over her arm and strode out, leaving Sam to tell Henderson off.

"You're really not very subtle sometimes, you know," she said.

"Fascinating," said her companion, his eyes still on the door that Maddy had just slammed behind her. "I wonder if the house is working through her, or if she's actually like that all the time?"

"Either way," said Sam, "I don't think it's going to do any of us any good if you piss her — or it — off, do you?"

"I prefer to think of it as 'winding it up so that it makes a wrong move'," he said, finishing his toast.

"Yes, well; first, you have absolutely no evidence that Maddy is anything other than a slightly petulant, over-imaginative nineteen year old girl, who doesn't like being bossed around, and in my experience there isn't a nineteen year old that does. Second, in your experience — which admittedly is greater than mine — is it actually possible for a house haunted by any number of terrible and upsetting things to make a 'wrong move'?"

"Now there I have to admit you have me," said Henderson, as Arthur began to tidy away the breakfast things. "And yes, I do get a bit bossy sometimes. Sorry."

"That's okay," said Sam. "Just be careful what you say. I'd hate to be the one carrying you out of here in little pieces."

"Better than carrying me out of here in one piece," he said. "For one thing I'd be far too heavy. Now, time to do some real exploring, I think."

Chapter Sixteen
The Music Room

The west wing began at a locked door, situated at the far end of the corridor off which the dining and drawing rooms were located in the main part of the building. The corridor had been panelled in rosewood but the door that halted their progress looked darker, older, and far more sinister. Sam resisted the urge to run a finger over the elaborate carvings of weird creatures in garish poses, some of which had talons that looked sharp enough to draw blood if she touched them.

"I'm sure I've got the key here somewhere," said Henderson, rummaging in the semi-darkness. For some reason the electric lights at this end of the corridor weren't working and Sam was trying hard not to think that it was because the house knew where they were going and was determined to have a little fun with them.

It took him three tries before he found the right one.

"There we go," he said, pushing down the cast iron handle.

The door opened with the kind of ear-splitting creak that no self-respecting haunted house would be without, and a shower of dust from the lintel greeted them as they peered into the darkness beyond.

"Do you think the lights will be working in here?" said the detective.

"Only one way to find out," said Sam, reaching in and feeling around until she found a wobbly switch. She jerked it up and down a couple of times until she felt a click and the passageway ahead of them was filled with a wavering light.

"Do you think they've got it on a special setting?" said Sam, trying to keep the tremor out of her voice. "You know: the haunted house dimmer switch?"

"Possibly," said Henderson, taking a step forward. "Although I suspect it's much more likely that this part of the house doesn't like the light."

"You know what I was telling you about saying the wrong thing at the wrong time?" hissed Sam, following him in. "Well, you're doing it again."

"Sorry," said Henderson absent-mindedly, taking out a penlight to inspect the walls more closely.

"Why didn't you use that to help you find the key?" said Sam as the pencil-thin beam revealed that the walls were panelled in the same dark wood from which the door had been fashioned. More worryingly, they also seemed to have been adorned with the same kind of carvings.

"I forgot I had it until I felt in my pockets just now," said Henderson in the kind of absent-minded way that Sam knew meant he was only half listening to her. "Look at these..."

"I'd rather not," said Sam even as she felt herself being drawn to what he was pointing at.

The carvings were similar to those on the door, but with the aid of Henderson's pen torch Sam was able to make out the designs in much more detail. Not that she was particularly happy to be able to; the wood panels were covered in tiny creatures no more than two or three inches high, all with teeth and talons considerably out of proportion to their bodies.

"Very pretty," she said with a grimace. "Although I imagine if one of those things was chasing you, it would trip up on its own fingernails before it had any chance of catching you."

"True," Henderson nodded. "Unless these folded shapes on their backs are meant to be wings. A shame there aren't any carvings of humans figures for us to get an idea of scale."

"What the hell are they doing here, anyway?" said Sam. "I thought this wing was meant to be the rebuilt part of some mental hospital."

"It is," said Henderson, getting to his feet. "But that's just the stone this part of the house is made from. We already know that Marx filled his house with items he hoped were charged with supernatural energy. Perhaps he found this panelling in a cathedral somewhere, perhaps they were carved by the inmates of the hospital, or perhaps..." Henderson trailed off, deep in thought.

"Perhaps what?" Sam asked, not sure if she wanted to know.

"Perhaps the house grew them to scare off trespassers," he said with a grin, before making his way further down the passage.

It wasn't long before they came to a door in the right hand wall. Henderson gave it a gentle push and then more of a shove before they were able to see the room beyond.

"I can hardly see a thing," said Sam.

"Yes, it is rather dark," said Henderson, walking over to the wooden shutters on the far side of the room. It took him a moment to work out how to open them and then, with creak of protesting wood, he was folding them back into alcoves in which they had probably not resided for many years. Sunlight flooded the room, illuminating swirling dust motes and gleaming off sticky cobwebs thick enough to make unidentifiable many of the objects they were matting. The purpose of the room was, however, still obvious.

"I wonder if that piano still works," said Sam

"Only one way to find out," came the reply.

Sam rolled her eyes as Henderson dusted off a stool upholstered in green leather and sat at the grand piano which stood in the middle of the room. He lifted the lid of the keyboard, and regarded the scarred ivory before him.

"I think it was Andrés Segovia Torres who said that the piano is a monster that screams when you touch its teeth," he said, his fingers poised.

"Quite possibly more often in some cases than others," said Sam, tensing herself for the ensuing potential cacophony. The attempted tinkling of a couple of keys caused her to relax a little.

"Not a sound," said the detective, much to his companion's relief. He hit the keys again, much harder, before he got up and lifted the lid of the instrument. "Completely empty," he said with a sigh.

"Obviously the casing of this particular piano was more important than having a working one here," said Sam, coming over to peer inside the instrument. "Has someone spilled brown paint inside it?"

"Possibly," said Henderson, "but, bearing in mind where we are, it's probably something else. I suspect this instrument was at some point used to hide a body." He turned to survey the rest of the room. "Well, seeing as we've found the music room without too much trouble, shall we see what else there might be in here of interest?"

In the far corner near the window was a harp, its strings withered and useless. A set of African drums yielded a groan of disgust from Sam as Henderson explained that the little bumps she could feel on the surface of each skin were probably the nose and lips of whichever unfortunate individual had had his face flayed to make it. A tiny, strangely-shaped violin had, in Henderson's opinion been made 'either for a monkey or a witch's familiar to play, possibly both'. A battered Bontempi electric home organ had the right hand side of its keyboard missing and had probably been used as a murder weapon. Sam didn't even go near the box of percussion instruments as she had no wish to hear Henderson's guesses as to what the castanets, maracas and football rattle had been made from.

"It's a shame, really," said Sam, looking out of the window at the forest beyond.

Henderson looked up from a table littered with bony-looking woodwind instruments. "What is?" he said.

"It's such a beautiful day outside, and this building is just fantastic architecturally. That someone should want to deliberately fill it with so many horrible things just seems even more wrong when the sun is shining on all of them."

Henderson came over to stand beside her.

"Well, we know *why* he did, and we also know that people who are desperate are capable of doing extreme and sometimes foolhardy things. That doesn't change if you have a lot of money; in fact often it's worse. Whatever William Marx brought to this house it's up to us to get rid of it. Or them."

Sam looked worried. "But that isn't what Sir Anthony wants us to do, though, is it?"

"Ah," said Henderson, finally realising where the conversation was going. "I know, but Sir Anthony is another very rich man and if it's one thing I've learned about very rich men, it's that they always think they can be richer. The contract we've signed with him says we're going to offer him proof this place is haunted. If during the course of our investigations we should by chance do something to stop it being haunted there's not much he's going to be able to do about it, is there? Especially as there's nothing in the contract about us having to ensure the building *stays* haunted."

"That actually makes me feel a lot better," said Sam. "For a moment there I thought were just going to find the ghosts and then run away."

"As if we were going to do any such thing," said the detective, putting an arm around her and giving her a brief squeeze. "Although I have a feeling that once the ghosts decide to show themselves, they'll do their very best to prevent us from going anywhere. If I were you, I would enjoy that sunlight while you can. I have a feeling after tonight this place is probably going to be drenched in darkness."

"You really are the master of being comforting one minute and then thoroughly discomforting the next, you know," she said.

"All I can be is my honest, simple self," said Henderson, brushing dust from his jacket.

"But not humble."

"Oh no, not that. You have to allow me *some* indulgences."

They propped the music room door wide open to allow some light into the corridor, which only served to show just how dirty and dust-choked it was. The next door down was on the left and demonstrated more strange carvings in the same style as the others, but this time in the form of row-upon-row of tiny human faces.

"I don't suppose those wide open mouths are meant to suggest that they're laughing?" said Sam with a grimace.

"Your guess is as good as mine," said Henderson as he gave the door a shove.

The room they found themselves in this time was huge, and its extent couldn't be fully appreciated until Sam had pulled the shutters back on one of three sets of double windows. The room appeared to stretch for the length of the wing. Set into the smeared walls at regular intervals were tiny lamps encrusted with dust, each one presumably intended to act as a light for whoever might be lying in the beds that had been positioned beneath each one.

"It looks like a hospital ward," said Sam. "There must be twenty beds here."

"Just down one side, if you ask me," said Henderson. "There's another twenty up against the opposite wall." He gave the nearest one a prod. The mattress responded by coughing dust at him. "I wonder if these are the original beds from the asylum or if he got them from somewhere else?"

"I would think they're the beds from Dorringborough," said Sam. "Why would they be anything else?"

"Oh I don't know," he mused, running his hand over the ironwork of the headboard. "I just have the strangest feeling that British hospital beds of the time wouldn't have had swastikas engraved on the finials."

Sam looked on as Henderson rubbed at the little mark on the right hand brass knob of the headboard. Now he had cleared the dust off, it was obvious.

"Do you think they all have them?" she said.

"Only one way to find out," said the detective. "I don't suppose you've brought a duster?"

It quickly became obvious that they didn't need one. The beds were of such a similar design, and the finials so exactly the same on each, that the discovery that every one of them possessed engravings similar to those found on the first bed was quite enough to convince the two of them.

"So where does that leave us?" said Sam. "Other than even more confused than when we started."

"Not confused, exactly," said Henderson, wiping his hands with a red cotton handkerchief. "More intrigued. I wonder which hospital he got them from, and why?"

"Maybe the beds at the asylum weren't in the best of shape," said Sam with a grimace.

"That's quite possible," said Henderson. "But even so, presumably these beds would have been used for German patients; the beds for their prisoners of war would have most likely consisted of wooden slats." He gave the bedstead nearest them a tap and was rewarded with the resonant clang of sturdy iron. "These are of a much higher quality, and of course the mere presence of any kind of decoration, let alone something as ornate as finials, is a testament to that. No, these beds were intended for the recuperation of German soldiers, which has me wondering why they should all have sufficiently terrible connotations to make Marx think they were suitable for his house of horrors."

"Perhaps they were all the victims of some sort of early biological warfare?" said Sam, immediately wishing she hadn't.

That's a very good point, was all she hoped he would say in the way of reply but unfortunately it was not to be. "Perhaps they all died horrible deaths from the kind of mutagenic agents that were being experimented with then. We all know about the use of mustard gas in World War One," Sam gave him a look that begged an explanation, "...but for those of us who don't, it was a substance capable of passing straight through your clothes and causing the formation of huge blisters filled with yellow fluid, so that the victims resembled an enormous walking bag of pus."

"I wish I hadn't encouraged you now," she said, knowing there was no stopping him.

"It was also carcinogenic," Henderson went on. "So just imagine what the effects might have been of something even more poisonous and faster acting than it. We know Hitler never used poison gas, but that needn't have stopped either side from developing something."

"Well surprise, surprise," said Sam, gazing down the aisle of dusty empty beds, "Another room filled with a history of suffering."

"I take it you haven't tried to sense anything psychically yet?" he asked.

Sam shook her head. "At the moment I honestly think it's too risky," she said. "Just like you, I want to get the measure of this place before I decide whether or not it's safe to open my mind to it. I think I'll leave that to Maddy for now."

"I must admit I'm quite surprised at her," said Henderson as they made their way out. "Or rather I have to say her actions make me wonder if she does possess any psychic ability at all. If you're worried about the possibilities of opening your mind even a little, I can't think what a séance might do to someone acting as the channeller. Perhaps she is stronger than you," he said with a grin.

"Or perhaps she's just full of shit," said Sam. "Don't forget that."

"I won't," said Henderson, realising as they walked on that they were coming to the end of the passageway. "Just as I won't forget that you don't hold a terribly high opinion of her."

"Oh that's just natural girly dislike," said Sam. "Part based on good reasons, like her being unpleasant to you and not listening to you, and part based on my own completely irrational intuition. But I promise I won't let it show. Much."

The corridor came to an abrupt halt and they found themselves faced with a panelled dead-end, where Henderson promptly crouched and began to tap at various strategic points.

"I wonder why it suddenly stops like this?" said Sam.

"Probably because there's a secret door behind this wall," was the reply. Any further attempts on Henderson's part to find the secret catch were curtailed at that moment by a scream from back the way they had come.

"Sounds like your least favourite person," he said, getting up and wincing as his back creaked.

"I suppose we'd better go and see what's wrong," said Sam.

"You never know," said Henderson, setting off back down the corridor at a pace. "Maybe some horrible thing has decided to show itself."

Sam was surprised to realise that for once she was almost as enthusiastic as Henderson to find out if it had.

Chapter Seventeen
No Way Out

It was a dead bird.

Or at least, Sam thought, the little chaffinch was nearly dead. As they watched, the tiny thing managed one further weak beat of a bloodied wing against the floor tiles of the entrance hall before lying still.

"It flew in here when I opened the door and just fell down," said Maddy, still shaking, as Jeremy also looked at it in horror.

"Is that what you saw happen as well?" Henderson asked him.

"What's the matter?" said the girl tearfully. "Don't you believe me?"

"Of course I do," said Henderson, "but I just want to know if that's what Jeremy also saw."

"I wasn't here," was Stokes' reply. "I was just getting my sunglasses from my room to accompany Maddy outside, when I heard her scream. I got here just before you two did."

"And you say it just fell in front of you?" said Henderson, taking a telescopic pointer from his inside breast pocket and extending it to its full length.

"Yes," said Maddy. "Oh God, what's wrong with it?"

He gave the bird a prod. For a moment nothing happened. Then, as they watched, the colour drained from the bird's plumage. With a faint crackling sound the tiny body collapsed in on itself, the blood which had leaked onto the tiles dried to a blackened sludge, and the entire carcass crumbled to a fine powder. Henderson tried hard to resist saying the word 'fascinating' out loud but found he couldn't stop himself.

"What the hell was all that about, Mr Henderson?" asked Stokes.

"That's a very good question," said the detective, wiping the end of his pointer and putting it back in his pocket. "Did it behave at all strangely before it fell?" he asked Maddy, who shook her head.

"It just came straight in here when I opened the door," she said. "Almost as if it was being chased by something."

Everyone looked towards the open doorway.

"We're all waiting for you to check it," said Sam.

"Yes, good point," said Henderson, extending the pointer once more and waving it in front of him as he approached the door. The others took a step back as he crossed the threshold and looked about him.

"Nothing out here that I can see," he said, waving the pointer in all directions.

"Does that detect supernatural forces?" Jeremy whispered to Sam.

"Oh no," she said. "But it has come in very handy for distracting things we would prefer to keep at arm's length."

By the time Henderson had come back inside, Alan and Helen had arrived and wanted to know what all the fuss was about.

"You probably wouldn't believe us if we told you," said Jeremy, who then proceeded to tell them anyway.

"Well there's nothing there now to suggest it ever existed," said Alan.

Henderson's ears pricked up at that.

"Very nicely put, Professor Pritchard," he said, regarding the highly polished area of floor where only a moment ago a bird had decayed to nothing before their very eyes. "I wonder if that is what happened, that this house somehow chased it in here so it could suck the life out of it."

"That's horrible," said Maddy.

"Yes," said Jeremy. "And besides, if it wanted to do a spot of life-sucking, why hasn't it done it to any of us?"

"Perhaps we're too strong for it," said Henderson.

"You mean too strong for it at the moment," said Sam.

Henderson nodded. "Well I didn't want to worry anybody but... yes, if I'm right, it probably means we have a more pressing deadline than the one imposed by Sir Anthony," He ran a hand through his increasingly unruly hair. "I wonder how long we've got?"

"Long enough to get out of here and never come back," said Alan, grabbing Helen by the hand, taking his car keys from his pocket, and making for the door.

The rest of them listened to the sound of a car engine attempting to be started.

"I'm keeping my fingers crossed, you know," said Henderson when Sam looked at him.

"What for?" said Maddy. "That they get away or that you're right?"

The car spluttered and coughed a couple of times before the engine died completely.

"That sounds like the cue to start walking," said Jeremy, doing his best to sound upbeat. "Even though Mr Henderson might not be right, it might be a good idea to check that we can actually escape from this place."

"How did you get here, Mr Stokes?" Sam asked.

"Train, then bus, then taxi," said Stokes. "I never learned to drive and I didn't want anyone to know where I was going.

Sometimes the best place to hide is in plain sight, although I have to say I was a bit distressed that no-one on any of the public transport I used recognised me."

"Perhaps they were too over-awed," said Sam, as the Pritchards returned. "But we have a car, which I'm sure Mr Henderson is about to go and try before we all get too worried."

Henderson gave Sam a look that she knew was a mixture of apology for having forgotten they even *had* a car, and disappointment that they were thinking of leaving. Even when lives were threatened, he did sometimes find it hard to leave a situation he found himself intrigued by. He left the house but was soon back.

"No luck I'm afraid," he said. "The battery's as dead as the Pritchards'."

"And as dead as we might be too if we don't get out of here," said Jeremy. "Anyone fancy a stroll?"

"I think we all do," said Sam, grabbing Henderson's arm. "We can always come back another time," she whispered to him, "but it's not really fair to keep these people here if they're this scared, is it?"

"I suppose not," said the detective before turning to the others. "Are we all agreed that we want to leave?" he said to the group.

"It's not so much that, as the fact that I'd really rather not die," said Alan. "At least if we knew we could get away..."

"...and perhaps if we found a garage that could fix the cars," said Helen.

"That's right," said Alan. "Perhaps there was some excessive magnetic disturbance during the night that caused the batteries to be discharged. I've certainly heard of supernatural phenomena that have been observed to do that."

"I don't want to leave either, Mr Henderson," said Maddy. "I think there is something here, and if we can communicate with it, then perhaps we can also reason with it."

"I'm not so sure," said Jeremy, heading for the front door "and if it's all the same to you I think I'll just take a stroll to the main gate, for the reasons Professor Pritchard has outlined. If anyone would care to come with me, they would be more than welcome. Anyone who doesn't care to come with me is even more welcome to avenge my death if something horrible grabs me before I make it there."

No-one made a move to stop him.

"I'll come with you," said Henderson. "I think it would be dangerous for any of us to wander off on our own. Once we're satisfied that it's safe, we can come back for the others. How does that sound?"

Maddy and the Pritchards nodded, while Sam insisted she come along.

"Only because if you're going to run into trouble I'd rather be there to help you," she said.

"Admirable, Miss Jephcott," said Henderson. "Shall we go?"

The three of them headed out of the house and began to make their way along the drive that curled around to the left and down the hill ahead of them. Jeremy led the way with Henderson and Sam keeping an eye out to either side behind him.

They were about halfway down the hill when Jeremy fell over.

"My dear chap," said Henderson, helping him to his feet. "Are you all right?"

"Fine," said Jeremy, rubbing his head. "Apart from feeling as if I've just walked into a rubber brick."

Henderson surveyed the open path ahead of him and gingerly took a step forward, and then another, until he found his progress halted by an invisible wall.

"Oh dear," he said. "This doesn't look good."

"It doesn't look like anything," said Sam. "What are you talking about?"

The detective put out his hands and took several paces to the left, then came back to the driveway and repeated the process to the right.

"There appears to be an invisible wall blocking our way," he said. "And I wouldn't be at all surprised if it extends right around the house."

Sam came up and gave the wall a prod. She recoiled as if shocked.

"Ow! Bloody hell! You might have said it was like an electric fence!" she said, rubbing her fingers.

"Obviously it has more of an effect on the psychically sensitive," Henderson mused. "That would explain why I didn't fall over. When you touched it, were you able to tell anything about the dimensions?"

"It's a bloody great perimeter wall going right round the house," said Sam, taking a step back and looking up. "I can't tell how high it is, which means it must be more than twenty feet. No idea how thick it is either but I suppose that doesn't really matter seeing as we've nothing we can ram it with if the cars aren't working."

"It's going all the way around the house, then?" said Jeremy, looking worried.

Henderson nodded.

"It certainly sounds like it, and I've never known Miss Jephcott to be wrong about such things before. Tell me, Mr Stokes, when you got here yesterday, were there any birds singing?"

Jeremy thought for a moment before answering, "I think so. I mean I'm not the kind of person who would normally notice something like that, but I don't remember there being any odd silence if that helps."

"It was deadly quiet when we arrived," said Sam.

"Exactly," said Henderson. "I wouldn't be at all surprised if once the house detected signs of human habitation within it, the life force was drained from every single living creature within a five mile radius to provide the energy to construct this wall."

"I don't see any bodies," said Jeremy, looking around.

"Well you wouldn't, would you?" Sam challenged. "Remember what happened to that chaffinch? It disappeared completely once it had died."

"Once it had been drained," Henderson corrected.

"So you're saying that us going into that house set off some kind of reaction that's resulted in this invisible barrier being put up?" said Jeremy, reaching out to touch it once more, but then thinking better of it.

"I am," said Henderson. "I suspect it's been under construction since last night and, now it's working properly, the house felt bold enough to give us a little scare just to inform us who is now in charge. What's more, I think we ought to get back to the house to warn the others before anything else happens."

They walked at a swift pace back up the hill and Sam's relief to find the other three still there was nothing compared to the joy expressed by Maddy, Helen and Alan.

Until, of course, Henderson told them what they had found.

"Are you saying that we're trapped here?" said Helen when he had finished.

"Well, the cars don't work and the exit is impassable," said Henderson. "I'd say that fits the description of us being trapped pretty well. Does anyone know where Arthur and his wife are? We ought to warn them too."

"They've gone into town," said Alan. "Said they'd be back later this afternoon to cook dinner."

"Looks like we're going to be eating tuna sandwiches after all," said Helen.

Alan turned to Henderson. "What do you suggest we do now, then?" he asked.

Henderson looked at Maddy with a broad smile on his face.

"Let's hold a séance," he said.

Chapter Eighteen
It's Séance Time!

The group's first formal attempt to communicate with the house took place later that evening, after a makeshift dinner made up of some of what they could find in the surprisingly well-stocked freezer and larder.

"I wonder why the Wakehursts needed to go into town, with all the stuff there is in there?" said Sam as they waited for Maddy to get the candlesticks from her room.

"Don't tell the others," said Henderson, stifling the onion soup that was threatening to repeat on him, "but I suspect they just wanted to be here as little as possible."

"What do you think they'll do when they find they can't get back in?"

"Well they might alert the authorities, and while it might make a very interesting item on the six o'clock news and encourage the attention of numerous researchers both reputable and disreputable, I very much suspect we're going to be on our own in here until events reach their natural end."

"You don't think Arthur and Philomena are going to do that, do you?"

Henderson shrugged and winced as a particularly unpleasant spasm of heartburn had its way with him. "I have a feeling if they come back to be faced by a twenty-foot-high invisible wall, they will probably run a mile and thank the Lord they're not on the wrong side of it," he said.

Once the dining room was finally converted into the kind of place that would do a practicing medium proud, the three sensitives (Maddy, Sam, and Jeremy, who despite his protestations was deemed to have more psychic powers of detection than Alan, to which the physicist had readily agreed) were seated in between the confirmed non-sensitives of Henderson and Professor and Dr Pritchard. In the centre of each place setting on the table had been placed a candle. The candles were ordinary, slim, white wax affairs which had been found after some not undue rummaging in the kitchen.

The candlesticks were something else altogether.

Maddy claimed to have found them in her room, and Henderson had not been the only one to wonder aloud why six pewter candlesticks adorned with engravings of taloned, rat-like creatures should have been so easy to find. "Unless of course," he said, "the house intended for us to find them."

Once the seating order had been decided upon, Maddy asked that they link hands, which was met with some disagreement from the rest of the group.

"It will help concentrate the power," she argued.

"True," Henderson agreed, "but if during the séance one of us was to receive, say, the psychic equivalent of a powerful electric shock, then we would all be affected. The same would go for possession as well. I think it would be a much better idea if we stick to just having the tips of our little fingers touching our neighbours. Then, if there is any sign of trouble we can sever the link at a moment's notice."

"But that could cause terrible damage to the medium," Maddy said.

"I know it sounds callous, but better that than the whole group being affected I'm afraid," Henderson replied and a vote from the group confirmed it. So despite Maddy's protestations, the six of them were now sitting in the darkened dining room, around the circular table that had been draped in the black cloth Maddy had found that morning, fingertips touching, and with candles lit. It had been obvious from the start that Maddy wished to be the individual who would try to channel whatever it was they had seen last night and no-one was going to argue.

Maddy took a deep breath and closed her eyes.

"We need to concentrate," she said.

"What on?" Helen asked.

"On what we saw last night," was the reply. "What you yourself saw. Ignore any descriptions or suppositions other people may have made and concentrate on your own personal experience. Remember the shape, the colour, the degrees of light and shade in what you saw. Remember how it appeared and the way in which it moved. Remember how it came to you, how it faced you, and what you saw in its depths. Remember each stage in as much detail as you can, and then reach out with your mind and call to it."

Maddy began to breathe deeply. Sam looked around the table at the others to see that they were doing the same. She had no wish to remember the squat, hairy, evil-looking thing she had seen the previous night, so rather than concentrate on that she did her best to think about something else.

But it was no use. A shadow was forming on the ceiling. In between the light cast from the flickering flames beneath, in the spaces where the light didn't quite reach, something was taking shape. At first, it was dark and there was only the merest hint of its presence, but as it reached beyond the safety of the darkness and began to spread to the pools of firelight, and as that natural light began to dim, so the shape began to achieve a whitish luminosity.

"It's working," Maddy hissed, her eyes still tight shut. "It's working!"

Sam threw Henderson a look, but she took his returning glare to mean she shouldn't disrupt what was happening, at least not now.

The shape was still on the ceiling but now it looked more solid, and certainly bigger than what they had seen on the previous evening. As it began to descend it also began to veer towards the head of the table where Maddy was sitting, her breaths becoming deeper and more frequent, the movement of her chest keeping time with the gentle undulations of the shifting shape as it floated towards her. Almost without realising what she was doing, Sam broke the connection. It seemed to make no difference at all. The shape drifted downward until it was almost touching the slight form of Madeleine Calverton. Then, with a quick dart, it covered her face and neck. The shimmering entity remained for a few seconds before seeming to vanish by dissolving into the skin of her face.

Maddy's eyes snapped open.

"How delightful of you to invite me back," she said in a voice totally unlike her own. "Of course," the not unpleasant basso continued, "I have had the pleasure of becoming, shall we say, acquainted, with individuals such as yourselves in the past, but I've never actually been formally invited before. How very novel, and I must say, quite unique."

This speech was followed by silence from the group, most of whom were stunned that their efforts had yielded any result at all.

"Who are you?" Henderson eventually asked from across the table.

The thing inhabiting Maddy turned to look at him.

"How splendid!" it said. "A man who is neither afraid of what I am nor why I might be here, but instead wishes to know more. Are you quite sure, young man, that you *do* wish to know? I can assure you that individuals more powerful than you have died for less."

"And I can assure you that it is a very rare occurrence indeed for me to be referred to as 'young man'," said Henderson, crossing his legs and leaning forward to better observe exactly how Maddy's features had changed since the entity had taken possession of her. "I take it, then, that you are far older than any of us?"

"Older than all of your ages combined and much more!" Not-Maddy replied, the thing appearing to be shifting and moving just beneath the surface of her skin, quivering a little at that almost as if it were chuckling.

"Older than this house, then?"

"Much older. Thousands of years older," was the reply.

"So you were here even before it?"

Not-Maddy folded her arms and leaned back in her chair. "I was not brought here, like so many of the sad elements of this dark place, if that is what you mean by your question," it said. "I have been here since long before this building, in which you find yourselves this evening, was constructed."

Henderson narrowed his eyes. "Can I therefore take it that you are of the stone ring that used to stand upon this site?" he said.

Not-Maddy smiled. "It was a way of communicating with me, yes."

The detective looked even more interested. "Well, I have to say that your modern day English is remarkably good," he said.

"You would prefer I spoke to you in Aramaic?" said the voice before reeling off a sentence in an ancient language none of those assembled could understand. "Or Old Norse?" More words tumbled from Not-Maddy's mouth.

"That's all very impressive," said Henderson, "but not being familiar with either Old Norse or Aramaic, I'm afraid I can't verify that you're speaking either of them."

Not-Maddy fixed the detective with a gaze that suggested it was less than pleased.

"What would you prefer, Mr Henderson?"

"Oh, perhaps a little classical Greek?" he replied. "I can still just about get my head around that."

Not-Maddy thought for a moment, then took a deep breath and said, "ο φόβος είναι ο πόνος που προκύπτουν από την αναμονή του κακού."

Henderson frowned in deep concentration. He was silent for a minute before he looked up at the possessed body of the medium once more.

"Oh, very good," he said. "Aristotle, I believe, and a very apt quote at that."

"He was one of those whom I guided," said Not-Maddy with an unmistakable hint of pride.

"If you were in ancient Greece, how on earth did you end up here?" Henderson asked in the manner in which a pre-war public school headmaster might ask an errant schoolboy why he was out of bounds.

"How I became tied to this place is of no importance to you," said Not-Maddy, "but I am pleased that you understand my warning at last."

"What did she say in Greek?" Sam hissed from his left.

" 'Fear is pain arising from the anticipation of evil'," said Henderson, not taking his eyes off the undulating form of Not-Maddy Calverton. "Is that what we should prepare ourselves for?" he asked the figure. "Fear and pain?"

"Those, and far worse if you do not leave," she said. "Only by the power of the girl in front of you am I able to warn you. Those who have come before you have not been so lucky."

"We can't leave," said Henderson. "There is a barrier all around this place."

"You have the means to traverse that barrier within your grasp," said Not-Maddy. "Only time and your own abilities will prove whether or not you are worthy of the opportunity to use them."

"You mean you're not going to tell us?" said Henderson, obviously trying hard to keep the annoyance out of his voice but failing miserably.

"If you cannot work out such a simple thing for yourself, then you are scarcely worth saving," said the voice. Henderson was about to reply, when Maddy's face contorted and the voice of the thing possessing her became a strangled squawk.

"It is already here!" it said, swaying Maddy's head from side to side and then turning it to look at each individual in turn sitting at the table. "One of you... one of you is not who they claim to be!"

"What?" said Henderson.

Maddy was pulled to her feet. Her right arm outstretched, pointing into the darkness behind them. "One of you has already been taken by this house... replaced by the evil that has come to reside here. In time it will take more, in time it will take all of you, then nothing will be able to stop it, and then it will go... beyond."

With that, Maddy fell forward across the table, knocking over two candlesticks and landing on the wood with a heavy thump. Sam ran for the light switch, as the others did their best to revive the girl they had just seen speaking with the voice of an unearthly creature.

Helen took a tiny brown bottle from her bag and wafted it beneath Maddy's nose. The girl twitched and then resumed consciousness with a bout of coughing.

"I think she'll be all right," said the doctor. "But we'd best get her somewhere she can lie down for a while."

"She probably won't remember any of it, do you think?" said Alan as Jeremy and Helen helped the girl back to her room, closely followed by Samantha.

"Quite possibly not," said Henderson, taking out a Mont Blanc fountain pen and commencing to tap it against his teeth. "But I can, and I'd say whether or not Maddy remembers anything is hardly our greatest concern at the moment, is it?"

"Well," said Pritchard, scratching his head. "It was all a lot of nonsense, wasn't it? All that stuff about knowing Aristotle and having been around forever. The girl's just had a bit of funny turn if you ask me."

"On the contrary, Professor Pritchard," said Henderson as Sam came back in to say that Maddy was all right, just a little shaken, "whether or not whatever spoke to us has been around forever or was just this house playing with us, there is one thing of which I am convinced. Something is coming, Professor, something powerful and evil that intends to consume us and then move beyond this house to cause heaven knows what carnage, and the bit that really worries me is that apparently it has already started."

Part Three

The Very Worst
Place to Stay

Chapter Nineteen
Trouble on the Hill

"What did it mean, 'One of us has already been taken'?" Jeremy Stokes chewed a fingernail and looked up from the drawing room fire. Henderson had suggested they convene somewhere *other* than the dining room to discuss everything that had just happened. Stokes had left Helen to get Maddy settled, and the doctor had joined them once she was happy that the sedative she had given to Maddy was working, and the girl was sound asleep.

"The spirit that possessed Maddy was suggesting that one of our group has already been possessed by the malevolence that is inhabiting this house," Henderson was on his feet, the better to address the group and, Sam suspected, to keep order.

"Well that's nonsense!" said Alan with a snort. "We're all of us just the same as when we came here. Except Maddy now, of course," he said, a worried look crossing his face.

"If what the entity that Maddy channelled said is true," said Henderson, "I very much suspect that the possessed individual would look and act in exactly the same way as before."

"You think she really did it, then?" said Stokes. "She wasn't making it up, putting on a silly voice, or anything like that?"

Henderson's face was grave. "Not that I would ever dream of pulling rank, but I do know my job, Mr Stokes. Whether or not Maddy possesses any psychic ability I still don't know. But something just spoke through her. The question is whether or not we believe what that something told us."

"Possession isn't all spinning heads and other nasty stuff," said Sam.

"Exactly," her colleague nodded. "Plus, if we *do* have a case of possession here, we have no idea when it took place. For all we know, it could have happened before we all met each other for the first time."

"You keep saying 'if,' Mr Henderson," said Alan, stroking his chin thoughtfully.

Henderson sat down and nodded. "That's because despite the classical training of whatever it was that spoke to us, I am not yet convinced that it was anything other than some part of the entity that lives within this house playing with us, trying to confuse us and make us mistrust each other, and by doing so prevent us from working as a team to get rid of the bugger."

"Or buggers," said Sam, to which Henderson agreed.

"That's all very interesting, Mr Henderson," said Jeremy, "but what if it was trying to warn us? What if one of us is plotting behind our backs? And what about what else it said? 'In time it will take more.' That means any one of us could be next."

"Or that we are in more danger from suspecting each other than if we believe what it said," said Henderson, trying to keep order. "What is most important of all here is that we don't panic."

"What should we do?" said Helen. "Thanks to what just happened, we're all loaded with nervous energy. We might as well try and find something positive to do with it."

"I would suggest we devote our energies to trying to get out of here," said the detective.

"It did say the means were at our disposal," said Jeremy.

"But it might also have been lying," said Alan.

"I know," said Henderson. "But even so, I think it would be a good idea if we continued the search we were conducting of the house and grounds before we were so rudely interrupted by the house giving us a demonstration of its power."

Jeremy went over to the window.

"I don't fancy going out there in the dark," he said.

"I didn't mean now," said Henderson, doing his best to make his voice calm. He took a pocket watch from the depths of his jacket and snapped it open. "It's nearly one o'clock now. I would suggest we all get to bed and in the morning we finish exploring this place. Does anyone have any better suggestions?"

"No," said Alan, putting his hand up, "not at the moment. But I do have a question. Why did you look at your watch when there's a clock over the mantelpiece?"

"I trust it more than something that belongs to this place," said Henderson as he snapped it shut and put it away. "And now it's probably time for bed."

"Should we barricade ourselves in?" Jeremy asked.

Henderson pondered that for a moment. "Probably best not to," he said. "I mean, while it may help to stop something coming in through the door, if it comes in through the window it'll take us that much longer to get in and help you, won't it? Stop looking so worried, Mr Stokes. I have a feeling this house has rather tired itself out for one night."

"Darling," said Helen to Alan, "perhaps you and Jeremy could make sure you both get back safely to your rooms while I have a quiet word with Mr Henderson about my new patient."

When the two other men had left, Helen came and sat close to Henderson. Helen made sure the footsteps outside had retreated before she began.

"I know I told the others that Maddy was sleeping peacefully," she said, "and she is, now; but I was wondering if you'd be good enough to come and take a look at her."

"Of course," the detective nodded. "What is it that you're worried about?"

Helen shook her head. "I'm not sure," she said. "It will probably sound very strange to you, but sometimes as a doctor you get a sixth sense about when something is wrong. Over the years I've certainly learned to trust mine, and I have to say I think there's something very wrong with Madeleine Calverton. I don't think it's physical, at least not in the way that I would classify it, but since we saw that thing moving under her skin…"

"She hasn't looked normal?" said Sam.

"It sounds silly, doesn't it?" said Helen. "And for all I know it may be that I'm just still spooked after that bloody séance, but my gut instinct is telling me you should come and have a look. If you don't mind."

Henderson gave a big yawn, denied that he was tired, and then followed Helen to Maddy's bedroom, with Sam in tow.

Maddy was lying on her bed, still dressed in the gown she had worn for the séance.

"She was too tired to take it off," Helen explained, leaning over the girl and gently shaking her. There was no response.

"Well, you said you'd given her a sedative," said Sam.

"Only a very short acting one," said Helen. "I don't like using the things at all, but she desperately needed calming down. She shouldn't be as unresponsive as this, though."

"That's not what you were worried about, then?" said Henderson.

"No," said the doctor, "this is something new. What I was worried about was her right hand."

Henderson knelt beside the bed and, very carefully, examined first the girl's palm, then the dorsum of her hand, and finally her thumb and fingers.

"I can't see anything obvious," he said.

"You're not looking closely enough," Helen whispered. "Check her index finger again."

Henderson took another look. Sure enough, on the very tip of her finger was a greyish discoloration. Tiny black threads were extending from it and beginning to encroach on the soft pad of her finger.

"Goodness me," said Henderson, gently replacing the girl's hand by her side, before turning to face Helen. "Well done Dr Pritchard, very well done indeed."

"What is it?" Sam asked.

"I have no idea," said Helen. "And to be honest, if someone came to my surgery with that I'd probably dismiss it as nothing to worry about. But we're not in my surgery. In fact I don't really feel as if I'm even in the real world anymore."

Sam had been asking Henderson, but she bit her tongue back from saying so.

"It would appear that our ectoplasmic friend has left a little bit of him or herself behind," he said, taking out a tiny magnifying glass. "It doesn't appear to be spreading," he said, peering at the lesion through it. "But you will tell me if anything changes?"

Helen nodded. "I'll keep a close eye on her," she said. "And I know I'm going to regret asking this, but is there anything in particular I should look out for? She's not going to transform into some huge bloodsucking monster, is she?"

"It's unlikely," said Henderson, "but who can say? The thing I'll be most interested in is if that spot changes. Also, if she wakes up let me know; I'd like to be the first to talk to her if that's all right. Are you going to stay here for the night?" Helen nodded. "Good. Not too tired?"

"I can manage the night," she said with a smile.

"Good girl," said Henderson. "We'll see you in the morning, if not before."

"Do you have to be quite so charming?" said Sam once they were back in the corridor.

"I've found it gets better results and is far better for morale," he replied. "Your point being...?"

"No point at all, really," said Sam with a sigh as they approached the staircase. "Are we off to bed then?"

"Well you certainly are," he said. "I want you to be well rested and ready for psychic action tomorrow, if you feel up to it."

"Oh, I'll be fine," said Sam. "We really need to get out of here now, don't we?"

"Well, we at least need to know that there is a way out," said Henderson. "As for whether we should leave before looking into things in a little more detail, I'm not sure."

Sam put a foot on the first step.

"Are you going to stay down, then?" she asked.

"Well, after all the excitement I have to admit that my mind is racing too much for me to go to bed just yet," Henderson admitted. "I think I might just take a look through some of the books in the drawing room, in case there are any clues to be gleaned."

"You believe the thing that possessed Maddy tonight, don't you?" she said. "You think there is a way out of here hidden in this house and now you're thinking about not sleeping until you find it." She laid a hand on his arm. "It's not good for you, you know," she said. "You should get some rest too."

"I will eventually," said Henderson.

"I don't mean half-collapsed over a pile of books when you finally can't keep your eyes open anymore," she said. "I mean you probably need a good night's sleep as much as I do. We all need you to be on top form tomorrow as well."

"I promise that I'll be fine," said Henderson.

"That's not what I want to hear," said Sam in her best 'I'm saying this for your own good' voice. "Promise me you'll spend an hour or maybe two, but that after that you'll definitely go to bed."

"I'll try," said Henderson, looking sincere.

"No *try* about it," she said, poised to slap his hand. "Promise!"

"All right, I promise," said Henderson with a sigh and a smile. "And for your information I still don't know what to make of what we saw tonight. Part of me says that most likely it's the house, which has now sucked sufficient energy out of the living things around it to be able to interact with us, and it's just beginning to enjoy itself. The other part... well, we know this house was built from a stone circle, and I suppose it's possible that some entity connected with it could have somehow become tethered here."

"But why should it want to warn us?" said Sam. "Or even communicate with us?"

Henderson shrugged. "Perhaps because the only way it can be released from here is for this house to be destroyed, but it can't do it by itself — it needs our help."

"If it needs our help that badly, why didn't it tell us how to get out of here?" said Sam.

"Because if we're not the kind of people who are capable of working it out for ourselves, then we probably don't have a hope of vanquishing whatever it is that lives here, and if we were shown the way out we would just leave, quite possible allowing the evil that has been tied here until now to leave with us."

"And that can't be allowed to happen."

"No," said Henderson. "Absolutely not."

"So," said Sam, trying not to sound too overwhelmed, "we either find a way out of here and in doing so vanquish this house of its evil and release the spirit of the stone circle, or we end up trapped here, possibly forever and definitely at the mercy of something really horrible."

Henderson nodded. "If, of course, we believe what we were told. If the house is just playing tricks with us, then all our efforts may be hopeless anyway. But that shouldn't stop us from trying, do you think? Sleep well."

As Sam watched her colleague wander off to rummage amongst as many books as he could before he finally fell over from tiredness, she figured the one thing she wouldn't be able to do was sleep. As it turned out she was quite right.

The house was not yet finished with her for the night.

Chapter Twenty
The House Strikes Again

Sam was about to make her way upstairs when she was stopped by an attention-getting cough from behind her. She turned to see Jeremy Stokes poking his head out of his bedroom door. From his nervous expression Sam guessed he had been waiting for Henderson to leave and had probably been watching the two of them bid each other goodnight. The thought of being spied on didn't put her in the best of moods.

"Can I help you with something?" she said, trying hard not to sound annoyed.

Jeremy came out of his room and closed the door behind him. "I was wondering if I might have a word," he said.

"What about?" A moment ago Sam had felt wide awake but now all she wanted to do was get to bed.

Jeremy looked around. "I'd rather we went somewhere a bit more private, if you don't mind?" he asked.

Sam's expression darkened. "Well if you've your bedroom in mind, you can forget it. I've met men like you before and if you think that just because you're on the television you can —"

"No, no." Jeremy was already waving his hands in a gesture of surrender. "That's not my intention at all, and I can understand you'd feel uncomfortable if I took you there." He glanced at the front door. "How about outside?"

There didn't seem to be any harm in this. Sam nodded and followed Jeremy out through the front door.

It was a warm, clear night and the star-studded sky was a welcome respite from the claustrophobic atmosphere of the house.

"That's Venus," said Jeremy, pointing to the brightest star Sam could see.

"How do you know?" she said.

"How do you not?" he said with a grin. "I thought that was the kind of thing everybody knows."

"Well I don't, I'm afraid," said Sam, shuffling her feet. She let out a sigh. "I don't suppose you smoke do you?" she asked.

"Me?" Jeremy looked surprised. "No. Why? Do you?"

Sam shook her head. "Not really," she said. "But every now and then I get the craving, and this is definitely one of those times."

"Well I'm sorry, I can't help you," he said. "I would if I could, though."

They stood for a moment, staring up at the heavens. Eventually it was Sam who broke the silence.

"So what was it you wanted to talk to me about?"

"I just get the feeling we've got off on the wrong foot," he said. "I know it doesn't look good — big television star who makes money from old ladies who just want to talk to their dead husbands one last time, but I meant what I said back at the studio. I really do think I'm helping make people a little bit happier."

"And making a lot of money into the bargain," said Sam, her voice colder now.

"That's a side effect," said Jeremy. "Admittedly a very nice one, but a side effect all the same. I mean, you wouldn't find me in banking or running a multinational corporation."

"You probably wouldn't have the talent," said Sam, wishing more than ever for the cigarette she knew she could not have.

"Probably true," said Jeremy. "But I just wanted you to know that I do care about the people I help on my show. Don't you know anyone who might benefit from the sort of thing I do? Who might, under the right circumstances, end up a little bit happier just from me saying the right words to them?"

Sam paused at that, remembering her mother and her last visit, that stupid teapot and the biscuits they shared. For a moment she thought she felt a tear, then she remembered she didn't do that sort of thing, certainly not while working and certainly not while standing next to a reprehensible television psychic like Mr Jeremy Stokes. All the same, she had to admit...

"All right," she said, turning to face him. "My mum loves your show and if she met you it would probably make her day, if not her year. But that doesn't change how I feel about what you do."

"I didn't really expect it to," Jeremy replied. "But I just wanted the chance to make it clear to you that I'm not actually the monster you seem to think I am. All I've ever wanted to do with my life is make a difference to others. That's what I hope I'll be able to do here, but so far I've felt worse than useless."

Sam felt a pang of sympathy at that, but it was overridden by her suddenly remembering what Jeremy's actual psychic gift was. Her voice shook as she said, "Look, you haven't brought me out here because you've seen my death have you?"

"Oh good Lord, no," said Jeremy.

"Or Henderson's?"

"No," he said again, "and I haven't seen anyone else's death forthcoming either. But it's not the most reliable of gifts, not like what Maddy seems to have."

Even in the twilight Sam bristled at mention of the girl's name, before telling herself to forget it. "I know," she said. "All the things she says she feels and I haven't picked up on a bloody thing."

She couldn't see it but she could hear Jeremy's smile in his voice. "Well it's nice to know there's one other person here with psychic powers that aren't one hundred percent reliable," he said.

"True," said Sam. "But I bet the two of us together could probably give Maddy a run for her money."

"I'm sure we could," came the reply. "Thanks for the chat. I hope we can at least be friends a little bit for the rest of our time here."

"Sure," said Sam, "and who knows? If Henderson doesn't come up with something soon we may be here forever."

"Scary thought," said Jeremy as they went back inside. He glanced towards his bedroom. "I don't suppose you'd be interested in...?"

Sam shook her head but this time she laughed. "I think 'friends a little bit' will do for tonight," she said as gave him a gentle push in the opposite direction to her and waited until his door was closed before setting off for her own bed. She made it to the top of the stairs before the house was plunged into darkness.

She had no idea if she slipped when she reached the top step, or if something came up behind her and pushed, but the next thing she knew she was flailing for a handhold as she grabbed at the polished surface of the banister where it curved to form the balcony rail for the landing.

She knew there was something wrong when her fingers sank into it.

She yanked her hand back and managed not to fall over. Her fingers felt as if they had been pushed into cold dead clay and she rubbed them to try and get some life back.

When blowing on them didn't help either, she wished she still carried a cigarette lighter so she could see if there was anything stuck to them. She was just wondering what to do next, when the landing was flooded with a harsh silver light. Sam shielded her eyes, but not before she saw that she had stumbled towards the door that led to the first floor of the west wing, the floor above the one that she and Henderson had been investigating that day.

The west wing door flew open, the elaborate carvings on its surface digging into the plaster of the wall adjacent to it. Despite the unnatural brightness of the landing, the blackness beyond the door was impenetrable.

Sam tried to take a step back but found that she couldn't. Trying to call for Henderson, or indeed make any kind of a sound at all, yielded the same result. She dreaded what might happen next and her whole body tensed as she felt the same soft, pulpy mass that had caused her to stumble start to propel her, gently but firmly, towards the open doorway. She reached out again for the banister rail, but now it looked miles away. She did her best to dig her heels into the carpet, but even so she was moving inexorably towards the doorway.

Where she could now see something moving.

She tried to scream again, but managed nothing more than an empty dry croak. Now the blackness seemed to be trying to extend beyond the doorway, out onto the landing, and she realised that it was welcoming her.

Sam fought with all her strength but it was no use: any second now the snaking black tentacles would touch her and she would belong to the house.

"What on earth's the matter?"

The shape vanished, the silvery light dissipated, and the door was once more closed. Sam looked up from where she had fallen to see a very normal Henderson looking down at her where she had fallen.

Chapter 20: The House Strikes Again / **169**

"It looks as if you're even more tired than I thought," he said, holding out a hand to help her up. "Good thing I decided to check you made it back to the room safely or you might have been here until the morning."

"No," said Sam, shaking. "I don't think I would have been. Or if I had it wouldn't have been really me, if you see what I mean."

Henderson looked concerned as he saw how shaken up she was. "Are you all right?" he asked.

The response was a string of expletives, or rather the same one repeated at least ten times before she gave him a huge hug.

"Oh God, Henderson, thank you thank you thank you," she mouthed into his shoulder. "It nearly got me. If you hadn't come along then you might have had some serious rescuing to do."

"And I know how much you hate being the damsel in distress," he said.

She pushed herself away from him, quickly regaining her composure. "Too right," she said, wiping away tears. "You know I can look after myself."

"I do," said Henderson, his face still grim. "Which means whatever's given you such a shock is really something to worry about."

"I should bloody well say so," she replied, taking a few deep breaths. "But as I said, I really do owe you a 'just in the nick of time' moment."

"Well, remind me if things get really hairy," he said with a smile as he took her in his arms.

"What do you think you're doing?" said Sam, suddenly prickly. "I'm all right now."

"You're still shivering," he said.

"Well I have just had quite a shock, you know." He touched his cheek to hers. "Watch it," she said. "I'm not that shocked."

"I'm just checking how warm you are," he said. "In fact you're a good few degrees colder than the ambient temperature. We'd better keep an eye on that." He tried to stand back. "You can let go now, I've finished checking," he said. "But if it's not too distressing I'd be very grateful if you could tell me everything that happened while it's fresh in your memory."

"Oh, yes, sorry," said Sam, disentangling herself and giving him as detailed a description as she could of her attempted abduction by the house.

"You think that's what it was, then?" he said. "You were going to be absorbed or taken over?"

"That's what it felt like," she said. "I couldn't move, and it was as if the energy was being drained from me. And that horrible black thing — ergh!"

"The horrible black thing that was waiting behind here?" Henderson went over to the door and rattled the handle, causing Sam to jump. "Oh I wouldn't worry, from what you've described it obviously needs to alter the physical surroundings before it can manifest; all that stuff with the darkness, the strange light, the altered dimensions of the landing. It isn't strong enough to just pop up in front of us, at least not yet."

"Thank God for that," said Sam.

Henderson subjected the door to swift series of percussive taps over its surface, examined the carvings, and then rattled the handle once more. "I wonder it the key is on the bunch Sir Anthony gave us?" he mused.

"Even if it is, I really don't think it would be a good idea to unlock it tonight," said Sam. "I don't even want to go back to my bedroom."

"In that case, bring some blankets downstairs," said Henderson. "The divan in the drawing room looks rather comfy and I can keep an eye on you when I'm not too engrossed in something. And if I am, all you have to do is scream loudly and I can come running."

"And do whatever it was you did just then," said Sam with a smile. "Thanks. I would appreciate it tonight, if you don't mind. By the way, I never did ask; what did you do to save me from the trans-dimensional clutches of whatever black nasty was trying to get me?"

Henderson raised his hands. "I'm afraid I have absolutely no idea," he confessed. "At the moment I'm theorising that it's going after the more psychically sensitive people first, which probably puts me at the bottom of the heap. Maybe my steadfast resistance to such things scared it off."

"Your steadfast resistance to things has certainly been known to scare things off in the past," said Sam, "and not just supernatural ones, either." She ignored his puzzled look. "But if that's the case, then it narrows down the list of who might already by working for the other side."

"A nice way of putting it, as well as a very good point," said Henderson, nodding. "Perhaps we'd better check on the others before we ensconce ourselves for the night."

They made their way back downstairs and under the balcony to the corridor that ran beneath the passageway off which their rooms were located. The first on the right was Maddy's room, which they felt they didn't need to check again after so short a time.

"Which is exactly what this house would want us to think," said Sam.

"Another very good point," said Henderson, trying the handle. The door swung open to reveal Maddy much the same as before, lying on her back, her face looking more serene than Sam had ever seen it, her hands clutched over her chest.

"She seems to be behaving herself," Henderson whispered.

"Even if she is doing her best to impersonate one of those sculptures you see on the tops of tombs in churches," Sam replied as the detective crept into the room and examined Maddy's fingers once more.

"It doesn't seem to have changed," he said on his return, "which either means it's nothing to worry about, or the house has been so busy elsewhere it hasn't been able to concentrate its energies on her."

They didn't need to check the next room along as it was obvious that Alan and Helen Pritchard were busy having an argument before retiring.

"Where are you going?" Sam asked as Henderson went over to the opposite side of the passageway.

"Well they're obviously all right," he said.

"But don't you want to know what they're arguing about?"

He shook his head. "Not particularly. I get the feeling that it's something of a nightly ritual for them."

Sam reluctantly tore herself away from the door, and it was made even more difficult because she had just heard Helen mention Henderson by name.

"Not a sound here," said the detective, his ear to Jeremy's door.

"They're talking about you, you know."

"Are they?" said Henderson with a big grin. "How absolutely splendid. I suppose we'd better disturb him, just to be on the safe side," said Henderson, trying the door handle. "Let's just hope he doesn't keep his door locked."

But Jeremy did.

"You can hardly blame him after what's gone on tonight," said Sam.

Henderson agreed and rapped smartly on the door, after which he sucked at his knuckles.

"That'll teach you," said Sam

"I had no idea the carvings were so sharp," he said, as the door was flung open and a terrified-looking Jeremy peered around the corner. He flashed a smile at Sam and then went back to looking petrified.

"Sorry Jeremy," said Henderson. "We're just making sure everyone's tucked in for the night."

"Well," said Stokes in a nervous voice. "I was until you knocked on my door. Is there anything wrong?"

"Oh no," said Henderson.

"Nothing at all," said Sam.

"Then why did you wake me up? And why do you both look so worried?"

"It's part of our job to be concerned, Mr Stokes," said Henderson, "and after everything we've all been through tonight we just wanted you to know that we'll be just down the hall in the drawing room if you have any concerns."

"Like what?"

"Like for instance if you're disturbed by anything in the night."

"You mean like now?"

"No," said Henderson, "I mean like the sort of thing we saw during the séance."

"What you mean is…"

"He means if anything tries to kill you in the night, Mr Stokes," said Sam, a bit more severely than she had intended. "Now isn't that reassuring? If anything horrible comes into your room all you have to do is give a hearty yell and we'll come running from where we've been waiting just down there." She pointed towards the drawing room.

"Er… thanks," said Stokes. "Although I have to say I feel less reassured now than I did."

"I apologise if that's the case, Mr Stokes," said Henderson. "But I think that if anything does happen in the middle of the night, you'll be glad of our little call now. In fact, I'm sure of it."

As the door was slammed in their faces, Henderson let out a deep breath.

"Well I think we handled that one reasonably well," he said.

"You could say that," said Sam. "In fact you *would* say that. I would say that we've scared him so much he's probably going to be running up and down the corridor all night worrying about the monsters he thinks he's seen trying to get in through his window."

"Well at least we've achieved our objective. Mr Stokes, indeed all our companions, appear to be safe at the moment."

"Either that or they've all been got at by the thing that tried to get me," said Sam.

"You really are pessimistic at times, aren't you?" said Henderson.

"Only because I've been working with you for so long," she said with a smile. "Now you go off and get started on your books and I'll join you in a minute."

It was more like fifteen, but when Sam eventually came back down it was with a bundle of sheets and blankets.

"Where's the divan?" she said as Henderson stared at her open-mouthed. "What's the matter?"

"I had no idea you would be... changing clothes to sleep," he said.

Sam looked herself up and down and grinned. "Well a massively oversized т-shirt like this one is pretty much what I usually sleep in, and I don't want to mess up my clothes for whatever adventuring we have planned for tomorrow. So close your mouth, put your eyes back in, and get back to your books. I'm sure they're far more interesting than what I wear to bed."

By morning Henderson had found something much more interesting, but he had been with Samantha long enough to have learned that it was probably best to keep the fact that it *was* more interesting to himself.

Chapter Twenty One
Worse Things Happen at Sea...
Don't They?

"At least the electricity's still working."

It was early the next morning, the sun was just peeking over the horizon, and the five of them (according to Helen, Maddy was still sound asleep) all displayed signs of having had little sleep as they convened in the dining room. Breakfast consisted of coffee and toast, causing Alan to make his optimistic remark, before adding that it might be a good idea if he made some use of his detection equipment soon in case the power did fail. Henderson had agreed, but was still determined that they explore the house as fully as possible first.

"In that case we should stick together," Jeremy said.

"He's right," said Helen. "None of this splitting up, or being paired with someone you might not trust who might creep up behind you when you're not looking. If we're going to explore anywhere let's all go together."

"Fair enough," said Henderson, refilling his mug and passing the coffee pot to Sam. "Unless anyone has any objections, I would suggest we start with whatever is above this room."

"I knew you were going to suggest that," said Sam. Helen asked why. "Because that's where the thing that we've seen seems to have come from on both nights," Sam replied.

"Not necessarily," said Jeremy. "It's just come out of the ceiling."

"True," said Henderson, "but it does raise my suspicions that the room above this may have an important part to play in our investigations. No-one is obliged to come with us, of course, but that's where Sam and I intend to make a start."

"Did you find anything of any importance in those books in the drawing room?" asked Alan.

Henderson paused for a moment before replying, "Nothing that's going to make a blind bit of difference to what we do today." He saw that most of the toast was untouched and was going to grab another slice when Sam stopped him.

"If you get heavier, it'll be that much harder to run when the time comes," she said with an affectionate smile.

"I suppose you're right," he replied with a sigh before looking at the others. "Are we all ready to make a start then?"

Helen wanted to brush her teeth and Jeremy made the redundant comment that he wished he had a gun while they were waiting for her to return, but ten minutes later the five of them, with Henderson and Sam in the lead, were making their way up the staircase. When they reached the top they turned left, but not before Henderson had asked Sam if she could sense anything strange on the balcony this morning.

She shook her head. "Nothing," she said. "Except a vague smell of smoked cheese."

"Smoked cheese?"

"Yes, that's all I can liken it to I'm afraid. I went to a food festival in Weston super-Mare a few years ago and they had Bavarian smoked cheese that smelled just the same."

"I've been to Weston super-Mare," said Jeremy. "I wish I was there now."

"Oh come on," said Henderson. "It can't be as bad as all that." He looked back to Sam. "But nothing else? Nothing like last night?"

She squeezed his hand. "No," she said, "but thanks for asking."

Henderson had to try three different keys in the bunch he had brought from his room before he found the one that fitted.

"How come you were given all the keys?" Alan asked.

Henderson shrugged. "Perhaps there was only one set and Sir Anthony thought I was the most appropriate to take care of them."

"Or that he was the one most likely to get himself into some sort of mischief which would prove to Sir Anthony that something horrible lived here," said Sam.

"I think we already know that, Miss Jephcott," said Henderson as the key turned in the lock with a crunch that set her teeth on edge. It took a good shove to get it open.

To reveal the entirely empty first floor of the west wing.

There was no wood-lined passageway, no individual rooms, nothing that resembled the hospital ward or either of the dining or music rooms beneath. Henderson took a step inside and his footsteps echoed off the bare floorboards.

"Curious," he said, and his voice echoed off the bare walls.

"What were you expecting?" Alan asked.

"More than this," was the reply. "On the floor below we have a dining room, a room filled with bizarre musical instruments and what looks like a hospital ward for Nazis. I was expecting something a little bit more than just a huge empty space."

Sam could tell he was disappointed.

"It could be worse, I suppose," she said.

Henderson raised his hands, speechless for a moment. "After what you said happened to you last night I was at least hoping for there to be... something in here," he said.

"What happened to her last night?" asked Helen.

"Nothing," they said together.

"Well if no-one else is pleased about this great big open space, I have to say I am," said Alan, pushing his way through and taking several paces over to the first of the five broad windows that looked out over the driveway. He stopped and tapped a toe against the stained wooden boards near the windowsill. "I would say the dining room is about... here, wouldn't you?"

"Give or take a few feet, yes," said Henderson. "Why?"

"I was thinking of setting up a magnetic resonance field here, if it's all right with you," Professor Pritchard continued. "Just because we can't see anything doesn't mean there isn't anything here."

Sam could see Henderson was tempted to slap his own forehead but thankfully he prevented himself from doing so.

"Of course!" he said. "How very stupid of me. By all means, Professor. In fact, I think it would be an excellent idea. Might I ask one favour: that I be here when you switch it all on?"

"I'd be delighted, Mr Henderson," said Alan, far more animated now that he had something to do. He made his way past them to get his equipment.

"I think you've just made a friend there," Sam said to Henderson as they watched him go.

"Oh, my husband is so easily bought," said Helen, sounding tired. "All you have to do is show him a whiff of enthusiasm for his work and he's like an excited puppy."

No-one ventured to respond.

"I think we can safely leave Professor Pritchard to get set up here," said Henderson. "But while we're on this floor, why don't we take a look at what's opposite?"

The door to the upper floor of the east wing was as elaborately carved as its counterpart, but this one swung open easily once it was unlocked, yielding a dusty passageway with wood panelling similar to that which they had seen downstairs. Dust motes spun through the air, seeming to bounce off the sunshine pouring in through the curtain-less windows on the right. To the left were three doors, evenly spaced along the wall.

"Now this looks more promising," said the detective, stepping inside.

Sam could tell what the first room was meant to be as soon as they opened the door, but then the scuffed, scratched rocking horse did rather give it away. It regarded her with its solitary left eye as they entered the room.

"That's a grotty looking playpen," she said, regarding a battered example of its type lying next to the equine monstrosity.

"And fashioned from barbed wire," said Henderson after taking a closer look at it. "I wonder what on earth someone wanted to keep in there."

"Perhaps a very naughty child," said Helen from behind them.

"Either that," Henderson agreed, "or one capable of tearing apart anything that wasn't reinforced steel." He opened the top drawer of the cabinet that was under the window. "Very interesting," he said.

Sam tried not to imagine the squat crouching thing she had seen two nights ago tearing its way through the barbed wire of that hideous playpen. To distract herself, she came over to see that Henderson was looking at an assortment of pen tops, beads and other small items.

"All items with a history of causing choking to death, I expect," he said.

Sam raised a eyebrow. "You think so?" she said.

"Well I do, when one considers what's hanging up beside it."

On the wall to the left were three ropes. At first Sam thought that was all they were, but on closer inspection she realised they had been used for skipping. She felt a chill as she realised they had doubtless been involved in accidents that had caused the death of at least one child each.

"I really don't like this room," said Sam, shivering.

"I don't think there's a single living person who could like this room," said Jeremy, trying to ignore a board game that seemed to involve forfeiting body parts if one landed on the wrong square.

"Anything to feel?" Henderson asked Sam, who was trying her hardest to ignore the collection of bloodstained household implements in the corner.

"There's no way I'm going to lower my barriers in this bloody room," Sam said with a snort. "Let's leave, shall we?"

Even with the door closed, she could still feel the rocking horse looking at her.

§ § §

The other two rooms on the east wing's first floor were empty.

"I bet the carpets probably have a nasty history, though," said Jeremy.

"You're probably right, Mr Stokes," said Henderson. "So without further ado why don't we check the ground floor on this side and then Dr Pritchard can check on her patient while the rest of us give her husband a hand to set up all his interesting bits and pieces."

"My husband doesn't have any interesting bits and pieces Mr Henderson," said Helen with a wry smile. "Believe me, if he did I'd know by now."

Sam gave her a glare, which the doctor pointedly ignored as the group made its way back downstairs.

The ground floor of the east wing consisted of a mixture of the kitchens which they had already seen, a set of utility rooms, and one large room filled with what looked like furniture covered with heavy sheeting. The last room had been crammed with so many objects that it was impossible to take more than a few steps inside it.

"Should we check all this stuff out?" Jeremy asked, lifting the corner of the nearest sheet to behold an ancient-looking desk with deep scratch marks down one side.

"I don't think that's going to be feasible," said Henderson. "Let's just assume it's a junk room and leave it at that."

There was a crash from upstairs.

"That'll be Alan 'setting up' his equipment," said Helen.

"Do you think he would welcome some help?" asked Henderson.

"I'm sure he needs it," said the doctor. "As to whether or not he'll let you is another matter; he can be very protective of his funny little gadgets. Certainly more so than he is of his wife."

Henderson was about to say something when a warning squeeze from Sam to stop him from putting his foot in it caused his open mouth to utter a strange squawking noise instead.

"Are you all right, Mr Henderson?" said Jeremy.

Henderson coughed. "Fine, yes, thank you." He ushered them back towards the entrance hall. "Why don't we find out how Professor Pritchard is getting on?" As they walked, he hung back to whisper to Helen, who nodded and left the group.

"You didn't say anything silly to her did you?" said Sam as they climbed the stairs.

"I'd be interested to know your definition of 'silly'," he replied.

"Well for example, like saying she should stop making all those derogatory remarks about her husband. I wondered about it at first, but in all honesty I think they're made out of some kind of affection. Plus, I suspect they might be the only thing keeping her as calm as she appears to be at the moment."

"Good point," said Henderson. "As a matter of fact, I was asking her to go and check on Maddy and let me know immediately if there's been any change."

"You say that as if you're expecting there to be some," said Sam.

"Oh yes, if not now, then very soon," said Henderson with a grave face, "and I very much suspect it will be for the worse."

Chapter Twenty Two
Looking for Ghosts

Considering how much equipment he seemed to have brought with him, Alan Pritchard was remarkably fast at getting it all set up; so fast, in fact, that Henderson was moved to comment upon it.

"Oh, it's all relatively light stuff," said the physicist. He pointed to the laptop computer he had set up near the door. "That's actually the heaviest bit. The rest I was able to carry up here almost in one go."

Sam looked at 'the rest of it': six black metal cubes, each no larger than a matchbox, arranged in a circle on the floor beneath the window.

"I've taken the liberty of mapping out where the apparition from the other night disappeared from the dining room," said Pritchard, pointing to a series of chalk marks he had made on the floorboards, "and set up the magnetic field in the corresponding position as you can see. My plan is to vary the magnetic field strength and keep my fingers crossed that something will show up."

"What happens if you happen to have it on the wrong strength and something decides to float up through the floor?" Sam asked.

Pritchard tapped the laptop. "This will cycle the magnetic field so it's never on the same strength setting for more than three seconds. Hopefully that way we won't miss anything."

"Good idea," said Henderson. "When are you planning to turn it on?"

"It's working now," said Pritchard with a grin. He hit the space bar and the screensaver — a floating ghost that intermittently produced a little green speech bubble with the word 'Boo!' in it — vanished to be replaced by a black-and-white image of the area of the room being monitored.

"Very impressive," said the detective. "Now what?"

"Well, waiting, obviously," said Pritchard with a sniff. "People don't seem to realise that science isn't all laser beams and splitting the atom. Most of it is measured observation. Sometimes days and even weeks can pass before any kind of measurable result is achieved."

"Oh dear," said Sam, to be rewarded by a scowl from her companion.

"I fully appreciate that, Professor Pritchard," he said. "And in view of that, and in view of the fact that we have our own research to conduct, I hope you won't mind if we leave you to it?"

"I was expecting you might," said Pritchard. "But don't feel you're deserting me. I rather like this kind of donkey work. You sort of have to in my profession. Besides, I'm not expecting much to happen until it gets dark, which should give you a couple of hours if you fancy coming back to see how I'm getting on."

"Oh, we'll be back," said Henderson. "We just need to check on your wife's patient first."

§ § §

They were met downstairs by a concerned-looking Helen.

"Maddy's no better," she said. "In fact, I think she's getting worse. Much worse"

"You mean like 'coma' worse?" said Sam.

Helen was wringing her hands. "She's been unresponsive for so long I'm worried she may have *already* done that. No, what I mean is, she's begun to... change."

Henderson's eyes narrowed. "Change? What do you mean?"

Helen opened the bedroom door. "I think it would probably be better if you saw for yourself."

Sam and Henderson pushed past her. Maddy looked as if she was sound asleep, even if it looked a little odd that Helen had pulled the sheet up over her patient, who was still fully dressed.

"I thought it best to keep her warm," Helen explained.

"Fair enough," said Henderson. "So what exactly has changed about her?"

Helen paused before replying, "It's her hand."

"Her hand?"

Helen nodded. "The right one."

Henderson bent over Maddy, studying the girl's breathing. Sam thought she looked terribly pale. "Is it safe to look?" he asked.

Helen shrugged. "To be honest, Mr Henderson, your guess is as good as mine. I think so. I certainly don't believe her to be in any pain, if that's what you mean."

With infinite gentleness Henderson lifted the sheet.

"Fascinating," he breathed. "Quite, quite fascinating."

Maddy's right hand had turned black; not dark, or tanned, but black. Her skin had acquired the silver-grey sheen of polished coal. Other than the change in colour the hand itself looked normal, the darkness ending just above the wrist in snaking streaks of a paler grey that were just beginning to encroach on her forearm. Henderson extended a finger.

"I wouldn't do that if I were you," Helen cautioned, handing him a rubber glove.

"You're worried it might be an infection?" he asked.

"Possibly, but mainly it's to protect you from the cold." Helen held up a hand and Henderson could see a bluish tinge to the tip of her index finger. "I barely touched her and nearly got frostbite. Her unchanged skin is at normal temperature, but I wouldn't want her to grab me with that hand."

Henderson pulled on the glove and gingerly prodded Maddy's blackened skin. Even through the latex he could feel a biting chill.

"Could it be gangrene?" he asked.

Helen shook her head. "It's not any kind of gangrene I've ever seen. The tissues are viable, and if you prick her finger she bleeds. The hand is just... different. At the risk of sounding stupid, it's as if her hand is from another dimension. No, that really *does* sound stupid, I'm sorry."

"Don't be," Henderson got to his feet, "it's as good a guess as to why it's like that as any. And she's shown no sign of coming round?"

Helen dodged the glove as he threw it at the bin. "Nothing at all. She's still alive, pulse and respiratory rate are normal and her pupils respond to light, but other than that it's as if she's in a coma. Have you seen anything like it before?"

Now it was Henderson's turn to look baffled. "I'm afraid not, which makes me wonder if we should perhaps restrain her."

Helen looked shocked. "Whatever for?"

"He's worried that Maddy might be becoming a monster," said Sam. "Aren't you?"

"It always pays to take precautions," said the detective. "Especially now that we're one down and we still don't know anywhere near as much about what we're dealing with as I'd like."

"Even so," said Helen. "I'm not tying her to the bed; it's monstrous. We simply don't do such things in this day and age."

"Not in modern medicine perhaps," said Henderson. "But if we don't get her strapped down now, we may live to regret it later."

"Is he often like this?" Helen asked Sam.

"If you mean 'bossy', then yes," she replied before adding, "I couldn't possibly comment on the restraining thing."

"Besides," said Helen, turning back to Henderson. "We haven't got anything to tie her down with."

"I'm sure you can improvise," he said, looking around the room but finding nothing immediately suitable. "Just make sure you do before that gets any worse." He pointed at Maddy's hand. "My feeling that it's worse now than when I looked at it just a minute ago is my imagination, isn't it?"

Helen peered at Maddy's wrist. "No, Mr Henderson," she said, her face paling. "You're quite right."

"How can you be so sure?" asked Sam.

Helen took out a pen and indicated a spot on Maddy's wrist that was now as black as her hand. "Because the pen marks I made to indicate the extent of the discoloration have gone," she said.

"I wonder if we should amputate it," said Henderson, stroking his chin.

Helen looked at him in horror. "Oh, now you *are* being ridiculous!" she said.

"Really?" he said. "If a patient were suffering from gangrene, or had a limb so badly crushed it was beyond repair you wouldn't think twice, or at least you shouldn't do. This might be even worse. By the time it overwhelms her, she may be sufficiently in the grip of this house that she could be a threat to others as well as herself."

"You really are completely unfeeling sometimes, aren't you?" said Sam. "It's bad enough that you should suggest such a thing, but to expect Helen to do it to someone she has met and spent time with, to expect her to do that to a young girl with her life ahead of her, sometimes you really are unbelievable."

"The young girl in question may not have *any* life ahead of her at all if we don't do something drastic," Henderson replied. "In fact, none of us might. Acting radically now might prevent disaster later."

"It's irrelevant anyway," said Helen. "I don't have the instruments here and, even if I did, I wouldn't know how to do it. I'm not a surgeon and I never wanted to be. If I tried to take her arm off, she'd bleed to death before I'd even worked out how to put in a stitch."

"In that case," said Henderson, "thank you for being so honest. It probably wouldn't have worked anyway." He looked at Maddy once more. "I do think you'd better find some rope, though."

Helen shivered. "What are you two going to do?" she asked.

"Try and find out why she is the way she is," he replied, and then more kindly, "but don't worry, we'll be back to see how your patient's doing in a bit."

Chapter Twenty Three
Supernatural Intervention

Jeremy had followed Sam and Henderson into the drawing room.

"Did you actually manage to find anything the other night?" Sam asked.

Henderson grinned and took down a heavy volume from a high shelf.

"*Mrs Makepiece's Malay Masterpieces,*" Sam read the garish text above a picture of a smiling old lady holding a wok. "Are you proposing we cook our way out of here?"

"You can't beat a good green curry, but that's not what I want to show you," said Henderson, opening the volume to reveal it had been hollowed out and a much smaller, much more ancient-looking tome concealed within.

"Something tells me that book's bad news," said Sam.

"Me too," agreed Jeremy, "and I'm not even psychic."

"Books are like chainsaws," said Henderson, "neither good nor evil in themselves. It just depends on whose hands they end up in."

"What about that book we found in Widdendale Church?" said Sam. "The one that chased me up the aisle and tried to —"

"That was a different matter altogether," said Henderson, gingerly removing the old book from its hiding place. "I read as much of this as I could the other night. A lot of it is obscure gobbledegook but there is a passage which talks about supernatural barriers and how they can only be traversed by a vehicle of supernatural power itself."

"You mean like a ghost car?" said Jeremy.

"I mean something supernaturally charged. Quite possibly something conjured into being."

"And how are we supposed to do that?" asked Sam.

"That's the next step." Henderson looked at the shelves of books before him. "Keep your fingers crossed it's all in here somewhere, although I've no idea how long it might take us to find it."

"Do you mind if I help?" said Jeremy.

Henderson looked surprised. "Not at all, my dear chap. Just show anything to me that you think might be of interest."

"You look worried, Mr Stokes," said Sam. "Is there anything the matter?"

Jeremy shifted uneasily from foot to foot. "Well, I don't know if I should tell you this or not," he said.

"Out with it and then we can tell you," said the detective.

Jeremy still seemed reticent. "You remember the reason for me coming here? This weird psychic ability of mine that was starting to drive me insane?" They both nodded. "Well, when I looked at Maddy just now I felt absolutely nothing."

"So she's going to be all right, then?" said Sam.

Jeremy shook his head. "No, that's not what I mean at all. It was as if she didn't exist. Not as if she had died, or was going to die, but as if she didn't exists at all."

"The house has her," said Henderson. "I suppose we could have guessed that."

"I think what Jeremy is implying," said Sam, "is not so much that the house has her, but that the house *is* her, if that makes sense."

"And that's not all," he said. "When we were with Maddy and Dr Pritchard just now, I got a very strong feeling indeed."

"Of what?" snapped Henderson.

Jeremy bit his lip. "I hate to say this, but I don't think Dr Pritchard is long for this world."

Henderson ran a hand through his hair. "In that case, you'd probably be better off keeping an eye on Helen while Sam and I look through everything here, and if you sense the slightest danger you come and get us, understand?"

Jeremy nodded. "Good man. See you in a bit."

As Jeremy went off to check on Helen, Henderson turned to Sam. "Don't tell the others," he said, "but I don't think we've got much time left."

§ § §

Upstairs, Alan Pritchard had settled down to wait for results. He was glad he'd remembered to bring his old fold-out fishing stool which he found by far the most comfortable thing to sit on for this sort of work. He tapped a few keys on the laptop, just to ensure everything was working, and then settled back to watch the screen.

Every now and then there would be a tiny flicker of activity, but nothing substantial. It was only when the sun went behind a cloud that Alan realised there was something on the screen.

In the area being scanned, some tiny flickers of light were appearing: just for one of the three-second scanning intervals, then they vanished as the machine set itself to a different frequency.

Alan tapped more keys and adjusted the modulator so it remained fixed on the frequency that was yielding results.

As he peered at the screen the sun came out again, the extra sunlight obscuring what was happening. Alan crouched close to the computer and cupped his arms around the screen to block out the excess light.

There they were again. Alan counted five bobbing dots of light, like tiny stars moving of their own accord over the floor just above the dining room. Sometimes they would collide and bounce off one another, and each time they did they increased in size. Alan looked over to the patch of bare boards beneath the windowsill. Satisfied that there was nothing corporeal to see, he turned his full attention to the screen where the dots of sparkling light had now becomes blobs. Once they were the size of pennies, they stopped bouncing off each other and began to stick together instead, until eventually Alan Pritchard's laptop displayed a ball of light the size of a football floating over the floor.

A ball of light which was beginning to take on a shape.

Alan watched, fascinated, as four tiny bumps extruded themselves into limbs, as a tiny head developed from the light ball's upper aspect, and a pair of gossamer-thin wings emerged from the its back. A fairy? Alan chuckled. Wait until he told the others about this.

Meanwhile, over in the area being scanned, the area in the real room, something else was rapidly taking form. Sadly, Alan Pritchard was too distracted by what was happening on his laptop screen to see the two garish figures materialise as if from nothing. One was tall, female, sad-looking, and was obviously the mother. The other was a pathetic, crouching, hairy toad-like creature that did its best to jump up and down in excitement at the sight of the physicist but was prevented from doing so by the strong grip of its mother's hand upon its own. Unlike Alan's fairy, the materialisation of these entities was achieved in a matter of seconds, and so rapidly did they move that by the time he realised there was something wrong they were upon him.

§ § §

Sam and Henderson had barely made their way through one shelf of books when they heard the crash from upstairs.

"Sounds like our physicist friend might have found something," said Henderson. "Come on!"

They ran from the drawing room and reached the top of the stairs just in time to see the body of Alan Pritchard emerge from the west wing. Sam guessed it was just his body because he didn't acknowledge them, his face remained slack-jawed and blank, and because he walked in a way that suggested his unconscious form was being manipulated by something invisible.

"Don't touch him," Henderson said.

"The thought hadn't crossed my mind," said Sam. "Seriously."

They stood on the landing as Professor Pritchard shambled past them, his eyes pointed at the floor, his stiff-legged gait making him resemble a poorly functioning automaton.

"Where's he going?" Sam hissed.

"I don't know," Henderson hissed back. "Why don't we get after him and find out?"

They followed the teetering figure as it lumbered down the corridor, past both of their bedrooms, and coming to a halt at the locked door at the end of the passageway. It stood there for a moment, regarding the ornate carvings. The odd, bird-like movements of Pritchard's head suggested that something was using him to inspect every aspect of the door before his right arm was raised and his right hand, the fingers of which had been curled into a fist, was brought down against the wood. Very hard.

Pritchard's face remained expressionless as his arm was raised again. The second time his fist made contact with the wood, it was with such force that the teeth of the carved face dug into his flesh and, as his hand was withdrawn, Sam could see blood dripping from the beast's muzzle.

"Hadn't we better stop him?" she said.

"We could try," said Henderson. "But I don't honestly think it would do much good."

For a third time the physicist's fist beat against the wood, leaving blood on the carving and a heavier bruise on the man's palm. The next blow was accompanied by a sickening crunch as the bones in his hand broke. It made little difference to his attempts to open the door, however. Now the figure of Professor Pritchard began to beat the useless hand even harder against the wood, his expression impassive, the blood on the door now running from the carved wooden gargoyle's mouth in streaks. Sam was about to run forward to make the awful scene stop when a bolt of blue lightning emerged from the gargoyle's mouth and hit Pritchard in the chest. He staggered back a few steps, then lumbered forward once more and recommenced his hammering.

A second bolt of lightning emerged from the creature's mouth. This time Pritchard stayed put and the lightning, rather than knocking him backwards, was reflected off him and back at the door, which gave an ominous creak.

"Something is trying to get that door open," Henderson whispered.

"I had sort of guessed that, you know," said Sam. "I'm more worried about whether it's a good thing or a bad thing that's waiting behind it."

"I have a feeling we're going to find out soon," replied her colleague.

Pritchard had recommenced hammering on the door. Now the blue flashes were becoming more frequent and were being reflected back against the wood by his increasingly dilapidated-looking body. One final burst of light caused him to fall back a few paces, but not enough to prevent the energy from causing an almighty cracking sound to issue from the wood. Pritchard's figure stood there for a moment, regarding the smoke now issuing from the gargoyle's mouth, before collapsing in a heap.

Sam was about to run forward when Henderson stopped her.

"Look!" he said.

Professor Pritchard's body convulsed and twitched as, ever so slowly, the two ethereal figures Sam had seen at the séance emerged from it. The tiny hairy toad creature was now leaping up and down in excitement and the young woman in the black dress was doing her best to calm it. For a moment she looked up, caught Sam's eye, and then did the last thing Sam was expecting her to do.

She smiled.

Not an evil smile, or a smile of wicked triumph, but a proper, warm smile, tinged with sadness perhaps, but certainly containing no malice.

"I think they might be the good guys," said Sam as the woman took the creature's hand and the two of them began to drift towards the door.

"If they are, they've made a hell of a mess of Professor Pritchard," said Henderson. "Oh, and by the way, I hope it goes without saying that I can't see anyone."

"They're floating towards the door now," said Sam. "I can see right through them. It's the woman and the dwarf creature. Now they're passing through the door... Now they've gone."

Henderson ran over to the Professor and checked for a pulse in his remaining wrist.

"Nothing," he said. "Either Pritchard was dead when they took possession of him, or the trauma of what he's just been put through was too much for a human being to stand."

"Oh God," said Sam. "What are we going to tell Helen?'

Henderson got to his feet. "I'm not sure," he said. "It may be my imagination but his body seems to be getting warmer."

They both watched as the body of Professor Pritchard began to glow, first a pale pink colour, then a much darker red. Tiny wisps of smoke began to emerge from his shirt collar and the cuffs of his sleeves. As his clothes began to char, his body erupted into flames which burned furiously for a matter of seconds before dying down, leaving nothing but an outline of pale ash on the carpet.

"Now I really don't know what to tell her," said Henderson.

Sam looked back at the door. "I wonder what is in there?" she said.

Henderson went over and tried the door handle.

"I wouldn't bother," said Sam. "I tried it earlier. It's locked."

The door opened with a creak.

"Sometimes all it needs is the right touch," said Henderson.

"Oh, sure." said Sam. "Plus the efforts of two celestial creatures, some broken bones, half a gallon of blood and a death, that's all."

"Not all keys are made of iron," said the detective as he pushed the door open a little further. The tiny room beyond was in darkness, but he could just make out a stone chair in which something appeared to be sitting.

"Very interesting," Henderson breathed as he took a step forward. He looked back at Sam. who was still frozen beside the swiftly disappearing remains of the professor. "Don't you want to find out who it is?" he said.

"We should go and tell Helen what's happened," said Sam.

"It will make no difference whether we tell her now or in ten minutes," said the detective. "And ten minutes may make all the difference to whether the rest of us can or cannot get out of here."

"We promised we'd check up on her anyway." For some reason she could not explain, Sam felt terribly guilty about them not going back to see if Helen Pritchard was okay right now.

But Henderson was already preoccupied with the possibilities the room offered. "I'm sure she's fine," he said.

But she wasn't.

Chapter Twenty Four
Something Nasty in the Garden

Once Henderson and the others had left, the first emotion Helen Pritchard had felt was helplessness. She sat in the chair on the other side of the room from where Maddy lay on the bed, her breathing slow and deep, her pulse rate normal, and the skin of her right hand the colour of nothing Helen had ever encountered in her life. She allowed herself an audible sigh. She hadn't even brought any intravenous antibiotics she could administer. Her medical bag, sitting on the floor at the end of the bed, was filled with plenty of pills, and she had assumed anything more serious would be dealt with following a short ambulance trip to the local hospital. She had never imagined that she would be a prisoner in a house closed off from the rest of the world by a supernatural barrier, nor that she would have to deal with an unresponsive patient who could not communicate, take drugs, or give her any sign as to whether or not she was near death.

Unable to keep still, Helen got up and looked at Maddy's hand again. The blackness had now spread to above the elbow. She remembered what Henderson had said about amputating. *He might even be right*, she thought. It might be the only way to stop whatever was happening to the girl.

But if it was, she was the wrong person to do it. One of the reasons she had become a GP was because she had harboured no desire to cut into people with a knife.

She gnawed at her thumbnail as she gazed at Maddy's arm. She could almost see the darkness spreading through Maddy's flesh, like the very worst types of gangrene she had been taught about. This wasn't gangrene, though. As she had tried to explain to Henderson, the flesh was viable, just terribly cold. She had checked Maddy's radial pulse at the wrist, while wearing a rubber glove to avoid freezing her fingers, and it had been normal. If the limb was rotten she wouldn't have expected to find any pulse at all.

She sat back down and scratched her head. She felt powerless and it was maddening. The girl was only nineteen! What kind of a doctor was she if she couldn't save a fit nineteen-year-old girl? She dreaded to think what might happen if the darkness spread over Maddy's entire body. Would she die? Would the last fragment of normal skin being consumed by that hideous blackness signify the end for her?

"Are you okay?"

She hadn't heard Jeremy come in, but it was a relief to see him. Normally she was fine on her own, but this situation was anything but normal.

"Fine," she said with a brave smile. "But then it's not really me that we need to worry about, is it?"

"It's a very stressful time for everyone," said Jeremy as gently as he could.

"Is that the tone you use for your old ladies on TV?" she said.

"Sometimes," was the reply. "But that doesn't mean I'm being insincere."

"Of course it doesn't," said Helen. "I'm sorry. I think I'm still shaken up by what Henderson said."

Jeremy sat on the edge of Maddy's bed, taking care not to touch the patient. "That's probably why he asked me to come back in and check on you," he said.

Her eyes brightened at that. "He did?"

"Oh yes. Mind you, it might just have been a ruse to get me out of the way while the two of them searched through more grubby old books, but I think he's actually a bit more considerate than we give him credit for."

Helen nodded. "You're probably right, but I'm fine, so you don't have to worry."

"Is that your way of telling me you'd rather not have my company?"

Helen laid a gentle hand on Jeremy's wrist. "It's my way of telling you I don't want *anyone's* company," she said. "My husband's upstairs trying to detect God knows what, while I'm down here trying to cure God knows what else. I just don't feel I'm the best company at the moment and I'll feel even more uncomfortable if you stay."

"Fair enough," said Jeremy, looking at a loss. "Everyone seems to have their work cut out for them, except me."

"If I were you, I'd enjoy it while you can," came the reply. "I have a funny feeling things aren't going to stay quiet here for long."

Jeremy peered through the window. The sun was still high in the sky and the weather looked impossibly nice. "I think I might take a stroll in the garden," he said.

Helen joined him and peered through the glass. "The tangled undergrowth, you mean," she said. "But it's as reasonable a thing to do as any. Have fun." She looked back at the prone figure on the bed. "Because, believe me, there's not much you can do in here, and I can do nothing quite easily for the two of us."

"All right," said Jeremy, who had only been joking, but now sensed there was no getting out of his decision. "But I promise I'll stick close to this side of the building so if you need anything just holler, okay?"

"I promise I shall do more than just holler," Helen beamed, "I shall positively scream."

As Jeremy left, closing the door behind him, Helen lifted the sheet to see the darkness had reached Maddy's shoulder and realised she felt like screaming anyway.

§ § §

It wasn't until Jeremy had got out of the house that he realised how badly he had been suffering from claustrophobia. Still very much aware that he was a prisoner, he nevertheless delighted in the cool, fresh air and the feeling of sunshine on his face. As he circled round the front of the house he could see Sam and Henderson through the drawing room window, already knee deep in books, the detective looking as happy as a five-year-old with a new toy box, Sam looking far more as if it was a job of work she wanted to get done as quickly as possible. As he watched, something caused them both to put down the books they were looking at and leave the room. Perhaps they had decided to check on Helen themselves, he thought. Well, if he was needed she could tell them where he was.

He trudged round to the back of the house. As promised, the first thing he did was to tap on the window of Maddy's bedroom. Helen jumped and then responded with a smile once she saw who it was. There was no sign of Sam and Henderson, though, so presumably they must have gone to see what Helen's husband was up to.

At a loss as to what to do and not wanting to go back into the house just yet, Jeremy began to wander idly between the tombstones, stopping from time to time to make a half-hearted effort at reading the inscriptions. He only understood why he was having trouble when the inscription on one, that was rather less lichen-encrusted than the others, revealed that the epitaph was in German. Jeremy frowned. He knew little of the language but enough to know that was probably what it was. A brief inspection of the other more legible stones revealed the same thing. Perhaps Marx had had the coffins of some particularly evil German family brought over and reburied here to contribute to his house of horrors? The surnames were all different, though, so that made no sense either. And while the dates of birth differed quite widely, the dates of death all fell within the early nineteen forties.

Jeremy would doubtless have ruminated further in this had his concentration not been broken by a streak of blue lightning emerging from one of the first floor windows. It hit the grave marker next to him with such force that the stone was knocked over. Jeremy backed away as another bolt of electricity was unleashed, this one hitting the ground and setting fire to a small patch of grass. He looked up at the window it had come from. Presumably Professor Pritchard had found something, and Henderson and Sam had gone to investigate. He was about to make his way back to the house to see what was going on, when there was a scream from Maddy's room.

Jeremy ran to the window to see something getting out of Maddy's bed, something as black as coal, its skin indistinguishable from the black dress it wore.

Something which had grabbed Helen by the wrist.

Jeremy turned to get back to the house to be faced by his next shock of the moment.

The ground was moving.

It was worst where the lightning had struck. There, and next to the toppled gravestone, the ground had actually split apart causing ripples which were making the surrounding surface undulate as if the ground had a life of its own.

Or as if something was trying to get out from beneath it.

As a skeletal hand emerged from the cracked earth next to the fallen gravestone, Jeremy wished he hadn't had that thought, especially as more hands were now beginning to appear, thrust up from the earth and in some cases from between the heavy flagstones that seemed to be causing little impedance to the progress of the rotting cadavers which were now pulling themselves out of the ground.

Jeremy hadn't seen many horror films, but he had seen enough to know that the one thing one does not do in such a situation is wait until the creatures that can potentially kill you are in a position to do so.

So, he took a deep breath and he ran, dodging skulls that tried to gnaw at him, pushing aside fragments of cloth that he realised with horror were the scraps of uniforms adherent to desiccated torsos and generally running faster than he had ever done round to the front of the house. Once he was inside, he slammed the door and was about to look for something with which to form a barricade, when there was another scream from Maddy's room.

What were the others up to?

Jeremy grabbed the telephone table and wedged it under the door handle before running to Maddy's room where the door was now open.

Helen was lying on the floor.

Her neck was crushed, and the thing that had crushed it now looked up from her lifeless body at its next potential victim.

"It didn't hurt," the blackened thing that had once been Maddy said with her voice. "It felt good. Let me show you."

Chapter Twenty Five
Something Very Nasty in the House

Something was sitting in the chair.

At first Sam thought it was a dummy — part of a department store manikin, or even the remains of some stage prop left to rot and gather dust. But not even the thick layer of cobwebs that matted the thing's face could disguise the fact that the desiccated corpse she now beheld had once been human. She could guess what Henderson was going to say even before the words left his mouth.

"My dear Sam," he said. "I give you Mr William Marx."

"Part of him, anyway," said Sam with a grimace. "I wonder where his hands and feet have gone?"

"I very glad you asked me that," said the detective, shushing Sam's "I'm not" with an upraised hand as he took his telescopic pointer from his inside pocket and poked at the spot where the withered forearms touched the chair. And joined with it.

"His hands and feet haven't gone anywhere," he said. "They've fused with this throne."

"That's a bit of a grand name to call what he's sitting on, isn't it?" said Sam, trying hard not to sneeze as Henderson disturbed more dust.

"Not in the slightest," he said, rapping on a corpse-free part of it to be rewarded with a distinctly non-woody sound. "Hear that? I don't know of many common or garden chairs that have been fashioned from stone, do you?"

Sam was about to say "Maybe a couple of garden ones," and then thought better of it. "It must have taken a fair few workman to get that up the stairs," she said instead.

"Oh I don't think they had to," Henderson replied as he got on his hands and knees and blew away dust from the throne's base. "I think this goes right through."

"I beg your pardon?"

"Right through. To the foundations." Henderson regarded her quizzical look. "Do I need to explain this for the hard of thinking?"

"You need to explain it to *me*," said Sam. "You can choose to do it before or after I give you a slap." She lowered the hand she had just raised with the obvious intention of leaning on the throne's right arm when Henderson stopped her.

"I wouldn't do that either," he said. "You're liable to get a nasty shock."

"Of the psychic kind?"

"This time," said Henderson with a grin. "Now listen carefully. This house was built on a stone circle, right?"

"Using the stones as foundations," said Sam. "We know that."

"Ah yes," said Henderson. "But what we didn't know until now was that not all the stones were taken down. One of them was left standing."

Sam's eyes sparkled as realisation struck. "And a throne was sculpted..."

"...out of the very top of it — yes!" Henderson clapped his hands with glee. "So you see, what we're looking at is just the pinnacle of a standing stone, one that passes through this house and into the foundations and thus makes contact with the other stones in the circle, the ones that were laid on their sides as part of the foundations before the house was built."

"Why?" said Sam, still trying to ignore the silent third party's empty eye sockets and in particular the way they seemed to regard her with amusement from a head that resembled a partially deflated football.

"Well, you know how lightning conductors work?" Sam nodded. "Well not like that at all." Henderson avoided her glare. "Quite the reverse, in fact. I think Marx filled this house with items that could act as very powerful generators of psychic energy, and the stones in the foundations were meant to act as a sort of receiving system; a bit like a radar dish."

"With everything getting more and more concentrated as you got towards the middle?"

"Precisely. And where do you think the middle might be?"

To Sam that *was* obvious. "We're looking at it, aren't we?"

Henderson was nodding far too vigorously for Sam's liking. It usually meant there was the chance of something awful happening. "All the psychic energy would be concentrated and sent up through this, so that whoever happened to be sitting here would get an immense blast of what the house had gathered."

Sam tried again to take her eyes from the withered corpse in the throne but it was no use. "With the ultimate purpose of what, exactly?"

Henderson shrugged. "Well I don't think his intention was to get himself fused to the chair. I wonder if the shock killed him, or if he just couldn't move and so he stayed here until he starved to death."

"Or he stayed here because he wanted to," said Sam. "You know, like the rat in that experiment that would rather press the button wired to the pleasure centre in its brain than eat or do anything else. Maybe sitting here Marx got what he wanted: his view of the afterlife. Maybe he got to see his wife and daughter, perhaps even speak with them." She coughed and looked around her. "You know, I'm still amazed that someone who was essentially a wide-boy during the war years could have got himself into such a situation. I feel a bit sorry for him, really."

"Well don't," said Henderson. "Since we've been here, I've been getting the strongest feelings that our Mr Marx was a little bit more than just a simple gun-runner. In fact, if I was a betting man, I'd place odds on that he knew all about this sort of stuff before the war even started. It just gave him more of a chance to exercise his skills."

"You mean he was into all the old 'Black Magic' stuff?"

Henderson nodded. "If you want to know what I'm thinking..."

"Not always," said Sam, "but this is one of the rare occasions where I'm going to say 'Please, go on'."

"Thank you. Well if you want my guess, I believe William Marx was a Black Magician who, amongst other things, probably experimented on his own daughter. When the war came along, he sold his skills to the Nazis in return for more experimental subjects it would seem they were happy to let him have."

"You mean their own men?"

Henderson nodded. "And, it would seem, the hospital beds they had died in. Of course we can't say whether he did whatever he needed to over in Germany or here, but he obviously had their hospital beds brought here after the war, so they must have been important too. Perhaps the soldiers were killed in the line of duty, but the Nazis were anxious for them to be up and about and fighting again, and Marx was keen to dabble in necromancy." He paused. "Thank heavens that didn't work."

"Why not?" said Sam.

"Corpses who met their deaths in violent circumstances are the most difficult to get rid of once they've been reanimated. It must be something to do with wanting to cling onto the life you were once denied, I suppose. Anyway, certainly all of that would explain how after the war he was able to amass such a concentrated quantity of psychic energy in one place."

"Just to talk to his wife and daughter again," said Sam. "Perhaps he wanted to repent."

"I don't think he actually wanted to see them again at all," said Henderson. "I think their being here might even be a bit of an accident, like the beneficial spirit of the stone circle Maddy was able to conjure up, which was then presumably cast out by something far nastier that now has possession of her. I do think they are who you've seen, by the way, and I think the reason they got that door open for us was because before we defeat Mr Marx, we have to face him."

Sam was still having difficulty coming to terms with what Henderson had said. "So he didn't want to see his family again?"

Henderson shook his head. "Anything but, I should imagine. I don't think that's why he built this place. That was just an excuse, a story in case anyone should want to know more. In fact, I wouldn't be at all surprised if the bombing of Bristol, and in particular of Marx's own house, was actually part of the deal he struck with the Nazis in return for his summoning up supernatural aid for them. His mistakes wiped clean, or at least that's probably how he saw it."

"So what *is* all this for?"

"Oh the usual: immortality, endless power, dominion over life and death. Looks as if it all went a bit wrong, though, and the house was left to rot. A failed experiment by one of the world's many incompetent Black Magicians. I wonder what was going through his head as he sat there?"

"Actually," said Sam, "I could probably tell you if I just laid a hand on..."

"Don't!" Henderson yelled. But it was too late. As Sam's slim fingers came into contact with the stick-thin right arm of William Marx, there was a blinding flash of light and Sam was thrown backwards. Henderson raced to her side.

"Are you all right?" he said.

"Yes," came the reply. "But thank you for bending so close you've nearly deafened me."

"Merely showing my concern, young lady," he said as he helped her to her feet.

"For whom, exactly?"

"A good question. It's not as if our elderly friend in the throne behind us can see."

There was a noise from the throne behind them.

"I wouldn't be too sure about that," said Sam looking over his shoulder. Henderson followed her worried gaze.

The motionless, desiccated, shrivelled-up figure was as wizened and as rotted as before, but now it was struggling to free itself from the stone. As they watched it began to wrench itself from side to side, the long-dead flesh that was fused to the throne tearing a little more with each swaying movement.

"He's going to be free in a minute," said Sam.

"He is indeed," said Henderson, "and I don't think it's a good idea for us to be here when he does." He turned to the door and pulled.

It refused to budge.

"In your own time, Henderson," said Sam.

Henderson tugged at the door again. Nothing. The corpse of William Marx had torn both stumps of its arms free and was now putting all its energy into releasing its legs.

"Anytime right now would be ideal," she said, keeping one eye on the writhing creature as she backed up against him.

"I am trying, you know," he said. "It's just that the door appears to be stuck."

One leg left to go.

"Why is it," said Sam, trying to get her fingers around the top of the door to help him, "that doors only seem to stick when there's some denizen of Hell only two feet away from us?"

"Isn't it always the way? I wonder if this has some kind of automatic locking device?" Henderson was rattling the tip of his pointer around in the keyhole in a pathetic attempt to manipulate the lock, when the corpse of William Marx finally freed itself.

"He doesn't look terribly happy!" said Sam.

"How can you possibly tell?" said Henderson as he struggled with the lock. "It's not as if he's got much of a face left."

"True," said Sam as the remains of William Marx shambled closer, "but the little bit of it that's still stuck to his skull looks awfully annoyed."

Henderson gave up and started banging at the door and rattling the handle. "Well, so would you be if you had no hands and feet," he said, glancing in Marx's direction. "But you know, for someone lacking the necessary means, he's doing a very good job."

"Unlike you, you mean?" said Sam, helping Henderson to hammer.

"This could be the end, you know," he said.

"Well if it is, I'd hate it for anyone who finds our broken bodies to think I wasn't at least helping," Sam replied as the door opened and they both fell through it and found themselves looking up into the startled eyes of Jeremy Stokes.

Chapter Twenty Six
The Power of Music

"Thank God!" all three of them said together before striding past each other.

"You don't want to go that way!" was the next thing they said in unison before Henderson pulled the door shut again and held onto the handle.

"I wouldn't worry about that too much," said Sam who answered Henderson's questioning gaze by raising her hands. "He hasn't got anything to open the door handle with, has he?"

Henderson shrugged and let go of the door. Behind it the muffled groans of a very angry William Marx could be heard, along with the faint rasping of rotted stumps against oak.

"Thanks for that," Henderson said to a bewildered-looking Jeremy. "You came just at the right time." He was about to lead Sam back down the corridor when Stokes snapped out of his shock.

"You don't want to go that way!" he cried.

Sam and Henderson halted, realising as they did so that the groaning, shuffling noises weren't solely coming from behind the door they had just closed. Not entirely. Sam ran to the balcony to see the rotting creatures from the back garden making their way up both staircases.

"I think we're really in trouble now," she said once the others had caught her up.

"Where did they come from?" said Henderson.

Stokes' surprised expression was presumably because he had been expecting Henderson to know. "Out of the ground at the back of the house," he said.

"Ah, so I was right," said Henderson as first of the shambling things reached the top of the staircase.

Jeremy looked at Sam, who responded with her quickest 'Believe me, you don't want to know' expression.

"Helen's dead," said Jeremy.

"So's Alan," said Sam. There was little time to mourn and they all realised the brief silence that ensued would have to suffice for the moment.

"So what do we do now?" said Jeremy. "We've got a horde of zombies in front of us."

"*Nazi* zombies," added Henderson.

"Nazi zombies, whatever," said Jeremy.

"And a very angry resurrected Warlock trying to get at us from the other direction," said Sam.

A long drawn out scream came from the direction of the throne room. They turned, Sam and Henderson expecting to be confronted by a very angry Necromancer's corpse. But it was not that.

It was the door.

The carved wooden gargoyle at its centre, still dripping with Professor Pritchard's drying blood, had opened its jaws even wider and was now emitting an ear-piercing shriek. As if in response, more screams could now be heard, sounding to Sam as if they were coming from everywhere. In her mind's eye she could see the carvings they had discovered all over the house becoming animated and joining in the chorus of agonised wailing.

"The house isn't happy," said Henderson.

Jeremy looked in horror at the first approaching zombie. "What are we going to do now?" he said.

"Into the bedroom!" was Henderson's reply.

"Why does it have to be my bedroom?" said Sam as he hurtled through the door with the two of them close behind.

"Possibly because I wanted the thinnest of excuses to come in here?" he said with a wicked smile, before turning to Jeremy. "Mr Stokes, if you would be so kind, could you see your way to barricading the door with whatever you may find to hand?"

While Jeremy did his best to drag a battered wardrobe in front of the door, Henderson ran to the window.

"It's quite a drop down there," said Sam.

"Indeed it is," said her colleague, looking down. "Tell me Sam, is there anything embarrassing in your bed?"

"I beg your pardon?"

"Anything embarrassing? You know — silly fluffy toys you can't do without, embarrassing pyjamas with 'Man Bait' written on them that you were given on some drunken girls' night out and actually found were so comfy and no man you ever brought home was going to see them so you kept them?" Henderson paused and regarded Sam's incredulous expression. "Nothing like that, then?"

"No," said Sam. "Absolutely not!"

"Excellent!" he said, dragging the duvet onto the floor and tearing the sheets from the bed. "Then it's time to replicate a scene beloved of bedroom farces and poor quality sex comedies."

"I hope you mean the old 'using the sheets to climb out of the window' routine," said Sam as she helped him knot them together.

"Of course," said her colleague. "What else?"

"I don't think this wardrobe's going to hold much longer," said Jeremy as a splintered segment burst inward and groping skeletal hands tried to clutch at him. He took a candlestick from the dresser and began to beat at the flailing claws, which turned out to be a lot more resilient than they looked.

"Never mind, my dear fellow," said Henderson, as he made sure the knot they had tied to secure the sheets to the leg of the bed was secure. "It's time for us to be leaving." He grabbed the sheet. "In the interests of safety I will go first. If the sheet fails to hold my weight then you'll have to find some other way out but at least you won't have been dashed to you deaths on the flagstones below."

Sam grabbed it from him.

"In the interests of not wanting to have to look at you splattered all over the flagstones below, I think I had better go first so that if it at least takes my weight for a little while I may survive to get to the bottom and can then find some way of distracting the monsters while you two get out of here."

Henderson looked at Jeremy, who was still doing his very best to stop the zombies from getting into the room and clearly didn't have time to enter into the argument.

"All right," he said, "but please be careful."

Sam gave him a tender smile as she climbed up on the window sill, squeezed herself through the narrow opening, and placed a tentative foot onto the stonework outside.

Which promptly gave way.

Sam fell, one hand gripping the sheet, the other clawing at the air until the bed linen became taut and she found herself swinging back and then forwards. She came to rest against the window of the music room and kicked at the glass. It cracked a little but refused to shatter. She was about to try again when she felt herself being pulled away from the window by an unholy force that lifted her as far from the building as the taut sheet would allow. Whether the force was for good or ill Sam didn't have time to consider as the glass of the music room window came zooming towards her.

"Can you see what happened?" said Jeremy, as they heard a crash and splintering noises.

"Samantha has decided to pay a visit to the music room," said Henderson, gathering up the sheet as un-dead hands began clawing their way through the holes they had managed to make in both the bedroom door and the wardrobe. "I suggest we pop down there to see if she's all right."

Henderson made sure Jeremy was safely at the bottom before attempting the descent himself. When the two of them were safely on the ground, he went over to the smashed window and peered inside.

"Miss Jephcott?" he inquired. "Are you all right?"

"I'm fine," said a muffled voice from within. "But my leg hurts and I'm stuck under the piano."

"Not to worry," said the detective, vaulting inside while taking care to avoid the splinters of glass still adhering to the window frame, "I'll be with you any minute... now." He crawled beneath the piano and began to pull at the wooden bar Sam's ankle had got stuck beneath. A much more cautious Jeremy followed to behold Henderson doing his best to dislodge his prone associate from underneath the instrument.

"It's all right," said Henderson, realising as he unhooked Sam's ankle that the position they were in looked somewhat compromising, "we work together."

"Not for much longer if I can help it," said Sam, getting to her feet and brushing herself down. She shot a glance at the door. "Hadn't we better barricade that?"

Henderson nodded. "Good idea," he said and looked at Jeremy. "Come on, give me a hand."

Together they manoeuvred the piano into position, getting it in front of the door just as something started hammering on it.

"Sorry we can't answer the door right now!" said Henderson, making a circuit of the room. He began grabbing musical instruments and passing them to the others as Maddy's voice resonated through the wood.

"There's no escape for any of you now!" she said. "You should let us in. It will be far less painful this way."

"I'm not so sure about that!" the detective yelled as he opened the lid of the piano and threw the instruments he was still holding into its gutted casing. He motioned to the others to do likewise.

"And why are we doing this?" said Sam.

"Damage limitation," explained Henderson as he took a notebook from his pocket and patted his pockets for a pen. He beamed when Jeremy handed him one.

"That's not exactly what I would call an explanation," said Sam.

"Do a lot of damage," said Henderson, scribbling furiously, "and thereby limit the nastiness that's brewing in this place. Now, on my word, I want you and Mr Stokes to climb out of the window, if you would be so kind."

"Why?" said Jeremy. "What are you going to do?"

"What are you writing?" said Sam as Henderson folded the paper up tightly.

"The lines from the twenty-third psalm," he said with a grin. " 'The Lord's my shepherd I shall not want, he maketh me to blow up evil haunted houses that should never have been built in the first place'."

"And that bit of paper's going to blow everything up?" said Jeremy, looking as if he did not believe a word of it.

"That, plus a few special words I've put on there that I'm not at liberty to divulge to anyone who hasn't been properly educated —"

"That'll be me, then," Sam interrupted.

"The word 'inappropriate' has crossed my mind on occasion during our time together," said Henderson, "but never mind that now. As I was saying, some Holy words, a couple of words of Real Power, plus a whole collection of supernaturally charged relics, which should all collide nicely to provide a whopper of an explosion. Needless to say, once I set it off I don't want to be fighting with you to get out of here so I shall ask you once again. Would you both be so kind as to climb out of the window?"

A blackened fist smashed through the door.

"I can see we are going to have to make you suffer," said Maddy in a voice now quite unlike hers. *But quite possibly similar to William Marx's*, Sam thought.

"Yes, yes I'm sure you'll do your best," said Henderson as Sam and Jeremy climbed back out the way they had just come. He made sure they were clear, lifted the lid of the piano once more, tossed the tightly folded piece of paper in and slammed the lid down.

For a couple of seconds there were no sounds other than Maddy's repeated and increasingly successful attempts to get through the door. Henderson backed away from the instrument but stayed inside the room.

"What are you waiting for?" Sam hissed.

"It doesn't seem to be working," said Henderson as the door splintered inwards and Maddy, her face now an unrecognisable mess of what looked like glistening tar, began pushing at the piano that was in her way.

"We want you, Henderson," she growled.

"That's the problem," said Henderson, "so many people do and sometimes it's just not possible to spread oneself as thin as everybody would like."

"Henderson, come *on!*" Sam shouted through the window.

Henderson shook his head and stared at the piano, waiting for a reaction other than the juddering that was being caused by Maddy's attempts to push it out of the way. Then his eyes sparkled with a brainwave. He dashed to the window.

"Sam, are you by any chance wearing the crucifix you brought with you?" he asked.

"I am," she said.

"And the Star of David?"

Sam nodded.

"Could I possibly have them? And any other religious symbols you might have about your person? I think my bomb in there needs something to spark its fuse."

Sam sighed and handed them over.

"But know I'm only doing this because if I don't I won't be needing them anyway," she said.

"Of course," said Henderson, rushing over to the piano and throwing his newfound items into the piano crammed with everything else he had already placed there.

For a moment Maddy ceased her attempts to move the piano.

The piano, however, kept juddering.

Henderson smiled as the instrument began to shake of its own accord. He licked the tip of his right index finger and looked very pleased indeed when he tapped the lid to be rewarded with the sharp hiss of evaporating fluid. After that he turned and dashed for the window.

"Well what are you two still doing here?" he said once he was outside. "That thing in there is heating up. Run away!"

"Where to?" said Sam.

Henderson looked up to see zombies approaching from either side of the building.

"I thought you said they'd followed you upstairs?" Henderson said to Jeremy.

"They did," was the reply. "Maybe this is some sort of second battalion."

Back in the music room the lid of the piano flew open. The crucifix flew out and landed on the wooden floor.

The piano stopped vibrating. Maddy gave it one more push and it began to shift away from the doorway.

"Damn. I hadn't reckoned on it doing that," said Henderson.

"What?" said Sam, keeping an eye on the slowly approaching un-dead.

"There's so much concentrated evil in that piano that it's starting to repel the opposing forces I've put in there. In a moment..."

The Star of David flew out, to be rapidly followed by a tiny scrap of paper.

"...that will happen. Which means we're in serious trouble."

"Why?" said Jeremy.

"Because the only way of getting my makeshift bomb to work now would be for someone to go back in there and physically hold in place the objects that bloody instrument has just spat out," Henderson replied. "And despite the fact that I really don't feel like dying today — or any day for that matter — it's starting to look as if this is how it all might end after all."

Sam laid a hand on his arm.

"Henderson, we need to go," she said.

Henderson seemed preoccupied for a moment.

"Go?" he said. "Yes... go. You'd better go. I have to... back... in there."

"No you don't," she said. "We've been in worse situations before, and we will be again. All we have to do is get out of the way of the zombies that are very nearly on us, and then we can think about what to do next."

"You are nearly ours!" screamed the Maddy creature from inside the room.

"No time," said the detective. "In the words of a once-popular song: it's now or never. And I've always been much more of a 'now' kind of person."

He made to climb back into the room when Jeremy Stokes stopped him.

"I thought maybe there might be an alternative," said the psychic, "but now I know there isn't."

"Precisely," said Henderson, "so if you would be kind enough to let me go, I can get on with saving the world."

"Not you, Mr Henderson," said Jeremy, "me. When you slammed the lid down on the piano that first time, I saw my reflection in its surface, and I saw what was going to happen to me."

Henderson stared at him aghast.

"You mean you…"

"I mean, it's time for me to save the world for a change, while you two dodge these things and get as far away from here as possible," said Jeremy, pushing him out of the way and climbing into the room. Stokes grabbed the items on the floor, dropped them back into the piano, held the lid shut, and rammed it as hard as he could against the open doorway.

"Run!" he screamed as Maddy reached for his flesh with a blackened claw.

"How long have we got?" said Sam.

"I've no idea," said Henderson, still looking lost. "I've never done this before. And we can't leave him."

Sam gripped his shoulders and put on her sternest voice.

"Look, usually it's you trying to convince me of this, but if we don't leave now we'll all end up dead. And if there's anything left of the evil that infects this place there won't be anyone around to fight it. The world needs you alive, Henderson, alive and well to stop any of this getting any further."

"No it doesn't," he said. For a split-second Sam wondered if he was admitting defeat until he took her hand and said, "It needs us."

They cast one last grateful look at Jeremy Stokes, the television psychic who had discovered the meaning of his life only at the point when it was to end. He waved them away with one hand, while he batted off Maddy's advances with the other.

They turned to find themselves entirely surrounded by the walking dead.

Chapter Twenty Seven
Taking Flight

"So what do we do now?" said Sam, as the zombies closed in.

"Let's see if this works," said Henderson, taking his notebook from his pocket again and scribbling something on it. He tore the page out and held it up to the creatures, who recoiled instantly.

"Fantastic!" said Sam as they began to make their way through the horde. "What does it say?"

"I've no idea," said Henderson. "It's a Tibetan chant intended to ward off the un-dead. Seems to be working, though."

Or at least it was until they reached one on whom the prayer seemed to have no effect. It reached for them, flailing its arms about in a desperate attempt to grab them.

"What's his problem?" asked Sam.

"No eyes," said Henderson, dodging the creature's blows. "It would seem they have to actually be able to see the words for this to work." He kicked it hard in the right leg, which crumbled to dust. The zombie leaned to one side and fell over. "Let's run for it before any more turn up, eh?"

"I wish you'd told me all we had to do was kick them," said Sam as they came round to the front of the house and started running down the driveway.

"I had no idea they were so friable," said Henderson. Behind them came an ominous rumbling like a dragon clearing its throat. They were halfway down the hill when a series of loud cracks caused him to push Sam behind the trunk of a great old oak. "I think she's about to blow," he said.

They crouched behind the tree and watched as the house began to vibrate in the early evening dusk. Tiles fell from the roof, the walls cracked and split, and the central tower began to teeter and fall backwards before resuming its position. Then it leaned forward, and then back again once more.

Henderson looked in horror at the shaking walls and the teetering tower.

"When's it going to explode?" hissed Sam.

Henderson's face was now deathly pale. "I don't think it is going to," he said, as they both realised the house wasn't falling apart at all.

It was laughing at them.

As they watched, bricks fell away from the front of the tower, leaving two gaping holes which could almost be eyes. Then, as it leaned towards them once more, the entire ground floor of the house split open lengthways, forming a vast mouth with granite teeth and lips of plaster.

They never expected it to speak, and when it did, it voice was so deep as to cause the surrounding countryside to rumble with every word.

"It is time for this little game to come to an end, Mr Henderson."

"It's William Marx," said the detective.

"It's a house," Sam breathed, still unable to believe what she was looking at.

"Well in fact, we're both right. It's William Marx *and* the house; a melding of bricks and flesh, plaster and blood, stone and soul," said Henderson. "And it's so obviously powerful that I must confess to feeling a bit scared."

"You and me both," said his companion. "Except I'm a *lot* scared."

"SILENCE!" roared Marx / the house. "I could crush you in an instant, but, sadly, were I to do that I would be damned for all eternity, such are the rules laid down by those who are, for the moment, more powerful than I. I have to fight you, and it has been tediously decreed that you are to be allowed weapons."

"Oh good, something to fight with," said Sam.

"I'd much rather we didn't have to fight at all," said Henderson. "I was all for running away. I mean it isn't as if it can go anywhere; it's a house."

"Neither can we," Sam reminded him. "We're trapped here, remember?"

"So choose!" bellowed the building. "Choose the instruments with which you will fail to destroy me!"

"He's a bit presumptuous, isn't he?" said Sam.

"Sign of insecurity," replied Henderson. "If you ask me, we're winning already."

There was a rumbling noise from behind them. To say they were surprised when they turned to see what it was would be an understatement.

Standing in the driveway was the most ornate black carriage Sam had ever seen in or out of a BBC costume drama. Her amazement was only matched by her heartbeat suddenly quickening at the sight of the four majestic black horses that had been attached to it to draw it.

"Where did that come from?" said Henderson.

"Oh, they're lovely!" said Sam, running over to calm the closest horse, as the rumblings from the house began to grow ever stronger. "But in answer to your question, I have no idea."

It was Henderson's turn to roll his eyes. "You weren't thinking about horses, were you?"

"No," she snapped, momentarily taking her attention away from her new friend. She eyed the sumptuous lining of the coach. "Were you thinking of that black velvet dinner jacket your tailor's making for you?"

Henderson checked over his shoulder to see the house shaking even more violently and paled. "I never think of *haute couture* when I'm working," he said.

"Liar," said Sam, making a circuit of the coach. "What about that red and white striped jacket you bought the other month after being inspired by the wallpaper in that haunted restaurant?"

"That was different," said Henderson, following her around to the other side of the carriage to see that she had discovered something. "What have you got there?"

"This is more of what I was thinking of," said Sam, trying to lift the heavy black sword she had found leaning against the carriage door. "Well, actually, I was thinking of some kind of gun, but at least this is something designed for fighting rather than running away," she gave Henderson a mock-disdainful look.

"I'm sure they're both going to come in handy," he said. "Now I suggest we use the carriage to get as close to the house as possible and then —"

His plans were interrupted by a cracking sound from further up the hill. They both turned to see something they knew they would remember until the end of their days.

The house was moving.

Not rattling or shaking or giving in to any random disturbances of the ground, but moving. As they watched, the wings of the house began to lift up, the brickwork cracked, came apart and remoulded itself. The black slates were multiplying, slipping from the roof to encase these new appendages giving them a scaly leathery look almost like...

"Wings," Sam breathed. "It's got real, actual wings. Henderson, that thing is going to bloody well fly. The house is turning into an enormous bird."

The face that had spoken to them was changing now as well. The flat frontage of the house was elongating and twisting, projections were erupting from it and fashioning themselves into ears, jaws, a snout, all covered with the scaly roof tiles as the thing the house had become gave an almighty roar and flame erupted from its mouth.

"Oh my goodness me; it's a dragon," said Henderson, rooted to the spot.

"Yes it is," said Sam "and we've got to get away." She pulled at his arm as the creature began to wrench itself free from its foundations. She looked at the carriage. "We've got to get away in a horse and cart that you dreamed up."

Henderson held up his hands. "Honestly this has nothing to do with me. I was thinking more along the lines of one of the cabbalistic tomes of Conrad von Holstein or Ludvig Prinn to help me conjure up something to help us. I think you'll agree that doesn't look anything like a dusty old book. I very much suspect the decisions have been made for us."

"Who by?" said Sam as the dragon finally tore itself free from the earth and from its life as a house amidst a shower of rubble and fractured standing stones.

"No idea," said Henderson, "but let's just hope they're on our side. Besides, I've always suspected that the supernatural barrier around this house can only be traversed by a supernatural vehicle and now we've got one. Which is handy. Now," he pointed at the coach. "You can drive one of these things can't you?"

"Do you mean a horse?" said Sam as the creature on the hill began to spread its wings to make its ascent.

"Well, yes, but preferably four of them," said Henderson, pointing to the driver's seat. "From up there," he added.

"Ah, well, seeing as that was what you meant, then, no — I have absolutely no idea," she replied.

Henderson looked bewildered. "Well, there must be a whip up there or something. Come on, up you go — it's not as if we've got time to stand around here discussing who can or can't drive one of these things." He gave her a nudge.

"I take it from what you're saying that you haven't the slightest idea either," said Sam, looking for a way to climb up.

"Exactly," replied her colleague. "Just as I have absolutely no idea how to use this sword." With a heave he lifted the heavy weapon up and did his best to wield it. It took both his hands. "But at least I can lift it up. Now when you're driving this in the expert fashion I have no doubt you're going to manage, I'm going to need you to keep the whole thing as steady as possible while I try and pierce our friend up there somewhere vital."

Sam could scarcely believe her ears. "What?"

The dragon beat down with its wings, creating a gust of wind that felt like a hurricane to the two tiny human forms shielded by the carriage.

"You are going to drive while I stand on top of the coach and do my duty," said Henderson, following Sam up the tiny ladder at the front of the coach. Sam took her place in the tiny black leather driver's seat and picked up the reins. The horses nickered and snorted in readiness. By her left hand lay a whip, but she had no intention of using that. Henderson was relieved to see that the top of the carriage was pockmarked with numerous grooved bosselations which would at least give some degree of a foothold. He looked up to see the dragon circling round to come in for the kill.

"Ready?" he called to Sam.

"Of course not," she called back to him.

"Then away we go!" Henderson raised the sword above his head, Sam flicked the reins, and they set off down the hill.

Chapter Twenty Eight
The Dragon Wing of Night

As the carriage rattled down the driveway and out through the gates the sun slipped behind the horizon, the last vestiges of daylight left the sky, and night descended.

"Good thing there's a full moon!" Henderson heard Sam shout.

"There shouldn't be," Henderson shouted back, doing his best to keep his balance. "But in terms of reality, I think all bets are off for the moment."

"Where am I supposed to be going, anyway?" As they reached the road, Sam pulled the reins to the left and, fortunately, the horses responded to her command and turned into the lane. The carriage rattled and bumped over the uneven road and Henderson imagined it was going to be as much a battle for Sam to stay in the driver's seat as for him to stay on the roof.

"Somewhere with a bit of space would be nice!" Henderson called back, wedging the tip of the sword into one of the grooves on the roof of the coach and leaning on it for a moment to gain some extra stability. He looked up. The light from an unnaturally large and bright full moon filtered between the branches of trees as they passed beneath. It was impossible to see the creature, but even above the rattling of the carriage wheels on the tarmac it was impossible to miss the regular rhythmic swooping sounds of its heavy wings. "We're probably safe as long as we keep under cover!"

A searing blast of flame reduced the expanse of hedgerow they had just overtaken to scorched embers. A belch of black smoke made them both cough as the carriage pushed through it.

"Or perhaps not," said Henderson as an oak tree toppled into the road behind them, blocking any chance of them going back the way they had come. He leaned forward and said, "Try to get to the main road and then hang a left. We should have more room to manoeuvre there!"

"Presumably there will be more chance of hitting cars as well!" Sam said, battling to keep the vehicle under control. Supernatural, or whatever they may have been, the horses were understandably spooked by what was happening. Henderson braced himself and waited until the junction appeared up ahead. Then he leaned heavily against the turn to stop himself from sliding off the roof.

It almost worked.

Part of the problem was having to hang onto the sword as well, which was why his foot skidded and he ended up flailing over the right hand side of the carriage, holding on with one hand while gripping the hilt of the sword in the other.

"Should I stop?" Sam cried.

Before Henderson could respond, a bolt of fire landed just to their right and turned a hay barn into a blazing inferno. "Just keep going!" he shouted

Henderson kicked at the carriage doors, finally gaining a foothold that enabled him to lever himself back onto the roof. Getting back into a standing position was another matter, however, and all he could do — for what felt like interminable minutes — was hang on as Sam guided the horses down the road. Eventually, he managed to roll onto his side and look up.

It was a beautiful evening, even if the arrangement of the stars was wrong and the moon was a worrying shade of copper. The smell of burning soon cleared to be replaced by the more pleasant odours of lush hedgerows and ploughed fields. Henderson wondered if all of this had been laid on just for them or if anyone who happened to be in the area was now witness to the most spectacular display of supernatural intervention into the real world in recorded history. Not that there would be anyone around to record it if he didn't get to his feet.

"There's another junction up ahead!" Sam yelled from the driver's seat. "And a much bigger road!"

"That'll be the dual carriageway!" he shouted back. "Try and turn left again!"

Sam did her best, but the horses were having none of it. Instead the black carriage and its four horses crashed across the central reservation before Sam could get them back under control. It was only when they saw headlights coming towards them that Henderson realised that once they had crossed to the other side of the road he shouldn't have kept telling her to turn left.

"We're on the wrong side of the road!" Sam screamed as a car shot past blowing its horn.

"Don't worry," said Henderson, placing his hands on her shoulders to help lever himself to his feet. "I believe there aren't any current laws regarding the use of horses and carriages on England's motorways."

"But we're in Wales!" she shouted, as two more cars weaved their way past and something enormous, winged and scaly overhead blasted them off the road.

"Why did it hit them?" Henderson asked.

"I don't know! Maybe it wants to make us as terrified as possible before it kills us. I have to say it doesn't actually have to try any harder where I'm concerned."

Henderson crouched low and held onto Sam's shoulders for balance.

"No, I'm serious," he said. "It had plenty of chance to get us as we were leaving the house but it kept missing, and the only times it's tried here is when other cars have gone past. I don't think it can see us."

"You mean we're invisible?"

"I think we've been provided with some protection by whoever sent us this carriage," Henderson replied.

"Wow," said Sam, giving the reins another tug, "a magic horse and carriage. I wish I felt a bit more like Cinderella."

"A pumpkin and some white mice wouldn't be of much help to us right now," said Henderson, getting to his feet, "but let's hope our fairy godmother's keeping an eye out for us."

Ahead of them loomed lights and an open forecourt. A large sign labelled 'Happy Henry Hedgehog's Hamburgers' depicted a rather terrifying cartoon mammal trying to consume a meat patty and chips while looking happy and contented at the same time.

"Try and pull in at that service station!" Henderson yelled. "And don't make any jokes about us not needing petrol."

Sam pulled the reins to the right and the horses went galloping up the slip road in the wrong direction.

Henderson glimpsed a range of expressions on the faces of those few late travellers who had found the need to stop for petrol, or even the food they hoped would make them smile with the same garish satisfaction as did the Happy Henry Hedgehog, while they beheld Henderson and Sam come crashing onto the forecourt with what looked like a Victorian hearse. The two people who were filling their cars with petrol sensibly abandoned the pumps, snapped on their vehicles' petrol caps and drove off at speed, possibly in response to Henderson and Sam's arrival, but more likely because of the enormous dragon that soared overhead. Those inside the restaurant were unable to see what was hovering above them and thus contented themselves to watch from behind the assumed safety of glass windows, munching on chips as they no doubt tried to guess at the conversation taking place between the attractive young lady driver and the strange man standing on top of the carriage waving a sword around.

"Henderson, why the hell have we stopped here?" Sam let the reins drop and as the horses panted, their visible breath thick in the chill night air, Henderson spoke while keeping his eye trained on the sky above him.

"It's the only place for miles around with any light," he said. "I can't fight the dragon if I can't see it and it can't see us."

"Isn't that a good thing?" said Sam. "As in can't we use this rather miraculous gift of invisibility to sensibly get far away it?"

There was a roar from above them.

"I don't think there *is* any getting away from it," he said. "So the best thing to do is fight while we still have energy left to do so." He jumped down from the carriage and almost fell over as he landed on the concrete of the forecourt.

"With just that sword?" said Sam, making to get down from the driver's seat.

"You stay there," said Henderson. "With luck you're going to be my escape route. And in answer to your question: no — I don't intend to just use this sword. I intend to fight fire with fire."

A blast of flame from somewhere up above hit the service station sign and reduced Happy Henry Hedgehog to a Miserable Molten Mess.

"You do realise we're in a petrol station, don't you?" said Sam. "And that if that thing blasts us any closer we're going to be toast?"

"I'm rather hoping it's going to be close enough to toast itself," said Henderson, "while you and I make our escape in our invisible getaway car. Now, if you don't mind, I'm going to try and lure it towards the petrol pumps. You get the horses ready and at my signal ride in front of me as fast as you can."

"That's not entirely true, is it?" said Sam.

Henderson looked confused. "What do you mean?"

"You said to drive *in front* of you. What you meant was drive *between* you and the massive dragon thing that will be coming straight at you and heading for where vast quantities of flammable liquid are stored and hope that I time it right."

Henderson nodded. "Exactly. See? I knew I didn't need to say all that, and I was right!"

Sam sighed. "I don't supposed there's any point in telling you to be careful or you might get killed?"

"I think there's a good chance we might get killed anyway," said Henderson, and now his face was grim. "So we may as well go down fighting."

Sam was about to say something in response but Henderson was already making his way towards the petrol pumps, dragging the sword along the ground and making as loud a scraping noise as he could, while watching to ensure the metal didn't start sparking against the concrete. Once he was at the pumps furthest away from Sam he ran out from beneath the covered awning and began shouting and waving his hands in the air.

"Mr Marx! Or whatever you are! Come and get me! I'm here!"

He almost didn't get to finish his sentence as the creature swooped over the awning and away from him, and a gust of wind threatened to throw him to the ground. Henderson steadied himself as he saw the monster circling round and beginning to swoop down. He signalled to Sam to bring the horses forward. The creature belched fire but it was still too far away to do any damage to the pumps. Henderson stayed his ground and picked up the sword. He waved it at the creature and did his best to impersonate a knight.

"Now I know how St George must have felt!" he shouted. The monster was coming in close to the ground and, as it approached, Henderson could make out every tiny scale on its snout. The harlequin pattern of its pupil-less eyes was just beginning to fascinate him when he realised the creature was taking in breath to strike again. He waved Sam on and then ran as fast as he could towards the creature. He lifted the sword into the air with both hands and threw it at the beast just as Sam drove the coach past him. The blade sailed towards the beast as if guided by an unnatural force.

For a moment, Henderson thought he had missed, as his body was engulfed in a warmth he hadn't known for many years. Not since the time when he had disposed of a dangerous artefact in a volcano and the subsequent interaction between cleansing flame and the sudden release of trapped metallic evil had caused it to erupt. He felt a similar heat now, one that singed his hair and probably did untold damage to his clothes. Then, suddenly, all was dark.

Did it boil my eyes? he wondered, before tiny dots of light above him made him realise they were back on the road again. He realised he had been holding his breath and, grateful that he had avoided scorching his lungs, he took several deep gasps as he hung onto the side of the moving carriage. After another minute had passed, he finally felt strong enough to climb up beside Sam. She greeted him with a smile and a nod but kept her eyes ahead of her as she guided the carriage back onto the road.

"Are you all right?" he asked.

Sam gave him another nod. "Pretty much paralysed with fear," she said, "but otherwise, I'm just fine. You do know how to make an exhibition of things, don't you?"

From behind them came the sound of a third explosion, louder and even more eruptive than the two that had preceded it. Black smoke erupted into the sky, accompanied by the stench of petrol fumes. Wide-eyed faces stared from the restaurant at the devastation on the forecourt.

"Well, you can't make an omelette without blowing up a few petrol tankers," said Henderson, permitting himself a look behind and noting with some relief that there didn't appear to be any movement in the blazing inferno that was all that remained of the fuelling area. "Hopefully that's the last we've seen of him."

"You always say the most inappropriate things, don't you?" said Sam.

"What do you mean?"

"Well I don't need a rear view mirror on this thing to tell you that my Sense of Something Extraordinarily Evil and Very Near is tingling like mad," she said.

Balancing himself on the roof of the coach, Henderson turned to look back at the devastation he had created. Devastation from which was now rising a thing of winged fire. With an unholy screech it took to the air.

"Oh bloody hell, I've created a phoenix dragon," said Henderson.

"Usually you'd be fascinated," said Sam, thinking of using the whip to try and make the horses go faster but deciding to use even more encouragement with the reins instead.

"True, but I have to admit I'm a bit distracted by the fact that it isn't dead."

"Well, you'd better come up with something fast," said Sam, "because not being dead is exactly what that thing is doing on our tail."

They felt a hot ungodly wind as the creature swooped over them once more.

"We must still be invisible to it," said Henderson. "Perhaps we should stop and think."

Sam tried to get the horses to stop but they were having none of it.

Henderson shouted in her ear. "I said perhaps we should stop and —"

"I'm trying to stop!" she screamed back at him "They don't want to!"

"In that case, let go of the reins."

"What?"

"Let go of the reins. Maybe they know where they're supposed to go better than we do."

Sam's fingers were like locked ice around the thin leather straps and she yelped with pain as Henderson prised them free. As she sat on her hands to warm them up the carriage pelted on down the road much faster than it had before. Soon the creature that was pursuing them was dropping back. There was no doubt that it was still coming, but the power of the driverless carriage had put enough distance between the two of them that Henderson and Sam were able to relax a little.

"Maybe we were never supposed to be up here," she said.

"What?"

Sam pointed downwards. "Maybe we were supposed to get into the carriage and be driven to safety. You know, like in *Dracula* but not, if you see what I mean." She shivered. "God, I'm freezing."

Henderson pulled himself forward to sit beside her on the driver's seat and put his arm around here.

"Any better?"

"Marginally," she said. "But stay like that anyway."

They said nothing for a few minutes, merely allowing the carriage to take them down the road, avoiding the few cars that always managed to pass them, however narrowly.

"You might be right," Henderson said eventually. "We probably are supposed to be sitting in the carriage. Which means we may have caused all that trouble back there for nothing."

"*You* might, you mean," said Sam. "I, as always, am merely your unwilling accomplice. At least that's what I'm going to tell the police if we ever get out of this alive."

"Always thinking of yourself," he said, giving her a playful nudge on the shoulder.

"Not really," she said. "Sometimes I think the safest place for you would be in a nice warm cell. No chance of you destroying a house or blowing up a petrol station there."

"As long as I could have a few books to read," he said.

"No," she replied. "Somehow you'd get some ancient magical volume smuggled in and the next thing anyone knew there'd be a gaping hole in the wall and a load of escaping prisoners, plus whatever horrible beastie you'd managed to conjure up by mistake."

"Oh ye of little faith," he said as she snuggled deeper into his shoulder. "And who, might I ask, would have smuggled the books in for me in the first place?"

She looked up at him. "You know I wouldn't have been able to put up with things without you for long. Life would be far too dull."

He gave her a squeeze. "Well, that's reassuring to know," he said. "Although having mentioned the police, I am beginning to wonder why we haven't seen them yet. That was probably the biggest bang this part of Wales has seen for years."

"Maybe for the same reason the cars keep avoiding us," said Sam. "They can't actually see us. They know there's something there but they can't quite put their finger on what."

"You mean we're as invisible to passers-by as we are to our friend up there?" said Henderson, looking up to see where the circling creature had got to. "Well it's a thought. It would certainly explain why we haven't been hit yet. But they could see us in the petrol station."

"Where it was light," said Sam. "I think this keeps us invisible as long as we stick to the shadows."

"Which means when the sun comes up we're going to be stuffed," said Henderson. "Any idea how long until daybreak?"

Sam shook her head. "No idea," she said. "But it can't be long: look."

She pointed to the horizon where the sky looked just the faintest shade lighter than the rest of the night sky.

"Do you know, if there wasn't a one hundred foot dragon chasing us, all this would be rather romantic," said Henderson.

"There's always something to spoil the moment, isn't there?" said Sam with an exaggerated sigh. "Well if we make it back home in one piece, I promise you the opportunity to try and recreate the mood. But I insist on lots of champagne."

Henderson smiled at her. "Let me assure you, my dear girl, that if we get out of this all the champagne you could wish for shall be yours."

Now they were thundering across a huge roundabout. Without pausing, the horses took the exit for the M4 headed west.

"Well at least they seem to know where we should be going," said Sam.

"I just wish we knew what we were supposed to do when we get there," Henderson added.

"Let's hope it doesn't involve the sword," said Sam as they pelted up the slip road to join the motorway, "seeing as you threw it away back at the petrol station."

Henderson turned round to see the fiery blob behind them still in pursuit. "Yes," he said. "Well, fingers crossed."

They settled themselves as best they could and let the horses take them wherever they were meant to be going.

Chapter Twenty Nine
The Suspension Bridge of Disbelief

They had been on the motorway for ten minutes when Henderson turned to Sam and said, "Do you notice anything strange?"

"You mean apart from the fact that none of the street lamps are working and that we haven't seen a single car?" said Sam. "In fact I was wondering when you were going to mention it."

The carriage rattled on under its own guidance, the horses showing no sign of tiring, which was just as well.

"We saw hardly any vehicles when we were on the other road, too," said the detective. "I'm just beginning to wonder whether or not we've been drifting in and out of reality."

"Staying in it just long enough to blow up a petrol station and endanger a few cars?" said Sam.

"Possibly," he replied. "I'm actually beginning to wonder if those were placed there for us as well. I just have the strangest feeling we haven't been in the real world for some time now."

"Since we left the house you mean?"

Henderson nodded.

"Or perhaps even before that. Wherever we've been moved to it's good to see it's a plane similar to our own."

Sam pointed at the winged beast still reassuringly far in the distance behind them. "And what about our constant companion?" she asked. "Is this his world?"

Henderson rubbed his nose and was surprised to find out just how chilly it felt to his fingertips. "I don't think so. I think we've all been transplanted elsewhere to fight it out,"

Sam nudged him. "I bet it was after you blew up the petrol station," she said.

"Yes, well if you wouldn't mind not going on about that, I'd be very grateful," Henderson said. "And besides," he pointed at the creature. "I may even have caused him some damage, even if it wasn't enough to kill him."

Sam tried to get more comfortable but it was impossible. "So what are we supposed to do now?" she asked.

"Well we don't have much control over where we're going, but I have a feeling it will become obvious when we get there."

For twenty minutes they continued down the deserted motorway, the distant horizon heralding dawn as a blush of pale crimson began to spread across the sky. It was only when the outline of concrete pillars and suspension supports appeared that Henderson sat up and began to take notice again.

"The Severn Bridge," he breathed. "I wondered if we might be headed there."

"What's so special about it?" said Sam.

"Apart from it being one of the largest estuary-spanning bridges in the country?" he said. "Anyway, I don't think it's the bridge itself that's going to be important, but rather what's underneath it."

"And what is underneath it?" said Sam.

The detective paused before delivering his answer as gravely and seriously as he could manage.

"Water!" he said, to be rewarded with a withering look. "I'm quite serious," he added. "Fire didn't work, but perhaps immersing the thing in salt water after a good roasting might be the way to get rid of it."

"And how exactly are we supposed to get it to go into the water?" she said.

Henderson looked uneasy as the horses began to slow down. "Well, maybe we're supposed to attract it," he said.

"Attract?" said Sam, looking around her. "How on earth are we supposed to do that?"

The horses came to a halt just as the road began to rise and become part of the bridge. Henderson looked behind to see the fiery blob which had been pursuing them getting larger. "They have to wait, now," he said.

"Wait?" said Sam. "Wait for *what*?"

"For our friend there to catch up."

Sam sat bolt upright in her seat and began to fidget. "You mean we're going to just sit here and wait for that thing to arrive so it can have *another* go at us?"

"I think the idea is more to drag it under the water," was the reply. "So I think it's about time we got off."

Henderson made to get up, changed his position, tried again, then tried for a third time, on this occasion making a loud straining sound before giving up. "It would seem we're not going to be allowed to leave," he said.

Sam struggled bound found she was firmly stuck to the seat as well. "Why not?" she said.

"Who knows?" said Henderson as the approaching dragon gave a bellow of triumph. "Perhaps we were given our chance and we failed. Perhaps we've seen too much and have to pay the price. Or, perhaps, whoever has engineered all this doesn't actually care about us at all."

Sam struggled against the seat with little success. "I take it you'd prefer the third if we had a choice?"

Henderson winked. "You're starting to know me really well," he said.

"Let's hope it's not all been a waste of time," said Sam as they both felt the searing heat begin to build behind them. With a jerk, the carriage started moving again; slowly at first, then more briskly as it began to gain momentum.

"I thought you said you didn't keep the sword!" Sam shouted as an ear-splitting roar came from above and one of the support pylons erupted into flames.

"I didn't!" said Henderson. "You saw me throw it away!"

Sam reached behind her. "So what's this, then?" she said.

Henderson grabbed the weapon. "Quite possibly our second chance," he said. He handed her the reins and indicated the horses. "Try and keep them from throwing themselves into the Bristol Channel for as long as you can," he said.

"Anything else impossible you'd like me to do?" said Sam.

Henderson got to his feet, free again now the vehicle was moving. He winked at her. "Wish me luck," he said. Then he climbed on top of the coach, lifted the sword above his head, and once again prepared to do battle.

And so the coach rattled across the suspension bridge pursued by the fiery creature, the beautiful girl at the reins trying hard to keep the horses to the outside lane, the man standing on the roof wielding the heavy sword doing his best to keep his balance.

The creature roared again, aiming a blast of fire directly at the carriage. Henderson had no time to think and so he reacted instinctively, bringing the sword across his body so that the flames came directly into contact with that instead. Bolts of fire made contact with the blade and were reflected back at the beast, which screamed in agony as the heat seared its already burning flesh.

"I think I've worked out how to do this!" Henderson shouted, waving the sword about.

"You *think*?" Sam called back.

"Yes!" he cried. "Or rather, no! The answer is not to think at all. Just rely on instinct and let myself be guided by whoever's trying to help us!"

A second wave of flame was met by another of Henderson's parrying blows. The creature roared again and began to rise above him. At first, Henderson thought it was retreating. Then he realised it was coming in for a direct attack.

"Brace yourself!" he shouted. "This one might be a bit tricky!'

"Oh good!" Sam yelled back. "I have got so bored of all those other easy attacks we've dealt with!"

As the beast began to plummet towards them — head first, clawed feet outstretched — Henderson suddenly saw it meant to pick them up. It was also only then, as the enormous left foot of the thing came towards him, that he was able to appreciate just how huge the creature was. He waited until the last possible moment, when the creature was almost touching the carriage, then thrust the point of the sword upwards into the leathery sole of the creature's foot with all his might.

The monster emitted a high pitched screeching sound and tried to shake the blade free. Henderson held on with both hands, using all his body weight to twist the blade back and forth as he felt his feet lose contact with the carriage. Henderson tried not to cry out as he was lifted high into the air, the beast ducking and swooping in its attempts to shake him off. He closed his eyes and wished for a miracle. When he opened them again he saw he was still high in the air. The closest thing to his flailing feet were the bridge's support wires thirty feet beneath him.

Henderson's flight through the air was soon to end, however, as the creature decided the best way to get rid of the agonising pain in its left foot was to scrape the sole against the side of the carriage. The detective braced himself as he was thrown against the door. The first couple of times caused a few bruises, but it was when he was thrown against the wood with such force that he heard it crack that he realised he was in some pain.

But it had also given him an idea.

The blade of the sword appeared to be well and truly wedged in the creature's foot. Henderson took a deep breath as he was swung away from the carriage. As he held on for dear life to the hilt of the sword he looked down to behold the black water of the Bristol Channel for an instant before being swung back into the carriage. This time the door splintered inwards completely and, as Henderson swung himself in, he manoeuvred the sword to jam the hilt under the frame of the now-open window. He let go and crossed his numb fingers.

The sword showed no signs of moving.

Unfortunately, the carriage did.

As Henderson did his best to climb back to Sam, he became aware that the entire carriage was lifting off the ground. The horses fell forward, still attached to the vehicle but now galloping frenziedly in the air as their hooves desperately sought purchase on something more substantial than the wind blowing down the Bristol Channel.

"What on earth have you done, Henderson?" Sam cried as they were dragged into the air.

The beast looked down at them, the carriage and its four horses now dangling from its left foot.

"I'm not sure," said the detective. "But I think it's time we were going."

There was a low gurgling sound as the creature took a deep breath in, presumably with the intention of incinerating the unwelcome addition to its left foot.

"And where, pray, are we supposed to go?" Sam screamed.

"The only direction we can," replied Henderson, taking her hand and kissing her on the lips. "Just in case I never get the chance to again," he said by way of explanation. Then he gave her an almighty shove and the next thing Sam knew the tangy scent of salt water was rapidly getting stronger.

They dropped into the estuary as the sky above them lit up with the fire of a thousand other-worldly dawns.

Chapter Thirty
The Wet and the Wounded

"Supernatural and *anti*-supernatural," said Henderson. "Or rather, supernatural matter and supernatural *anti*-matter. That's the only explanation I can think of. The house... dragon-creature... whatever it was... must have been made of one kind of energy, the coach and the sword of another, and when they stayed in contact for too long: KERBANG!"

"I have no idea what you're talking about," said the nurse, "but could I ask you to stay by your bed and not go wandering off like you keep doing? The doctors will be coming round in a bit."

Henderson stopped fiddling with the knot of the hospital smock they'd given him and wondered what they'd done with his suit. At least they'd put him in a nice quiet side ward with just the four beds, of which only the one he was in was currently occupied. He shielded his eyes against the bright morning sunshine and saw from the wall clock that it was a little after eight. Sam was in the female bay next door. As far as he was aware, she wasn't awake yet; at least she hadn't been the last ten times he'd checked.

"Mr Henderson?"

The detective looked up to see a brisk young man in surgical greens accompanied by a small entourage of staff. The man held out his hand.

"I'm Andy Murray, the A&E consultant. How are you feeling this morning?"

"As if I've swallowed about twenty gallons of sea water," Henderson replied, licking his lips.

Murray flipped open his notes and scratched at his closely trimmed blonde scalp. "Well according to this, that would be about right," he said. "What on earth *were* you doing with your friend in the Bristol Channel?"

"I suppose the best explanation is that we fell in," Henderson said, looking sheepish.

"Yes," said Murray, "I suppose it might be. Of course, I *could* suggest to you that you jumped."

Henderson looked shocked. "Jumped?"

"We get quite a lot of suicide attempts here, Mr Henderson, and a joint suicide pact isn't unheard of, you know. We've yet to get the story from your companion as she hasn't come round yet. She was unconscious when we dragged you both out, so I'm not surprised she isn't awake."

"She *will* be all right? Henderson said.

Murray snapped the file shut. "Oh yes, I expect so." He paused, as if waiting for something and when he didn't get what he wanted he said, "So?"

Henderson frowned. "So... what?"

"So was it suicide? We have a specialised counselling service here if you'd be willing to be seen."

"Thank you, but that's all right," said Henderson. "I can assure you it wasn't suicide on either of our parts."

"It might be worth a member of the psychiatric team seeing him anyway," murmured the nurse who had woken Henderson up with a glance at her charge, who, as far as she was concerned, was clearly unstable and liable to self-harm at a moment's notice and seemed to be incapable of focusing on the slightest thing for any length of time. She took the consultant aside for a moment and whispered in his ear. When Murray came back over, his face held the trace of a smile.

"Nurse Watkins says you've been mumbling about dragons and ghosts and all kinds of strange things," he said. "She thinks you might be a bit out of sorts." Henderson was about to say something but Murray stopped him. "That's fine," he said. "I might have thought the same, but one of my colleagues upstairs is into... all that kind of thing. He writes books in his spare time and he's as sane as you or I. Well..."

He gave Henderson an admonishing look. "You still have to explain why we had to fish you and your friend out of the Severn at five o'clock this morning."

"Research," Henderson spluttered.

"I beg your pardon?"

"You were quite right," Henderson said with a fierce nod. "I'm a writer... and Miss Jephcott is my typist," he added quickly. "She was helping me research my new novel but unfortunately things got a bit out of hand and we... er... fell in."

Murray seemed to be more satisfied with that. "Well, that does sound a bit more plausible than all that stuff about a 'horse-drawn carriage' that you apparently kept going on about in the ambulance," he said. "Either way, once you're feeling up to it, the police are waiting to talk to you."

Henderson paled. "Could you possibly do me a favour?" he asked Murray as the ward round was about to move on.

"That's very much going to depend on what it is," said the consultant, now starting to look a little irritated.

"Allow me to wait until Miss Jephcott comes round before talking to them. I'm hardly going to be able to concentrate on giving sane, rational answers to any questions if I'm worrying about her."

Murray thought about it for a moment, and then nodded, both to Henderson and to the rest of his team. "But once she's up and about, the two of you will be discharged," he said.

Twenty minutes later Nurse Watkins came back. "Your friend's awake now," she said, "and she doesn't look very happy."

Henderson made his way to the ward next door, where a bruised, disgruntled-looking Sam eyed him with vehemence.

"What's all this about 'Oh good, I'll go and tell your boss his typist is awake?'" she growled.

"There wasn't room for 'Investigators of Paranormal Occurrences' on the forms they gave me," said Henderson, unable to keep the smile off his face. "And I would just like you to know that I am so pleased to see you awake that I would hug you, but you do look a bit battered."

"Hug me anyway," she said, holding out her arms.

When they were finally finished, Henderson said, "I don't think I've ever felt you wince and smile so much at the same time."

"Well make the most of it, because I hope it's not going to happen very often," said Sam. "The wincing, I mean."

"Of course," Henderson replied before whispering, "Apparently the police are here, so if you fancy pretending to be knocked out for a bit we may not have to talk to them."

"Oh yes you *will*," said the uniformed officer who had appeared in the doorway.

Henderson resisted the urge to provide a time-honoured pantomime response and, instead, asked humbly if he might be allowed his trousers before he was to be interrogated.

Chapter Thirty One
A Coffee Shop in Cardiff

Two weeks later, Sam had her fingers crossed that nothing they might have told the police was going to get them into trouble with their employer. Henderson had suggested he face Sir Anthony alone, as the delicate matter of the death of the old man's grand-daughter might be better discussed between just the two of them. Sam thought Henderson was probably just trying to protect her from the old man's wrath, but she could understand why he had made the suggestion and hadn't put up much of a fight as Henderson had left her stirring a cappuccino at Morwen's Cake House in one of the shopping arcades off St Mary Street.

It was only after around ninety minutes, with two more coffees inside her — and the cakes starting to look perilously tempting — that she began to worry about him. She gave a deep sigh. Henderson should never have told the police they had been engaged in research for Sir Anthony Calverton, and Henderson himself had later admitted to her that he had mentioned their employer in a moment of panic, hoping it would add *gravitas* to what he had already told them.

She rattled her spoon against the inside of her empty coffee cup. Sir Anthony had probably arranged for the district Chief Superintendent (most likely a close personal friend) to be waiting when Henderson arrived, ready to cart him off for involving the reputation of a fine, upstanding industrialist in his paranormal tomfoolery. She took out her mobile, knowing even as she did so that Henderson didn't carry one. She stared at the screen, feeling more helpless than ever. If she ever saw him again, she was going to force him to get one. No arguments.

She was on the verge of going over to the Diverticulum Club — even though she knew it was likely she would be refused entry without a pass — when the detective appeared in the doorway.

"Henderson!" she said. "You are going to get yourself a mobile phone. No arguments."

"Do you mind if I get a cup of tea first?" he said quietly, ordering one at the counter and then changing his mind for an espresso with a shot of mint syrup instead.

"Yes I do!" she shouted, at last having an outlet to vent her frustration and determined that he wasn't going to get away without being told off. "You've been bloody ages. I thought you'd been dragged off somewhere."

"By whom?" he said, looking at her quizzically before munching on a biscotti he had neglected to pay for. He gave the little old lady behind the counter the money for the biscuit, said "Thank you, Morwen," then deduced from her confused expression that she wasn't the owner of the coffee shop, and then carried his drink over to the table.

"I'm fine," he said. "But I can see next time I'm going to have to take you with me. If I leave you alone, you obviously get terribly wound up over nothing."

"It is *not* nothing!" she screamed. The café's three other customers turned to see what all the fuss was about and Sam did her best to calm down. "We've had one of our most exhausting cases ever," she said, quietly enough so no-one but Henderson could hopefully hear, "we nearly drowned in the

Bristol Channel, and we got into trouble with the police, so I hope you can understand if I am slightly concerned that any of the terrible things we've had to face recently might have somehow sneaked back and got you while I wasn't looking."

Henderson sipped his coffee, apparently decided it was too hot for the moment, and put the cup down. "Well, they didn't," he said. "Now, have you calmed down enough for me to be tell you what has *actually* been taking place over the last hour and a half?"

Sam wanted to boil with rage at that, but she knew it would be pointless. Besides, it was very good to know he was safe. "Go on," she said as she tried to bend her teaspoon between thumb and forefinger to dissipate some tension.

"As you can probably guess," said the detective, "Sir Anthony had gone over the report we sent him last week with a fine tooth comb, so the first thing I did was to offer my condolences regarding the death of his grand-daughter."

"Good idea," said Sam, biting her lip. "But I suppose he went mental anyway?"

Henderson shook his head, still looking as if he had difficulty believing what he was about to say. "Not a bit of it. He said that was quite all right, and would I like to meet the girl who supposedly turned into a demonic entity during our adventure."

Sam frowned and bent the teaspoon harder. "Meaning?"

Henderson leaned back in his chair and folded his arms behind his head. "Madeleine Calverton — the *real* Madeleine Calverton — doesn't look anything like the girl we picked up on the road leading to William Marx's house. She has dyed pink and blonde hair, is twice the size, and could barely look me in the eye she was so shy."

Sam's eyes widened. "So our Maddy Calverton was...?"

"...a creation of the house; at least I think so." Henderson tried his coffee again and found to his delight that it was now drinkable. "I suppose I should have guessed, but it just goes to show that sometimes even the greatest minds can be caught off guard."

"But what about the séance?" said Sam, putting the twisted wreck of the spoon down. "What about the spirit that took her over? That *was* on our side, wasn't it?"

"Yes, I think it was," said Henderson. "I also think it wasn't part of Marx's plan, just like the ghosts of his wife and daughter weren't part of his plan either. And the more I think about it, the more we have all of them to thank for us getting out of there in one piece."

"Some of us didn't," said Sam, knowing that Henderson didn't need reminding. "Were Alan and Helen make believe too?"

Henderson shook his head. "No, they were real; and so was Jeremy. The real Maddy Calverton simply decided at the last minute that going to a properly scary haunted house was probably too properly scary for her."

Sam picked up her spoon again. "So what did Sir Anthony have to say about *their* deaths?"

Henderson took another sip of coffee. "Something along the lines of how both Alan and Helen knew the risks when they took the job and that the money he had paid them would more than compensate any surviving relatives, of which he understands there are few, if any."

"And Jeremy?"

Henderson's face fell even further. "As Sir Anthony quite rightly put it, Jeremy Stokes was my responsibility. I should have made it clearer to Mr Stokes what he was getting into, and if he died it was my fault."

There was a long pause, during which it felt to Sam as if the room shrank around them. It was only at that when Sam realised Henderson really wasn't himself at all. After what she felt to be a suitable length of time had passed she said, "I'm sorry for shouting at you."

Henderson reached across and held her hand. She squeezed it back. Tightly.

"I know," he said, his voice barely a whisper. "But I do feel rather bad about what happened to Mr Stokes."

"He did die saving us." Sam didn't know what else to say. "Stopping the zombie hordes and Not-Maddy who in fact wasn't even Maddy when we thought she was. This isn't meant to sound trite at all, but I have a funny feeling it's how he would have wanted to go. He spent his life giving meaning to others, and finally found a meaning for himself."

A single tear rolled from Henderson's eye. It was all she could do not to kiss it away. "You really are good for me, you know?" he said.

"No," she said. "Only as good as you are for me. And we've always known that in this job of defending the world as we know it from all the horrible things out there, that we're going to lose one or two along the way. Sometimes we just have to take solace in the fact that their deaths aren't in vain." She let Henderson finish his coffee and went and got him another one before saying, "So, Sir Anthony wasn't upset, then?"

"No," said Henderson. "In fact he was delighted. He'd had his men inspect the site and apparently the house isn't there anymore."

"I would have thought that would have really pissed him off," said Sam.

"He wanted evidence of either the existence, or the non-existence, of the paranormal," said Henderson. "There's no way we could have physically dismantled that house in the week we were given. According to the demolitions expert Sir Anthony consulted —"

Sam raised both eyebrows at that. "Demolitions expert?"

"Oh yes," said Henderson. "Our Sir Anthony is nothing if not thorough. Anyway, according to them not even half the house could be demolished and carted away in the time we had. Therefore, the complete disappearance of the house has to have been by supernatural means. He said it was the best evidence he could wish for." With that Henderson took an envelope from his pocket. "And he paid us. In full."

Sam's face lit up. "Oh, marvellous!" she said. "Now we can pay the bills."

"For the next year-and-a-half," said the detective with a grin.

"It also means we can have a well-deserved break," said Sam. "I know I've just had one, but you definitely need it."

Henderson looked as if he agreed but she could never be certain. "Well there's the Jeremy Stokes tribute show we've promised to appear on next week," he said. "The only other outstanding item is this."

He fished a bulky-looking A5 envelope from his outside jacket pocket. Sam eyed it with suspicion. "What's that?" she said.

"Well as Sir Anthony was shaking my hand for a job well done and writing me a cheque for an enormous amount of money, he mentioned some trouble he'd been having with another property of his that he bought a couple of years ago," said Henderson. Sam couldn't help notice he was finally becoming his old self again, which wasn't necessarily a good thing. "He says it's been standing empty because he can't get workmen to repair it."

Sam couldn't help but smile at this. "And I suppose you've said 'yes' to this already?"

Henderson nodded. "Honestly, it looks fascinating! I can't wait to give it the preliminary once over."

Sam looked at the envelope. "Am I allowed to know what it is?" she said.

Henderson took an ancient black and white photograph from the envelope and laid it on the table. "Marston Pier," he said, pointing to the blackened ruin stretching out to sea. "Very popular with Somerset tourists, right up until the mid-1980s when a fire gutted it. Since then there have been..."

"Wait," said Sam, so pleased to see the twinkle she loved so much back in his eyes, that she wanted to laugh out loud. "Let me get another coffee for myself. I have the feeling we're going to be here for a little while longer."

It was a lot longer, actually.

Acknowledgements

First and foremost my thanks to the ebullient, enthusiastic and ever-understanding Ian Alexander Martin, without whom this book wouldn't even have been a twinkle in my eye, and to Steve Upham, whose very fine Screaming Dreams outfit published *Against the Darkness*, and without whom the characters of Mr Henderson and Miss Jephcott would never have seen print at all. Thanks are also due to Ramsey and Jenny Campbell, in whose house I finished this book, despite Mr Campbell trying to distract me with such movie "gems" as *Sh!*, *The Octopus* and *The Man Who Turned to Stone*. My Dad researched the Welsh translations and both my parents have done a sterling job forcing the inhabitants of Abergavenny to buy the first book. Finally my thanks to Kate, who was convinced I could write this even though I wasn't, and who makes all the darknesses worth fighting.

About the Author

John Llewellyn Probert is the author of five short story collections, including the award-winning *The Faculty of Terror* and its follow-up *The Catacombs of Fear* (both from Gray Friar Press), *Coffin Nails* (Ash-Tree Press), *Against the Darkness* (Screaming Dreams) and *Wicked Delights* (Atomic Fez). Spectral Press has just published his novella *The Nine Deaths of Dr Valentine*. *The House That Death Built*, which you are holding in your hands (or robot claws if you're not of this earth) is his first novel.

He lives with fellow horror author Thana Niveau in the east wing of a Victorian gothic mansion that they feel should be haunted. Sadly, so far they have yet to see a ghost, but that might be because what goes inside the house is already scary enough. He posts regular movie reviews at his *House of Mortal Cinema* which can be found at www.JohnLProbert.blogspot.co.uk. News of his latest writing projects and an index of all his published work so far can be found at www.JohnLProbert.com.

WICKED DELIGHTS

A collection by John Llewellyn Probert

Wicked...
The book that sucks the blood from children

...Delights
The film that turns people into self-destructive
sadomasochistic obsessives

Wicked...
The lunatic asylum that steals souls

...Delights
The art exhibition of mutilated humanity...
where the exhibits are still alive!

John Llewellyn Probert's latest short story collection – containing
eighteen delicious selections across 352 delectable pages – mixes
the cruel with the carnal, the sadistic with the sexual, the erotic with
the outrageous, to bring you tales of a cuckolded husband's terrible
revenge, the television channel where you can pay off your debts
but at the worst price imaginable, the man willing to do anything to
improve his chances of success with the ladies, a marriage guidance
counsellor who goes to bloody extremes to prove her point, the
woman who will do anything to keep her family, and a city made
entirely from human bone. All of this, and the last Christmas ever,
just to make things even *more* cheery.

★ *Vividly creepy images... are all the more compelling when
rendered in Probert's breezy style.*

— **Publishers Weekly**

*Gruesomely amusing horror tales... crisp, screenplay-ready
narration laced with vivid imagery... his penchant for wily humor
and odd narrative twists... yields a genre gem.*

— **Carl Hays**, *Booklist*

*There's dark humour here, and unexpected poignancy — indeed,
the book is as full of surprises as the man himself. Horror is lucky
to have him.*

— **Ramsey Campbell**

Jacket-less Hardback: $39⁹⁹/£22⁹⁹ ‡ ISBN: 978-0-9811597-2-0
E-Book: $4⁹⁹/£2⁹⁹ ‡ ISBN: 978-0-9811597-7-5

CPSIA information can be obtained at www.ICGtesting.com
Printed in the USA
LVOW011252230413

330514LV00011B/340/P